DATING DR LOVE

RACHEL DOVE

Boldwood

First published in Great Britain in 2025 by Boldwood Books Ltd.

Copyright © Rachel Dove, 2025

Cover Design by Head Design Ltd.

Cover Images: Shutterstock

A CIP catalogue record for this book is available from the British Library.

Paperback ISBN 978-1-80483-620-0

Large Print ISBN 978-1-80483-619-4

Hardback ISBN 978-1-80483-618-7

Ebook ISBN 978-1-80483-621-7

Kindle ISBN 978-1-80483-622-4

Audio CD ISBN 978-1-80483-613-2

MP3 CD ISBN 978-1-80483-614-9

Digital audio download ISBN 978-1-80483-617-0

This book is printed on certified sustainable paper. Boldwood Books is dedicated to putting sustainability at the heart of our business. For more information please visit https://www.boldwoodbooks.com/about-us/sustainability/

Boldwood Books Ltd, 23 Bowerdean Street, London, SW6 3TN

www.boldwoodbooks.com

Dedicated to Marlene Rothwell
Beloved mother, grandmother
and great-grandmother,
always loved, forever missed

1

'I wonder if blocking your parents' email addresses is frowned upon these days. Is ghosting the people who gave you life a thing? Drew Barrymore divorced hers, right? She seems to be doing pretty well.'

'Err – excuse me? Did you ask me something?'

Chloe Henry blushed furiously, remembering that she wasn't alone on her lunch break. And that the man currently sharing her space probably thought she was weird. *Speaking out loud again. Great.* Sitting in the doctors' lounge grabbing a brief break from work, she scrolled through the half-dozen passive-aggressive emails her parents had sent her in the last forty-eight hours. Even the one from her sister was enough to make her want to throw her phone at the wall. She'd sent her a number for a Botox specialist, citing that at the last family dinner she'd 'noticed her deep frown lines'. The deep frown lines were caused by the ruddy dinner in the first place. And the fact that she'd felt so sick being there. Sunday dinners at her parents' should be sponsored by alcohol and wrinkle removers, quite frankly, like the American Superbowl. Their half-time show could be a therapist who specialised in dealing with family politics where the dinner wasn't the only thing that was roasted. Even here, at work, they were getting to her. Snipping little pieces right out of her soft, vulnerable underbelly. Lately, it seemed the only time she felt normal was when she was at home with her cat, watching her favourite shows and hiding from the world. Her couch was already calling her name as she turned to the guy and tried to pretend she hadn't just thought-vomited all over him.

'No, sorry. Talking to myself, you know. Nothing will drive you quite as crazy as family, am I right?' The agency doctor sitting to her right was looking at her as if she'd had some kind of mental episode. Which, to be fair, wasn't far off the mark. A good mental episode would almost be welcome about now. Maybe she could even get a day off out of it. Head to the beach or something. Anything other than work every hour she was awake. Even when she did sleep these days, her dreams were filled with work. The other night, she'd jolted awake after two hours of fitful sleep. Her hands were raised as if she'd been performing surgery on the rumpled sheets.

When the man next to her didn't even try to reply, Chloe felt herself needing to fill the silence. Which was typical of her lately. She was so used to trying to explain herself these days, she over compensated and generally made things worse. Her family triggered her need to defend her choices, which left her snappish, detached. Or it could go the other way entirely, where she felt the need to narrate her life to the people around her. Like now, when the anxiety bubbled out of her in word bile to a complete stranger. The need to be poised and professional at all times was grating. It drained her energy, acting like she was so 'on' all the time. Alert, ever watching for a keen observation or unkind word to hit her between the eyes like a silent sniper. These days, it felt like she was in *The Truman Show* and her family were the avid viewers. She didn't know who to trust. Who was a mere colleague and who was a paid actor in on the secret. The only time she was truly herself, no-one was there to see it. She was so tired of feeling the need to smooth over every aspect of the parts of herself she forgot to hide. *Yet you keep doing it. Stop talking, you're scaring him!*

She caught herself gripping her phone too tight and loosened her fingers. 'Or maybe not. Sorry. Again. Bad day. Bad week, actually. You know.' More silence. 'Or maybe you don't know on that score either. I'll shut up now.' *I wish I could shut up forever. Trying to appear normal is exhausting.*

The doctor raised a sceptical brow but said nothing, returning to his rather boring-looking ham salad sandwich. Sighing, Chloe closed down her email and returned to the article she'd been reading about Doctor Camilla Wainwright, a woman who'd gone through medical school with her. They had been at the same level, both obsessed with medicine and perfection. The cream of their class. Both set for stellar careers, accolades in their fields. The difference was, when they qualified, Chloe had defied her parents by going to work within the NHS instead of private practice, and Camilla... well, Camilla had gone into charitable work, jetting around the world to swoop in and save lives. Her smiling face beamed up at Chloe from the article. *National Geographic* had hailed her as a 'miracle worker', citing her initiatives in bringing cutting-edge surgeries to the furthest corners of the world. It made her sound like she was performing brain surgery in the middle of nowhere with nothing more than a spoon and some tape. Which, knowing Camilla, wasn't that far from the truth. Looking at those photos of her, something ached in Chloe's chest. The envy felt like heartburn, ravaging her as she took in the glossy spread of what *NG* had called 'the beautiful travelling doc'. To further emphasise the point, there was a photo of Camilla on a tropical beach, wearing a palm-leaf green bikini and a stethoscope. Yep, a fricking stethoscope around her tanned neck, like she was not only beach ready but life-saving ready too. Ugh. That tan. Even her nails were painted in a bright coral colour, long and perfect. Chloe couldn't remember the last time she'd done her nails or even been near any sunshine. Her skin tone would make a vampire do a double-take at this point. Camilla, in this photo, looked like she was glowing right off the page.

Chloe made a mental note to try the fake tan again, next time she had a day off. Or a day off which wasn't consumed by sleeping most of the day, watching TV and doing laundry so she could have clean underwear for her next shift. Who was she kidding? She'd end up buying more online instead, same as she had for the past month. It wasn't the laundry, the tan or the look that she envied so much. She loved her job, and the hours she put in were worth the sacrifices. It was the freedom that shone out from Camilla's sun-kissed face that she coveted. The look of a woman who lived life for her and no-one else. She looked, happy. Peaceful. Like she was doing what she truly wanted to do without anyone telling her she was off track. Chloe's mother had emailed her the link to the article, which was why the comparisons between them stung just that bit more. Still, she kept reading it, applying lemon juice directly to the fresh cuts each little detail slashed through her. Stupid, happy, sun-kissed Camilla.

In another life, they'd have been friends. The best kind, who pushed each other to be better. Chloe could still remember the way Camilla's eyes had narrowed when Chloe had introduced herself at the mixer they'd attended before their internship had started.

'Oh.' She'd pouted, looking Chloe up and down as if she was looking for the label. 'Henry, eh? One of *those* Henrys?' Camilla's family had money too, but they were bankers or hedge-fund types, not in the medical profession. The fact that Chloe was from a legacy medical family had obviously gotten out before she could even attempt to show people who she was and what she could do on her own. She'd worked just as hard as everyone else, but her surname held weight. Akin to a millstone, which she often felt like she was pushing in front of her. From that day on, it was like Camilla could see through her – her need to prove herself, to be the best. She also knew that Camilla assumed Chloe's drive and determination was arrogance, even when it couldn't be further from the truth. Chloe never corrected her, of course. What would be the point? She'd already formed her opinions, another chiselled mark on the stone she dragged around. She'd been a little more naïve back then, at the start of things. Hopeful that people would eventually see her for what she was, rather than who she was related to. She knew better now, was hardened against it for the most part, but she didn't forget it. Every look and snide comment was buried in her memory, popping up in her weaker moments.

She still remembered the punch it had elicited to her gut all the same. Of course, when your family quite literally has their name on the research buildings of some of the best medical facilities in the UK, it was kind of hard to hide your heritage.

'Er, yes,' she'd stammered, feeling small behind the shadow of her family. The walls of the mere moments ago friendly mixer closed in like bars on a gilded cage. 'I guess I am.'

'Legacy, eh?' Camilla had smiled. 'Must be... nice.' Her smile didn't even try to reach her eyes, and Chloe knew in that moment that her hopes for forming friendships and a normal career were futile. Wherever she went she would be Chloe Henry. Daughter of the great Archibald and Yvette Henry, little sister of Elizabeth. All pioneers in their respective fields and not a wallflower among them. Facts which only served to point out Chloe's differences in ever more glaring detail over the years. She didn't want the accolades, or the buildings named after her. She wanted to be herself – geeky and socially awkward, sure, but still her. Doing what she loved, making a real difference. Experiencing life without everything the Henry name brought with it. Which made her sound like a privileged brat, but in fact was quite the opposite. She ran her finger across the screen to read more of the article. There were more photos. Colourful, glossy insights into her former rival's seemingly perfect life. Camilla grinning outside a tent surrounded by fearsome-looking soldiers. Another one of her holding a small child, thick forest behind them. Camilla, standing on a deserted beach, a leather old-style doctor's bag in one hand as she looked pensively into the distance. *Okay, that one was a bit much. Come on.*

Yesterday, Chloe had spent three hours in surgery treating a guy who'd been stabbed for trying to avoid his car getting jacked from outside his own house. And the stabber had still nicked his car. And promptly wrapped it around a tree attempting to evade police. It had been a stunningly stupid move which had landed him in the adjacent operating room with her colleague operating on him to save his leg, which he'd mangled in the wreck. Chloe didn't exactly want to draw parallels, and she would much rather be treating Joe Public, but the article still struck a chord, nonetheless. It was the pure smug freedom that got her. They'd gone through the same journey, but their destinations in life couldn't be more different. The fact her mother had sent her the article link only made things worse. That silent recrimination beating the familiar drum of 'you're not good enough'. All through her training, it had been 'And how is Camilla doing?' and 'Well, I hope you beat Camilla.' As if training to be a surgeon was some Miss UK pageant. Even now, a *National Geographic* spread was something else they would use as a comparison. The next dinner with her parents was going to be about as much fun as taking a cheese grater to the face.

'Stupid Camilla,' she muttered, and ham salad sandwich guy gave her another odd look and moved to the next chair, putting his back to her entirely. Finishing her own quinoa salad with a sigh, she dumped her Tupperware container in her locker and went back to work.

'Doctor Henry, you can't have eaten lunch already?'

Chloe shrugged at her favourite scrub nurse as she got back to the theatres. She'd had the carjacking surgery and a splenectomy already today. This afternoon, she was pretty light on scheduled surgeries but, having to push a surgery to deal with the emergent case that had spilled over from the ER, she was looking at two more surgeries before she could dictate the post-surgical notes, deal with her administration duties and then think about what she had scheduled for the day after that.

'Yep. Salad. Checked my emails.' *Depressed myself thoroughly. Perhaps I should pause my* Nat Geo *subscription for a bit.*

Lizzie threw her a dubious look. 'Salad again? Girl, you need a pizza once in a while. Carbs are not the enemy. OR two is all set up. The patient is ready, but they have questions.'

Chloe nodded with a smile. 'No problem, I'll go up to the surgical ward now if we're all set. Did you speak to stores about the supply issue?'

'I did, but they said something about a backlog with distribution.' Chloe huffed. 'I'll chase again, but since you asked us to stockpile a couple of weeks ago, we're not in any danger yet.'

'Good, but please tell them that we need to have the supplies by the end of tomorrow at the latest. Ask one of the other nurses to do it if you need to, you're in surgery this afternoon.'

Brushing a stray strand of brown hair back into her tight bun, she headed straight up to the surgical ward. The second she hit the floor, she knew that the bosses were there. The bunch of suits near the nurses' station was a dead giveaway, in addition to the plastered-on smiles of the staff and the fact that Doctor Jeffries was also present. He was normally heading to the golf course at this time on a Friday, leaving the rest of the surgeries to her and the others while he did his 'admin'. Otherwise known as the back nine.

'Doctor Henry.' Dr Jeffries spotted her, beckoning her over to the crowd of trustees. 'Glad you could join us.'

Chloe felt her jaw pulse from the gritting of her teeth. If she had to work under this guy much longer, she'd need to wear a mouth guard. Between him and the dreams, her teeth were going to be stumpy little nubs before she was forty.

'Yes.' She smiled through closed teeth. 'I just completed my latest surgery, prepping for the next.'

He waved a hand at her. 'Sure, sure. Well, the trustees are here about the new changes coming to the department.' The suits were all looking at her, and she felt her pulse quicken. More changes? Like what? A sixty-hour work week would be nice, but she wouldn't bother holding her panicked breath.

'Changes, sir?'

'Yes.' One of the suits walked over, offering a hand that looked like it had been bathed in moisturiser. She was betting the closest thing this guy had gotten to cutting was his weaselly chin when he shaved. 'Todd Archer, HR. Nice to meet you.'

Taking his hand, she shook it firmly. Her parents had always told her a firm handshake said a lot about a person. The way his hand jolted under her grip told her a lot about him, too. 'Nice to meet you.'

'I hear good things.' Todd grinned, nodding at Doctor Jeffries. 'I thought the trustees would benefit from seeing how the department was working before we appoint the new head of surgery.'

Chloe's pulse thudded in her ears. *Oh my God, this is it. This is what I've been waiting for. Why I have taken all of the stress, the late nights. The running of the department for Doctor Jeffries while he perfects his handicap on the golf course and takes all the credit.* Now he was finally retiring, and she could actually do the job she was already doing, for the most part, but with the title and the ability to make real changes, and finally get out from the glare of his little minion too. She was surprised he wasn't here doing his best shmoozing act.

'Right.' She nodded, trying to look like she wasn't in the grip of a full-blown adrenalin rush. 'Well, I have patients to see, but if you need anything, do let me know.'

'Well, actually, we do have an event coming up that we would like you to participate in.' Doctor Jeffries was talking to the other suits now, and when Chloe looked over, she could swear he was pretending to swing a club. *Ugh, typical.* The board was a total sausage fest. She had tried to focus on the medicine, but it was hard when upper management was such a boys' club. With Doctor Jeffries leaving, it was now or never. If his protégé Doctor Carson got in, it would be more of the same. Worse, because Jonathan Carson was a smarmy git to boot. He treated her like his own personal PA whenever they were in company even though their job titles and pay grades were the same, and he stared at her boobs whenever she had cause to talk to him. She was not going through all this just to end up with that for a boss. Her and her breasts would rather walk out of the door and go cap in hand to her parents. Either option would be worse than chewing glass, and she wasn't going to go down without a fight. She plastered on her best amiable smile and shone it Todd's way.

'Event?'

'Oh yes.' Todd clapped his hands together. 'The conference, it's been on the calendar for a while but we' – he thumbed behind him – 'we thought it would be an excellent opportunity to showcase the new candidates, and we have heard good things about you, Doctor Henry.'

'From Doctor Jeffries?'

Todd blanched, and Chloe's heart stuttered in her chest. Of course it hadn't come from him.

'Well, er, Doctor Jeffries does have his own opinions about a candidate, of course, but we at HR do prefer to take into account the whole picture.'

'Right.' Chloe could feel her eyes narrowing. 'My surname, for example?'

To his credit, Todd at least tried to pretend he didn't know what she was referring to. For about half a second, before his mask slipped. 'Well, like I said, we do want to take into account all of the factors before we make a decision. I can email you the information on the conference. We will make sure adequate cover is provided for the department, of course.' *Nice.* That would probably mean more work to catch up on when she got back. Locums tended to leave things messy paperwork-wise, and the nursing staff were overworked as it was. She'd have to rearrange her scheduled non-urgent surgeries, minimise the fallout... and Todd was still speaking. She tuned back in. 'Maybe you can speak to your family. We are looking for some additional speakers if you—'

'I'll take a look at the information,' Chloe cut in. 'My family won't be in attendance sadly, but I am happy to give a talk of course.' She straightened the lapels on her lab coat to give herself a second to refocus. 'I'm sure you understand my parents are very busy people.'

Todd's megawatt smile flickered and dimmed. 'Of course, Doctor.' He offered her his baby-soft hand. 'I'll be in touch.'

'Thank you.' She nodded, gripping his hand just a little tighter than she needed to. 'I'm looking forward to the opportunity.'

Todd returned to the wall of suits, just in time for Doctor Jeffries to give him a slap on the back. Chloe watched them for a moment, all big bellowing laughs and inside jokes. She felt the hollow in her chest widen into a chasm as she thought of the hard work she'd done, and the effort she still had lying in wait, like obstacles in her path. She'd been waiting for this so long. For Doctor Jeffries to finally announce his retirement, for her to take her shot at running the department she'd been looking after for the last few years. This was it, her chance. She didn't want to be part of the boys' club; she wanted to rise above it. Change things. Prove to everyone that she wasn't just a Henry. That she was a doctor in her own right, and worthy of the job. She wanted it so badly she could taste it. If she had to ace this conference, rub shoulders with the suited and booted, she would do it. She would finally get out from under her family name, and out of their shadow and into the light.

'Doctor Henry, to the surgical suite. Doctor Henry, to the surgical suite.'

She sighed at the tannoy announcement, took a glance at

Doctor Jeffries, who was still holding court without a care in the world, and turning on her heel, headed back to work. Another few hours and she would be home. She could celebrate with an early night, before getting right back to it tomorrow. Once she got this out of the way, maybe she'd have more time for some fun. The nurses were always asking her to go out for drinks; maybe she could make it more than an annual thing for once. She could travel, see the world beyond the hospital or her place. Read those books she kept buying but never got around to reading. A date might be nice, although finding someone who didn't balk at her ambition or her family might be asking too much. Someone not in the medical profession. A real-life man, with a different job and the ability to talk about something other than surgeries or patient outcomes. At this point in her life, a nice meal with a cute guy was about all she could hope for. It didn't have to be anything world-shattering. An orgasm without batteries would do it. If she got the job, she would have space. Opportunities to do something for her without having to run it up the flagpole to the many puppeteers pulling her strings. Maybe, just maybe, she could finally do what she wanted in all aspects of her life. And then she could figure out the rest.

2

TWO WEEKS LATER

'You're killing me here, Logan! I hope you know that. When I stroke out, I'll be sending you my private medical bills. I'll make sure I get the best care too, so get that TV money of yours ready.'

'It's not that bad.'

'Not that bad? You're kidding me, right? I'm getting calls from all the major news channels, asking for a comment on the fact that the biggest TV star in Britain is a huge lush and a slut!'

'Hey! No slut-shaming. Besides, I wasn't with any women last night. A couple of them tried to come home with me, but I shook them off.' If he'd been seen taking a woman home, he would have bigger problems right now. A few had chatted him up in the club, but his heart wasn't in it lately. They wanted the TV star, not him. He was tired of empty, meaningless encounters with faceless females, had been for a while. The whole club scene was getting a little tiresome, if he was honest with himself, but there wasn't much else to fill his time with. There was only so much gym he could stomach. His friends were all in the biz, superficial acquaintances at best. Being famous since he was a teen had alienated him from his old school buddies. The irony that he was so lonely while everyone thought him a party boy was funny most of the time. Not so much now he was pushing thirty. To be honest, sometimes he kind of wished he was getting up to some of the things the media insisted he was doing. At least then he'd be actually getting something out of it. These days he couldn't even have a night out without being accused of sleeping with anyone he was standing next to. He had been caught out last night, sure, but he had gone home alone. Like he always did these days. Just because women were snapped throwing themselves at him, didn't mean he was out there with his catcher's mitt. If someone had sold a story to the tabloids, it was all BS. Right now, the only woman he was in a relationship with was the fifty-five-year-old cleaner who came to his place twice a week, and she was happily married and didn't own a TV. Which was one of the reasons he'd employed her in the first place.

Throwing back the covers, Logan dragged his hungover body out of bed and headed to his huge bathroom. His voice echoed in the sleek tiled space. 'Whatever crap they are tattling, it will blow over. The season's wrapped. We have a while till the promo starts. The gossip rags will sink their teeth into something else before we know it. I'll just lay low.'

'Oh yeah,' his agent scoffed in his ear. Logan rolled his eyes, hitting the speakerphone button and squeezing paste onto his electric toothbrush. 'Like last night? I have photos of you coming at me from all angles, Logan. Very unflattering photos of you stumbling out of the Hooky Lounge looking like you drank half the damn bar.'

'Oh... riiigghht.' That was what those flashes were. He figured sneaking out the back way into a waiting car had helped him escape the paps. Obviously not. He tried to remember, but the whole thing was pretty hazy. 'Well, it was just a celebration, you know. For the wrap.'

'The wrap party was three days ago, Logan. You mean to tell me that you've been partying since then? Do we need to talk rehab?' Logan shoved the brush in his mouth, letting the noise drown everything out. He caught his reflection in the mirror, wincing at what he saw. His apartment had the best lighting, especially in the bathroom, but even that couldn't get rid of the green tinge to his skin, or the dark eyebags. Reaching into one of the drawers, he pulled out some eye masks and stuck them under his puffy eyebags. If he went out today, the last thing he'd want was to get snapped again looking like death warmed over. His thick, usually luscious locks were wrecked. He had glitter stuck in the clumps, and the hair gel he'd slicked through it the day before was now sprinkled through his strands like a cheesy dandruff ad. 'Logan, do I need to make a call or what?'

'No,' Logan huffed. He was getting pretty sick of people having opinions about him enjoying life. Weren't they the ones who had moulded him in the first place? 'I don't have a problem, Pete; I don't need rehab. And if any sniff of that kind of rumour gets out there, we'll be dealing with a much larger problem. I have the casting call to think about, and—'

'Logan.' Pete's tone dropped off a cliff. 'At this rate, you get caught up in one more scandal and I won't be able to cast you anywhere. Have you not seen the news this morning?'

Logan winced at himself in the mirror as he rinsed his mouth of toothpaste.

'I said I didn't see the paps – geez—'

'Not your news, dipshit. Belinda Jenkins. The shit is hitting the fan for her, which means your ridiculous shenanigans are not going to fly any more.'

'What?' Throwing his brush down on the counter, Logan headed to his lounge and flicked on the widescreen TV. The news channel came up, and he didn't need to put the volume up to know what was going on. The headline on the ticker tape at the bottom said it all.

Network executive's husband in cheating scandal – creator of *Doctor Love* files for divorce after telling photos released.

Logan turned up the volume, a sense of foreboding roiling through him as the newsreader turned to her co-host.

'This is bad news for the network, really. We have the star of *Doctor Love*, Logan Broderick, seen out most nights, with the drinking and the various women around him, and now the creator's husband is photographed in flagrante with another woman. Given that the show is marketed as being a cornerstone of drama, romance and yearning, I think the fans are going to have a hard time with all this. It really looks like what we love to see on the screen does not translate into real life.'

'Right?' her colleague said almost gleefully. 'I mean, half the world is in love with Dante Love, but Logan is definitely not husband material. Belinda must be feeling pretty embarrassed right now, especially given that she's spoken so openly over the years about how her inspiration for some of the best romance storylines on screen was inspired by her own marriage.'

'Exactly. It looks like Belinda is really having trouble keeping the leading men in her life under control.'

'Shit,' Logan cursed. 'This isn't good.'

'Exactly. Shit,' Pete echoed. 'Belinda is pissed. I've already had her on the phone this morning, threatening not to renew your contract. She said, and I repeat this verbatim, "Tell your star to get his crap together and keep it in his pants, or I will send kill pages faster than he can zip up." She is out for blood, Logan. This isn't good at all. I'm trying to do damage control, but it's make or break time. Having the main star on her show being out all hours, drinking, draped in ladies? It's not a good look, and now her husband's been caught stepping out, your news is tied right in with hers. I calmed her down once, but now she's in the firing line with the media, it's going to take more than a few apologies.'

The supple leather of his couch squeaked as Logan sank down into the cushions. 'Okay, so how about a fruit basket then? Flowers?' Flicking through the channels, Logan stopped when he saw his own face pop up. A rerun of one of his best episodes, when Dante Love not only took down an angry patient in the A & E waiting room but also saved the life of one of the show's scrub nurses by performing brain surgery. With a broken arm, no less. The ratings had been golden for that one. Maybe he should remind Belinda of it, how pivotal he was to the show.

'Flowers?' Pete screeched back. 'You'd have to send her the fricking Chelsea Flower Show to get out of this without consequences. We need to get out in front of this, go dark.'

'Go dark?' Logan felt whatever colour was left in his cheeks drain away. 'No, Pete. Don't make me do it. I can't.'

'Oh, you can, and you will. The whole world saw you in that club with a load of women last night, half cut. You were photographed coming out with women. The exact opposite of your character, who is a goddamn saint and basically a pin-up for any woman with half a brain and a romantic yearning for Mr Perfect. Dante Love is not the type to be sucking face with models and peeing off hotel balconies.'

'That happened once, and I told you – I woke up and thought I was in the bathroom.'

'Yeah, you mentioned that. I keep covering for you, Logan, but lately, it's getting too much. The optics are not good, whichever way you slice it, and while you aren't Dante Love, he is linked to you. When photos like these come out, the press brings the other persona into the equation. Which means more press for the show, and lately, yours is not good. Belinda is not about to stand another scandal for your sorry ass, not after her own life blew up. I'm telling you right now. Even going dark might not cut it this time.'

'But what about the film? With all this press, I don't want to lose it. It's my next step; I was made for that movie. I want that role. It's what we've been working towards for years!'

This is not good. I've really messed up this time. The irony is, I have been trying to distract myself from the stress of waiting to hear about the role, and now my stupid distractions might cost me the thing I need to get people to see me differently. Of course, I can't tell Pete that. Because like the rest of the planet, he only sees what the media does. A cocky actor with no attachments, doing whatever the heck he likes. Because the press cast me in that role a while ago, and I never bothered to correct them.

Pete's sighs were his tell. When he sighed like he was taking a breathalyser test, it meant he was well and truly mad. 'Yeah, well—'

'I mean, they're going to still send the contract, right? We'll still get the movie?'

'Logan—'

'So I can't go dark, okay? That's the worst possible thing I could do right now. It makes me look guilty if anything. No, I say we ride this out, like normal. They wanted me before this, you said so yourself. Auditions are soon. I was planning to be seen out exercising, you know. I had that combat trainer lined up, and I thought we could be seen out in Hyde Park, showing how much effort I was putting in for the physicality of the shoot—'

'Logan, I can't even get the studio to return my call, let alone talk about the casting. A few shots of you flashing your six-pack with some ex-squaddie personal trainer is not going to slide you into the biggest war epic since... since the last damn war epic! It's set in World War Two, and the hero is a dedicated officer pining for a girl back home. Not exactly a match for your playboy image, is it? Mr Get Pissed and Bang a Girl in Every Port is not the lead actor they're going to be chasing. Going dark is the only choice if you want to have a contract for anything. Don't forget, we haven't signed on the dotted line for the new season yet. Dante Love can quite easily fall down a mine shaft, Joey.'

Logan winced at the *Friends* reference, when one of the main characters, an actor called Joey Tribbiani, got a little too cocky with the writers of the show he was part of, and the next thing he knew he was being killed off and written out of the show by the very same. And he was a doctor on the show too. The parallels were scary right now, especially since it was something they'd joked about when they first got the deal for Dante Love. At the time, it was funny because it seemed impossible that it would happen in real life. Now, Logan could practically see the lift doors looming in front of him.

'Shit. Okay, okay. I get it, I messed up again. I'm sorry. But what can we do? You know what the press are like! They make up stories where there are none anyway. Even if I stop going out they will still try to find dirt. This Belinda thing is big news, and if they can tie me in with that they are going to keep coming. Belinda won't believe I've changed, Pete. No-one does.'

'So change her mind. Show the real you for once.'

'Yeah right.' *I don't even know who that is any more. Why*

should anyone believe it when I don't? I never set out to be this guy. I don't even do a fraction of the stuff I get accused of, but what's the point in telling them that? Me sitting home every night reading lines doesn't sell their papers or get their subscribers clicking those boxes. It hit him again, a fresh wave. *The people who know the real me are not here any more. My point of reference is gone forever.* 'Pete, you know for a fact that I am not out there doing a lot of the crap they think I am, and you still think I'm messing up. How am I supposed to convince everyone when you don't buy it? What am I supposed to do, start crochet? Instagram-live me sitting on the couch on my own every night?'

'Well, you joke but that's not exactly out of left field. You're not a bad guy. I would have dropped you a long time ago if I thought you were the man everyone else does, but even I am starting to get tired of the playboy persona, Logan. We need people to realise that you're not as bad as they make out, but it will take work. Discipline. Which, aside from your work ethic, you don't seem to have much of these days. It's your downtime you need a babysitter for. With the Belinda scandal, you are going to be roasted over the coals all over again. The optics are not going to convince any studio that you are stable enough for this kind of leading role. It's going to be a box office smash, and they won't take chances on the lead. Your character Dante is a faithful doctor, pining for a woman he can't have. Just like the film character. Which did mean you were a sure thing, before this. You were first pick, but the radio silence is scary. They are probably casting their net out there already for an alternative, and we can't afford to let them sign someone else while you pull your finger out. We need to play that angle IRL for once.'

'Angle?' Logan frowned. 'I'm not pining for anyone, Pete. I don't even bring women home any more. I got over all that.' *When I'd finally pulled myself out of my grieving hole of mourning the mother who'd raised me. The woman who had been at every audition, driving me to classes, and cheering me on. It was just the two of us back then, and she looked after me. When I hit the big time, and she needed to be the one looked after, I was there. For all of it. Used my money to make her life better. Get her the best healthcare, the freedom to focus on her health and not worry about money or working to make ends meet for once. When she passed, I was lost. And yeah, I didn't handle it well. Let outside influences 'cheer' me up. What else could I do? I didn't want to talk about it. Couldn't talk about it. Keeping her out of the media was always important, and her death didn't change that.* The press never knew about Logan Broderick and the wonderful parent that had been taken too early. Pete had earned his money there. They'd crafted this persona of a confident young actor with seemingly no back-story. Distracted them with titbits of nothing. Beautiful women on his arm. Half-naked photo shoots. *Who cares what he's thinking or going through – look at those washboard abs!*

After the funeral, there was always a party to go to. A red carpet to shimmy down. Dante Love was the character he hid behind till his antics pushed Logan out from behind his shadow, like a dastardly alter ego. Numbness and distractions saw him through the worst of it, but when he finally got his shit together and the noose of grief loosened from his neck, the die was already cast. The world had seen him work through it in all the wrong ways and never even saw his hidden pain. It had solidified the mould they'd cast for him as the partying lothario, and by the time he'd realised it, it was too late to convince them otherwise. *Once the pretty boy, always the pretty boy. He doesn't have serious stuff going on. He's here for the fun.*

And dating? Pfff. Not. A. Chance. The type of woman he would have wanted to take home to his mother if she were still here was not looking his way. Not beyond a passing glance or a judgemental side-eye. He rattled out a sigh that gave Pete's a run for their money, feeling his mood darken. Maybe he was kidding himself. Perhaps his time had run out. He should have put paid to this earlier, instead of leaning into it. The mantra he'd repeated to himself – *Fine, I'll be who they think I am* – was running through his head, but this time it sounded like a warning bell. He wasn't going to go down without a fight. Not when he was so close to getting the movie role he'd always wanted to play and finally proving to everyone that he was a serious actor and not a one-trick pony. Dante was his breakout role, but he didn't want to stop there. He had more to show people, more roles he longed to sink his teeth into. Most of all, he wanted to be the man his mother had raised again. A man worth taking home to meet the family.

'I'm not just going to sit in some hole and let them bury me, Pete. I'll stop the bar stuff. It will blow over when they have nothing to photograph, right? No skeletons in the closet. Seriously, if they think someone out there is going to have fresh dirt on me, they'll be digging a long time.'

'Thank God for small mercies,' Pete muttered under his breath. 'We need to play this just right. The angle is quiet bachelor, Logan. Pulling a Dante is the only way we have a chance. Don't be seen with any other women, I mean it. If you see a granny in the street, walk the other way. You need this, Logan. One more scandal and you'll lose more than the movie.'

As he looked at the muted headlines flashing across the screen in front of him, Logan's usual rebuttal died on his lips. The media were ready to flay him alive. Women's groups were coming out saying that he was a toxic male, judging by the tweets scrolling down the right-hand side of the newscaster. Belinda and her husband flashed up on the screen, and the husband was being lauded as a killer of romance. A frustrated growl dropped from his mouth as he saw the truth of what his agent was saying. He was in trouble. This time, he couldn't get out of it with a cheeky grin and a press release.

'Okay, fine. So what else? An interview maybe? Set my side of the story straight?'

'What side of the story? Pictures don't lie, Logan. You have no defence. They will never believe that you're some lonely bachelor while you're out there living it up. The Dante Love persona is in the bin right now, covered in shame and body glitter. No, no interviews. You need to lay low. Like, way low.' Pete's voice drifted off, and Logan swallowed hard. He knew what it meant when he got like this. It meant those sly cogs in that brain of his were turning, and usually, it meant what came out of his mouth next, Logan would hate.

'I'm booking you a hotel for a couple of weeks. Off the beaten track. Out of the city. You can hole up there while I deal with this shitstorm. Take your scripts, learn your lines, stay off social media. In fact, stay off the internet full stop. I need you to disappear, Logan.'

'But—'

'No buts. No whining, no phone. I mean it. Start packing. I'll send you the details and the name I booked you in under.'

'Thought I couldn't use my phone,' he whined childishly.

'Cute,' Pete shot back, in a tone that implied he found it anything but. 'Stay off social media. Don't even order take-out. I'll send a car in an hour. Be ready. And Logan?'

Logan's sigh rattled his hangover. 'Yeah?'

'This is your absolute last chance. Don't fuck this up.'

* * *

Peeling off a note from the wad in his pocket, Logan thanked the porter for bringing his bags to the door. 'I've got it from here, mate. Thanks.'

'No problem,' the chirpy guy beamed back. 'Enjoy your stay, Mr Broderick. Wife's a big fan.'

Logan pulled down the peak of his hat lower while trying to slide the key card into the lock to get away.

'Thanks, mate, but it's McHenry here.' He waggled his finger in a circle in the air. 'Privacy. I'm sure my agent told the hotel what would happen if the press found me here.'

The porter's face dropped. 'Oh – oh, course, Mr McHenry.' He recovered when Logan flashed him a grateful smile. 'Your secret is safe with me.'

Tipping his cap at the man, and sliding another twenty in his hand, Logan watched him leave and sagged with relief. He was supposed to be incognito here, which was why he was in this Cornish version of *The Shining* hotel in the first place. It was well off the beaten track and hosting some kind of medical thing all week, which meant it was busy but not full of holiday-makers. Alan said he should blend in where possible, but the fact his baseball cap and sunglasses hadn't even fooled the porter wasn't the best start. The reception staff hadn't looked twice, but there had been a queue, mostly full of arrogant doctors who were moaning about various things that Logan didn't give a crap about. He'd been handed a key without a side-ward glance, and the porter had been only too happy to help a customer that wasn't being a nuisance. Pulling his suitcases behind him through the door, he felt relief wash over him the second the door clicked shut. Maybe this was a good thing, being here. For one thing, he could work on the script for the film role he wanted and not think about what the gossip maga-zines were saying about him. On the way over he'd defied Pete's rules and took a peek online. Thirty seconds in, he wished he hadn't bothered. His agent had downplayed the shitstorm he was in if anything. With the Belinda cheating scandal, Logan and his partying ways were being trounced on the net. He read one article that said Belinda should stop writing perfect men, since she had the opposite in her life. The hashtag #Logan-whatadick was trending, and the horrendous play on his surname was enough to make him stop reading for the rest of the journey. Perhaps he should have taken that role in the horror franchise he'd passed on earlier in the year. Playing a deranged serial killer might actually have worked in his favour career-wise. Sighing, he left his cases by the door and went to explore his hiding hole.

The hotel room was smaller than he'd expected. He usually had suites, but he was supposed to be flying under the radar. It was smart, given that he was deep undercover. Peter really did think of everything. He just hoped that the eager porter would keep his mouth shut, or he'd have to move again. Till then, this was home.

He could see a little lounge area through an archway to the left. To the right of him was a large king-size bed, and in the centre a door which he assumed to be the bathroom. He assumed it was the bathroom because he could hear running water. *Wait, what?* There was steam coming out from under the door. With one ear to the door, he listened. The shower was on.

'What the hell?' he muttered under his breath. He was just about to open the door when his phone rang in his hand. Pete's name flashed up on the screen.

'Hello?' A strangled-sounding female voice rang out from the other side of the door, and the water was abruptly cut off.

'Shit,' Logan cursed, hitting the reject button. 'Er, hello?'

'What the hell are you doing in my room?' The woman

sounded pissed, shaky, and he could hear frantic shuffling from the other side of the door. 'Get out now! I'm calling security! I have a scalpel!'

'A scalpel? Why the fuck do you have a—'

The words died in his throat when the door to the bathroom came flying open. Emerging from the steam like some kind of crazy banshee, a towel-clad wet-haired ball of rage shot out, heading straight for him.

'Get out! I have a weapon!' she screamed, a half second before she barrelled into him, just as he was making a run for the door. Soapy-wet limbs collided with his tracksuit-clad chest, and Logan was enveloped by wet tendrils of fruit-scented dark brown hair.

'You're in my r— Jesus, how are you so strong?' Logan's hands reached out and grabbed for anything he could to stop his fall as the screaming woman in his arms grabbed his hair by the root and yanked. 'Argh! What the hell are you doing! Stalker!'

'Stalker? Stalker? You're a hotel room invader! Get the hell out!' Logan's back hit the door frame, the same second he pulled on the garment in his hand. 'Get off!'

'What the hell is this?' Logan's words died when he realised what he was holding. 'Oh my God, it's your...'

'Towel!' she shrieked, giving his hair another yank as she released it to grab for the towel. Too late, because Logan got an eyeful of creamy skin and a body that he wanted to see more of. A lot more, judging by the way his lower half reacted. Apparently little Broderick still functioned even when accosted by a naked intruder. 'My God, are you insane?' Now she was back in the towel, Logan took her in properly for the first time. She was insanely pretty, even angry and wet. A cute button nose, which was currently scrunched up in disgust, sat atop a pair of plump pink lips. Her eyes were a piercing light blue. Piercing because she looked like she was about to cut through his head with the laser-sharp glare she was throwing at him. She shook her head, as if she couldn't believe what she was seeing. She was looking at him like she couldn't believe he was standing there. Which was normal, he guessed, except the fact she was in his room and obviously there for a reason. Did stalkers take showers while waiting for their prey? Was that a thing? 'Why are you here?' she demanded, her look incredulous as her eyes scanned him from head to foot.

He just about managed to form words. 'I think I should be the one asking the questions. What are you doing in my room?'

'Your room? This is my room!' She stamped her bare foot on the carpet, jiggling her covering loose.

'Er... towel.'

'Shit!' she squeaked, wrestling to cover herself. Not before he saw more of his attacker, parts that made his groin clench. *God, Logan, look away!* Logan felt like his face was on fire. He locked his eyes to the ceiling, trying to tamp down the adrenaline and weird arousal he was feeling. For a room infiltrator, she was very cute. It was disturbing in more ways than one. She was muttering to herself, the words a flustered torrent. He thought he caught the word 'hallucinating', and his eyes widened. *Yep. Definitely disturbing.* She kept muttering, her gaze flicking from him to the room in rapid succession. He tried to make out what she was saying, but it was just a string of squeaky murmurs.

'What?' He felt the flick of moisture, the thwack of her hair as she whirled around the room. The whole time, he could hear her inner monologue. 'What are you saying? Are you on medication?'

'What?' She glared at him. 'I'm... No, I'm not on medication! How dare you! What are you, some kind of tribute? A clone?'

'A clone? Tribute? What are you talking about?'

She wasn't listening, too busy pacing the room and speaking in tongues. Or she might as well be, because he couldn't make out a darn word. 'Where is my phone! Why are you still here? Get out of my room!' Her eyes zeroed in on the door behind them. 'Security!'

'Hey! Sshhh!' He took a step towards her, thinking better of it when she tried to karate-chop at him with her non-towel-holding hand. 'Quiet!'

'Oh, don't you dare shush me!' She poked him in the chest, and meeting her eye, he saw she was shaking. He could see a tattoo peeking over her left shoulder, a blur of colour as she side-stepped him and bolted. He went to grab her, just as she got to the door. *Big mistake, Logan. What are you doing? Unhand the crazy lady, stupid.*

'Wait! Don't call security, I can't be seen—'

'Get the hell off me! Put me down!'

She kicked backwards and connected with his knee. He almost went down but managed to lift her off the ground, one arm wrapped around her waist, the other trying to block the door. 'I'm not a psycho, okay? I didn't know you were here! This is my room; it's been booked through my agent. I can explain everything, if you just calm down! Wait!'

He whirled her around, his arms tight around her waist. She tried to kick him again, and without thinking, he lowered one arm and lifted her fully into his arms. She froze.

Shit. 'I'm sorry!' he said, panicking. 'I mean you no harm, I promise. I'm not a crazy stalker!'

'Oh yeah,' she huffed, her chest heaving. 'Says the man who just wrestled me half-naked! Put me down!'

He did it immediately, holding his hands up in surrender. 'I mean you no harm. I promise. This is all a misunderstanding.'

He reached slowly into his back pocket for his wallet. 'Here,' he panted, pulling out his driving licence. 'I'm Logan. I'm staying here. That's all.' He pulled out his key card. 'See?'

She eyed him for the longest time after scanning the licence. An odd look crossed her features as she deflated, just a little. If she recognised him, she didn't say it. Usually when people saw him, they called him Dante and were only too eager to say hello. This one, she was looking at him like he was wearing a space suit and had just landed from Mars. 'Logan,' she said slowly. 'Broderick. You're... Logan.' She ran her eyes up and down him slowly. 'You're staying... here?'

'Yes,' he confirmed, pushing his wallet into his back pocket. It was wet. His hat had been knocked off some time in the melee, and his T-shirt was soaked down the front. 'I didn't mean to grab you; I just didn't want you running out of here half-naked and screaming. I'm kind of laying low.' She was looking at him as if he had two heads. He was trying to ensure his eyes didn't stray from hers. It was more difficult than he thought, given that all he could smell was the fruity scent of whatever she had used in the shower. She blinked a few times, her face a picture of shock. He could see it now. *TV lothario arrested in Cornish hotel attack.* 'Pete is going to murder me for this.'

'Pete?' she croaked, as if she'd just woken up.

'Yeah, he's my—'

There was a loud knock at the door.

'Er, Mr McHenry?'

Before he could do anything, the towel-clad woman was reaching for the handle.

'No!' he started, stepping forward to block her path. He

tried to grab her, panic at whatever was behind the door over-riding all sense of proprietary. 'Don't open...'

She wrenched open the door. The porter was standing there, eyes wide. And he wasn't alone.

'...the door.' Logan sighed, just before the flash of a camera went off.

3

'This can't be happening. The stupid porter let a pap in right to your door. Jesus, we should sue the hotel.'

Three hours later, they were sitting on opposite sides of the couch glaring at each other as Logan's agent Pete wore a hole in the carpet pacing the floor in front of them. His hair, or what was left of it, was sticking up at all angles in a halo around the back of his head. Given that he'd just arrived via a bloody helicopter, Chloe shouldn't be surprised, but it was jarring to look at. The second after the cameraman had taken the photos, Logan had kicked the door shut and got straight onto his phone. She'd been stuck here ever since, too scared to leave. Too shocked to speak. When the agent had choppered in, his hair had been the first thing she'd taken in over the last few hours of awkward silence. Even with everything she'd just experienced. Logan Broderick. Logan Broderick had been in her hotel room. The real Logan. The man she'd watched for hours and hours on her TV. When she'd gotten over her terror at having a man in her room and realised it was him, she still didn't believe her eyes. For a moment, she thought her brain had finally cracked from the pressure and he was some kind of hallucination. Or a doppelgänger. People had tribute acts posing as them, right? Body doubles. But no. He was the real McCoy, standing in her hotel room and staring at her as if she had just parachuted in from the ceiling. Hours after she'd been reading articles about him being out with multiple women, he'd walked right into her hotel room. Had held her against his beefy chest and almost taken a beating, which was not how her usual fantasies involving him went in her head. Not only that, he'd seen her naked. *Naked!* Her cheeks flushed as she remembered him hoisting her into his arms in her little white towel. She wanted to die all over again.

'This can't be real,' Pete said again, pacing another length. *Just what I was thinking.* 'This is the worst news! After everything Belinda said, now this? Tell me, Logan, do you have a death wish, because this can't be your life right now!'

'Well, it is,' Chloe huffed, pushing thoughts of naked body parts and strong arms firmly out of her panicked thoughts and reminding herself of the reality of the situation. The fact that she'd been photographed looking decidedly un-doctorlike. 'And you need to do something about it.' Her hair was dry now, sticking out in wavy angles. She was fully dressed, not that it mattered. Her towel, and its contents, were all over the internet. In the shots, she looked flushed, her wet hair around her shoulders, the towel only just covering her modesty. Logan, his body flush to her chest, his arm around her. They were both looking into the camera lens, looking every inch the guilty pair. *Oh God. How is this happening?* It was everywhere, on every gossip page. Her gut clenched when she thought of the conference. Her parents, seeing those photos. Her sister would be laughing her head off somewhere in London right now. Logan Broderick. And her. Together. Right after he'd been seen photographed with yet another flock of women. The fantasy was definitely not living up to the daydreams in her head. He was no Dante Love, she reminded herself. *I am not a fan.* Shock gave way to panic. 'I have a week to stay here, and I can't have this in my life!'

'It's not that bad,' Logan started, but she cut him off with a glare. 'Okay, it's pretty bad, but it's just a misunderstanding. You were in the shower in my room—'

'My room! It's my room, and you walked in on me and scared me half to death. You ripped my towel off, and—'

'You ripped her towel off?' The agent, who looked like a slightly taller version of Danny DeVito, slapped Logan on the back of the head. 'What were you thinking? I told you to keep it in your pants!'

'I did keep in in my pants! It was hers that were off!'

'Hey!' Chloe leaned across the couch to slap him too, but he dodged it. 'Why are you here, anyway? Don't you belong in TV land or something?'

Logan quirked a brow at her, and for a second he looked so deliciously handsome that she forgot he'd not only seen her naked, but now they had been photographed together at the door to this very room. Her with tousled wet hair. In the arms of Logan Broderick, none other than Doctor Love. With his strong arms around her and his shirt all wet from her... well, naked soapy body. *Dear God, kill me now.* It was only a few hours ago that she'd been sitting on the train from Manchester, going over her conference pack and reading the latest gossip about the man sitting on the couch across from her. More news that had disappointed the image she'd crafted in her head of the TV doctor. She loved *Doctor Love*, and whenever she read about the man who played Dante lately, the surer she was that being single wasn't quite so tragic. *Talk about meeting your heroes.*

'TV land?' Logan rested one long leg over the other. *Hmm, manspreader. Figures.* 'And what does that look like, exactly?'

'I don't know. Fancy parties, soulless huge apartments full of naked women.'

His grin widened. 'Well, correct me if I'm wrong but this room had a naked woman in it.'

'Oh, don't you even go there! I'm a doctor,' she told him. 'A proper real-life doctor. I could kill you half a dozen different ways with a scalpel and no-one would be any the wiser.'

'That's what the scalpel thing was about,' Logan muttered to himself as Pete paced a little faster. 'I've got to say, I am a little relieved.'

'Keep muttering to yourself and I'll add more to that list.'

'I didn't hear that,' Pete cut in, pausing to stand between them, hands on hips. 'You're really a doctor?'

'Yes.' She nodded. 'I'm here for the medical conference; I'm presenting a talk later in the week. This was my chance to shine, earn a promotion.'

'What type of doctor?' he asked, his face changing from panic to something that looked almost calculating.

'A real one!' Chloe huffed. 'A general surgeon. I'm trying to be the head of my department...' She trailed off, picturing the boys' club she was up against and what they would make of this. 'Well, I was, until this.' She sank back into the couch cushions, wishing they would swallow her up with the lint and the crumbs from previous guests and hide her forever. 'My parents are going to love this.'

'This isn't my fault,' Logan cut in. 'You were in my room!'

Chloe picked up one of the oversized cushions and volleyed it at him. 'Will you shut up about the damn room! My career is over! It's all right for you, Doctor Dickhead! You live like this anyway! I'm practically a damn nun compared to you. Do you realise what this means for my reputation? My future? Everything I have been working for is riding on this. If I don't get that promotion I will never get the life I want!'

'Reputation. Nun.' Pete was pacing again now, repeating random words from her speech.

'Why are you repeating everything I'm saying? Aren't you supposed to be off somewhere, trying to delete the internet?'

'Delete the internet, sure,' Logan scoffed, ducking when another cushion sailed past his head. 'I'm pretty sure if that was a thing, lots of people would have done it before now.' He pouted at her. 'And Doctor Dickhead, really? You don't even know me!'

'I don't need to know you. I read; I have a brain.' She was not about to tell him she was a fan. Not a chance. He would love that, she realised, and his arrogant nonchalance coupled with the fact that he'd just shot her chances of pulling off her life plan made her dig her stubborn heels in. She would rather die than give him the satisfaction of knowing she was a superfan. Which after today, and what she'd read about his private life lately, she was decidedly not.

'But you've read about me.' He smirked. 'Dante fan, huh?'

She shot him the deadliest glare she could muster. 'Don't flatter yourself. The nurses at the hospital have your poster pinned up on the noticeboard in the staffroom. The fact that you're a star on the biggest medical show on TV doesn't mean that you should try to pork everything in a five-mile radius, you know.'

'You watch the show?' he asked, a little smile forming. She narrowed her eyes. *No way am I telling him I'm a fan. I was right on the money about him being a walking ego.* She was not telling him a thing. Not. A. Chance.

'Of course not,' she refuted. 'I don't have time for all that.'

'No time for the best show on television? What do you do for fun then? Read medical journals? Sharpen your scalpels?' He waggled his eyebrows. 'Let me guess. You sneak into hotel rooms to steal the fancy complimentary shower gels.'

4

I actually want to murder him. How can someone so brilliant on screen, so romantic, be such a colossal douchebag? She could feel her blood pressure rising with every flick of his brows. She had thought that the media stuff about him might only be half true, but the way his agent was panicking, and the way Logan was being so nonchalant about the whole thing, was definitely making her rethink things. Her panic was behind the wheel right now, and anger was the chosen destination.

'I work, jackass. Some of us don't spend our time licking shots off supermodels to get our rocks off.' He turned to stare at her, his lips parting on his beautiful face, but she raised a finger at him. 'I don't want to hear it.' She folded her arms and turned away. 'And,' she added, whirling round to grab another pillow to throw at him, 'for the record, you need new writers, because from what I've heard, your character sucks!'

'Oh, hang on just a minute.' Logan scowled, trying to grab the cushion. She tried to yank it back, pulling him with it. 'My character is one of the best loved on the show! The fans love me, and... Let go of my cushion!'

'It's not your cushion,' she yelled. 'This is my room! My room, my cushion!'

He yanked it harder, pulling her practically into his lap. 'Will you stop fighting me, you wildcat!'

'I'd rather be a wildcat than a pussy chaser!'

'Pussy chaser! You don't even know me!'

He pulled her again, and she ended up straddling him. Her libido, already awake from the tussle earlier, flared to life. She could feel the strength of him beneath her, the imposing build of him right under the most sensitive parts of her. She barely held in her surprised gasp which felt suspiciously like a moan and tunnelled back into her fury to snuff out the sudden sexual frisson that roiled through her. At first, he looked just as surprised as her. *Did his pupils just dilate?* He'd grabbed for her, his hands kneading the side of her hips as if he didn't know whether to pull her closer or push her off. Then he squeezed, and her breath died in her throat.

'See?' His voice was gruffer when he spoke. Deeper. 'Wildcat.' When he followed it up with a long look at her lips, her body seemed to forget how to move again. Pete coughed from somewhere behind Logan, and the cloud of lust that had descended puffed back into conscious thought.

Infuriated that she'd let her mind wander when everything was such a mess, she ripped the cushion from his grasp and gripped it between white-knuckled fingers. 'I don't need to know you, everyone knows where you dip your wick, and now the whole world thinks I'm one of them! God, I could kill you!' She shoved the pillow over his face just as Pete piped up.

'That's it! That's the plan!'

'Mmmffff?' Logan said from under the pillow.

'What?' Chloe paused, trying to suffocate her unwanted visitor, and Logan pushed the pillow off. 'What's the plan?'

Logan went to stand up, taking her with him like she weighed nothing and depositing her on the sofa beside him. She hated the part of her that wanted his hands back on her body. His heat and hungry eyes devouring her like fire. Was he breathing as hard as she was right now, or was she just imagining it? *He's a professional woman-chaser, Chloe. Zip it up.* Logan ran a distracted hand through his hair as he glanced from Pete to her again, his eyes hooded. Or that could have just been a trick of the light in the room. She had just tried to smother him with a feather pillow. Her doctor brain registered that it was far more likely that he had allergies, than be experiencing the physical response currently thundering through her at his close contact. He shook his head, turning back to his agent when she dropped her own gaze to the floor. 'You're really going to delete the internet?'

Pete threw them a look. 'If I had those kinds of skills, I wouldn't be standing in this hotel room watching the two of you fighting like toddlers over a toy. Or whatever that was.' He tapped his tongue against the back of his teeth. 'I can't get rid of this, but we can spin it. I can't pull this story back, it's out there.' He said this to her, and Chloe sagged down in her seat, while Logan gathered his breath. 'But what I can do is spin this into something different.' Pete grinned, and Chloe could practically hear the cogs in his brain whirring. 'Something that I think would benefit both of you, something believable, but we need to be on the same page.' He pointed two stubby index fingers at them. 'And the same room.'

Logan was looking at his agent now, and Chloe watched him. She saw the moment his confused expression turned to grim understanding. 'I don't follow,' she mumbled, looking from one to the other, waiting for one of them to enlighten her. 'What's the plan?'

Logan met her eye, wincing before turning back to Pete. 'You're not serious. Pete, I don't know about this. We'll kill each other. She'll never go for this, and even if she did, the press won't buy it.'

'Oh, I'm deadly serious.' Pete folded his arms. 'We talked about restoring your reputation. Well, she's your best shot. Beautiful, accomplished, normal.'

'No,' Logan said, shaking his head. 'Not a chance. Pete, I mean it. No. We can't do this. Not involving her. I'll just take the hit. Tell the truth.'

'Logan, I love you, but we both know they will never believe that, even if it is the truth.' Pete shook his head. 'Belinda is going to fire you. After this story, there is no way I can save the new contract. The film will be off the table. For good.' He pointed at Chloe. 'She is your redemption story. The woman by your side to show the side of Logan the press never wants to see. We spin this right, and we get everything. Redemption, the new contract, the movie.'

'Spin what?' Chloe cut in, suddenly wary as she watched Logan's grim expression, at total odds to Pete's almost giddy smile. She felt like she was back with her parents while they discussed her as though she wasn't standing in the room. The familiar out-of-control feeling cooled the ardour she'd felt mere moments ago. Whatever they were plotting was pointless. It was already over, right? The hopes for a normal life were now about as easy to grip as the wisps of smoke from her dumpster fire of a previously private life. She'd officially entered the Twilight Zone. 'How can you spin this, exactly?' She nodded her head in Logan's direction and had to look away again the second she clocked his cheek muscles tic. It was both maddening and sexy, which was a pretty accurate description of the man as a whole. 'The news channels are already painting me to be some kind of sleazy hook-up. How are you going to fix that exactly? Those photos are out there forever now. They will follow me around. Patients will have seen them!' Her breath was puffing out in shaky huffs, her old friend anxiety ramping up to uncomfortable levels. 'I had a good reputation. Now the conference attendees are going to think I was... was...'

'Hooking up with me,' Logan huffed, his jaw tight with tension. *Je-sus. He had no right to make angry look so fine.* 'I get it, wildcat. You don't need to remind me. I'm a bad apple, and you're Eve.'

Pete shot her a smile that made a snake oil salesman look like the more honest bet. 'Good analogy, as it goes, but Adam is what we need to be aiming for. Which is why the two of you are going to work together. A united front. A partnership. No!' He was practically vibrating with excitement. 'A love match. We say that Logan was here for you. He came to Cornwall to spend the week with you. We tell them you've been dating a while. Casual, you know the drill. Dating on the down low. But the recent media attention caused problems between the two of you. Hell, I can even fabricate a little tiff, which would explain Logan's recent benders.' He started clicking his fingers in rapid succession. 'Yep, that works. Definitely puts a different slant on the bar-hopping amping up again since the season wrapped. It's juicy, lovelorn. It's perfect.' He was doing some kind of beautiful mind thing right now, not even talking to them. Chloe risked a glance Logan's way, and his guarded frown told her she wasn't far off the mark. 'This is the story. You've been casually dating under the radar. Super-secret, but the distance and both of you having demanding jobs, having to hide your relationship, it took its toll. You broke up, and Logan was heartbroken. We say that Logan hot-footed it here to win you back, and you're now back on track. Together again, trying to make it work because you missed each other. Cue the press barging in to your hotel room. The photos were the press encroaching on a tender moment, not some hotel hook-up.' He narrowed his eyes at Logan for that part. 'A committed relationship. Strong, solid. Young love's dream, all wrapped up in a doctor-meets-TV-doctor bow.'

'Love's young— Wait, what?' Chloe jabbed Logan in the arm. 'With him? You want me to go out, with him? Pretend we're together? No. Not a chance will people buy into that. He's been photographed in the press with other women!'

'Yes, but none of those women have ever come forward to say they were actually involved with Logan. We all know that photos don't always tell the true story. Without any of the women coming forward, we can definitely make this believable.'

'They wouldn't talk,' Logan seethed. 'Because I haven't been with any of them. Being in a club with me doesn't mean they were *with* me.'

'I'm not with you!'

'Well, I have seen you naked...' Logan's smirk made her want to jump out of the window. This couldn't be happening. People wouldn't buy it. Her stomach definitely was though, because his 'I've seen you naked' statement made it flip over. Shame it was caused by a man who infuriated her so much she was starting to question the whole 'do no harm' code. Once again, she felt the anxiety threatening to spill over and moulded it into venom.

'I will slaughter you,' she spat with gritted teeth. 'One more word...'

'Yeah, yeah. Scalpel, mysterious ways. You said.' He chuckled, running his hand down his jaw. She noticed his trademark clean-shaven look was looking a little worse for wear. Could it be that this scandal stuff actually bothered him? He didn't exactly look relieved about Peter's little plan either. She was used to being managed, but at least every decision wasn't pored over by complete strangers on the internet. People who didn't even know her judged her, but at least it was to her face. Logan had the world commenting on his every move. She couldn't imagine living his life. She hated any attention, and the little taste she'd had today had only confirmed that. It was all such a mess. Her parents and her sister had already called her half a dozen times, and she'd turned her phone to silent. She'd rather perform surgery on herself without anaesthesia than speak to any of them right now. Looking at Logan now, he looked a little... defeated. 'You have to be kidding with this, Pete. Even if the press did buy this, we can't pull it off. The two of us? It would never work, fake or otherwise. It's too much to ask.'

'My sentiments exactly,' Chloe huffed, feeling an odd sting in her chest at how alarmed Logan felt at this idea. Which was fine, because that was normal, right? She fancied him, of course, but he wasn't exactly in her league, right? She'd seen the women in the photos, and none of them looked like she did on one of the rare nights out she actually dressed up to go to. Film stars and her didn't exactly mix. What did she want, him to be happy about the prospect? She sure wasn't. Just because she'd seen him on her TV for years didn't mean she knew him any better than the readers of those articles did. And the way she was around him? She couldn't endure that for a whole week! She felt so weird around him. Uncharacteristically strong, with a side of sharp tongue. He made the hairs on her neck stand on end, and it was all kinds of frustrating. She found herself wanting to climb him like a damn tree and then verged between wanting to kiss his lips off or claw his stupid sexy eyes out. Confronting was a good way to describe it. Horny was another. The man was a walking, talking trigger for just about every part of her she didn't know existed. Trust the one person to pull her out of herself to be a man who was so different from her in every way imaginable. They were worlds apart in everything. It was a truly bad idea, because if she actually had to go through with this, she was going to combust – one way or another. 'No-one will believe this.'

Pete was vibrating with tension, his fingers flying across a tablet screen he'd produced from nowhere. 'Really? Well, someone obviously found out who you are, because look at the public reaction.'

He thrust the screen at them. Chloe's eyes narrowed in on the top hashtag on the site and fell silent.

#Dantefindslovedoctor

There were others too. Dirtier ones, most of them puns on bedside manner.

'There's so much of it,' she breathed, scrolling with increasing horror. 'Wow. Graphic too.' Some of the fantasies she'd had about Dante/Logan were mentioned by users, along with a few she hadn't even thought of.

'What?' Logan grabbed for the tablet, ignoring her returning swat as his eyes ran up and down the screen. 'Jesus. What's a reverse— Never mind. I get it.'

Chloe blushed furiously. 'Yeah, well, according to the internet, you're definitely getting it.'

Logan's head snapped to hers, and they held each other's eyes for a moment that felt far too sexually charged for the situation. She cleared her throat, crossing her arms over her waist to cover her discomfort. And her nipples, which currently felt like they were poking out of her clothing. Logan made a weird noise and licked at his lips before returning to scrolling.

'They seem to like the idea of us together.' He side-eyed Pete. 'They're really buying this? Yesterday I was a dick.'

'Only yesterday?' Chloe muttered under her breath, but Logan ignored her. 'It's just a hashtag.'

Logan snorted. 'It's a lot more than a hashtag, sweetheart. This stuff is out there.'

'Still.' She held up a finger at Logan to cut him off. The middle one. The sweetheart comment had worked well to tamp down her raging libido. He was gorgeous, till he opened his sexy mouth. She thought of her parents to remind herself that she needed to stay firm. Get out of this situation and Pete and Logan out of her room. 'It will be gone tomorrow. They'll move on eventually.'

Pete's grin was predatory. 'Maybe, but not without the damage following you both. We can make this benefit both of you if we play this right. This is the hot news item right now, and with the other stuff, it's going to leave a stain if we go silent. I've already had every media outlet worth a damn asking me for comment, an exclusive. Logan, I was coming here to fire you as my client, but actually, I think this is our ticket to the big time.'

'You were going to fire me?' Logan's voice was thin, reedy. 'For real?'

'I told you what would happen if you messed up again.' His gaze slid over to Chloe, who was looking between the two of them, trying to translate their conversation. She swallowed when his grin turned into a smirk. 'I think that an arrangement could be very beneficial to you both. I know you have a lot to prove this week, Doctor Henry.'

The pause before he fully named her had Chloe on instant high alert.

'Is that right?' she said, trying to feel him out. He couldn't know anything, could he? 'And what makes you think that? I thought you didn't know who I was?'

'Well, I wanted to see you in person first, before I said anything. I have my sources, and I know you have a lot riding on this week.'

Yeah, sources that had no doubt knew everything about her. Her family, why she was here. She hated that he was right. This week was her chance to prove herself, to show everyone what she was made of. If she made head of department, her family might just let up on her. Let her live her own life. Or that was the plan.

'I know how important this conference is for you, your career,' Peter continued. She couldn't help but glare at him. She knew he was going to be another person trying to control her. He had his client to protect, after all. He didn't care about her, just the way he could use her for his own ends. She swallowed down her irritation. Glancing across at Logan, she expected him to be gloating. He wasn't. He looked like he felt sorry for her. A flash of guilt tinging his sympathetic expression. She didn't know which was worse. 'We could help each other here, Doctor Henry.'

'Really.'

'Really. I know that this conference you're taking part in is important for your next step. Head of department at Manchester General?'

'How do you—'

Pete waved a hand at her. 'Oh please. Finding out about you was pretty easy. Committed to work, legacy child. No relationships. No real social media profile. My team spoke to a couple of people at the hospital you work at and they had a lot to say about you. Not a lot about a social life, but they did let us know about the job you've been working towards. This conference is your chance to prove yourself.' He pointed a finger at Logan, who was watching their exchange with a tight look. 'I think dating a megastar might just be the ticket. Imagine the good press for the hospital, with your face at the forefront. They'd be nuts not to hire you after this.'

'I... I...' *No way. Not a chance.* This was the exact opposite of what she wanted! Being here, getting this job, was supposed to be about her merits. Her talents in the job. Stepping out of her parents' shadow and coming into the light, on her own. 'I don't think getting pictured in a towel with television's man-whore of the moment will get me the promotion I've been working towards for the past few years.'

'Nice,' Logan cut in. 'Judgemental much?'

'Sorry,' she huffed. 'I can't help it. This whole thing is... a lot.' *You're a lot actually. Quit pushing all my buttons. Especially the one in my pants.* She shook her head, trying to focus and get her head out of the dirty thoughts swirling around her. Again. This man made her crazy in more ways than one. His eyes undressed her too much, body and mind. He hadn't just seen beyond the towel today. She had a feeling he'd looked right into her head for some insane reason. Which was bullshit, obviously. Did anyone see the real her? No. It was just the jarring mental image of having a living, breathing Dante Love in front of her, she tried to remind herself. She was still trying to dissect the two apart, working out which vein fed which artery. Either way, Logan Broderick was not the only issue here. He was just the latest obstacle standing in between her and the life she was desperately trying to live. 'I'm just... trying to get my head around this, but this is not a good thing for me, by any means.'

Her voice cracked, and she blinked hard to stop the frustrated tears from spilling out. 'I might as well go home. It's over. My bosses are all about keeping women in their place, and now this is all over the press, well – it's just not worth bothering any more.' She thought of Camilla, halfway around the planet and loving her life. Living her dreams on her own terms. Her photos a world away from the ones of Chloe plastered across the internet. 'Thanks for the nightmare, Pete, Logan, but I'm going home.'

She was halfway out of her seat when Logan's hand clamped onto her wrist. She was too distracted by the sparks that flew from his skin to hers to take her hand back.

'Wait,' he said, softer than she'd heard him speak before. 'You're really going to leave? It sounds like this job's important to you.'

'It is!' She almost sobbed but managed to pull herself together enough to pull away. 'It was, but it's done with now. I should have known better. I have no chance of being taken seriously now, and I'm damned if I'm going to spend the next week being the butt of their macho jokes. It was bad before, having to prove myself to people who were not worth my time, but now? It will be unbearable.' Logan's eyes on hers were the only thing stopping her from tearing up. That assessing look across his features folded into grim resignation.

'I think we should do it,' Logan rumbled. 'Pete, can we make this happen, for real?'

'What?' Chloe whipped her head around to Logan, but all she saw in his face now was steely determination. 'We can't do this. What are you talking about?'

'Look.' Logan claimed the spot next to her on the couch. His hand reached out to hers, which were now clasped tight on her lap. She watched the movement, bracing herself for the sparks that she knew would come. Found herself excited to feel his touch again, if only to prove the last time was a fluke. A trick of the mind caused by the stressful events of the morning. He stopped at the last minute, steepling them together instead. Her own hand twitched in response. 'This mess is kind of my fault. Let me fix it. Pete's right. If we spin this our way, we can both come out of it with what we want.'

'How? We don't even know each other! People will see straight through it.'

'Not with me behind the wheel.' Pete clapped his hands, grabbing the tablet. 'I can sort the hotel staff; cancel the room you had booked.'

'This was my room,' Logan interjected.

'Er, no. This was Chloe's room. Reception's mistake, it turns out. Henry, McHenry? You were booked a suite next floor up, but we'll get rid of your reservation under the fake name. Make it look like you were supposed to be here the whole time.' He held up a finger, stabbing the air. 'Ah! Got it. We'll leak that the suite booking was a ruse to fool the paps! More believable that way, especially if we're going for the whole Logan-coming-here-to-make-up-with-you narrative. People love a good love story, and it explains away why you were in here in the first place. Doctor Henry was mad about you partying, you came to make it up to her.' His eyes were gleaming with excitement. 'Logan Broderick changes party ways for the love of a good woman. Perfect.'

Logan and Chloe spoke together.

'That's terrible!'

'That's good, I suppose.'

They huffed at each other.

'We don't have a choice,' Logan mumbled. 'What about the photos? It looks a bit like we were panicked.'

'Oh course you were!' Pete squeaked. 'Picture it. You came here to surprise your girlfriend but the press got wind of it, ruined your romantic moment. We can make a point of that too, saying that they ruined a work event and that Chloe is understandably upset. You can make a statement, expressing your regret that Chloe was dragged into this and had her privacy violated. Show that protective alpha male side of you off. I'll write one, get it out there. In the meantime, the conference starts tonight, right? Drinks?'

Chloe was still reeling from her life being released in a statement when the words sank in. 'How do you... Oh, right. You're some kind of weird spy.'

'I got a copy of your itinerary, yes.' He turned to Logan. 'Drinks tonight, a few team-building events tomorrow and Sunday, followed by a few lectures and the presentations. There's an expo on Thursday, with exhibition stands, a lot of reps arriving for the day to plug their latest medical devices and whatnot.' He focused on Logan. 'Doctor Henry has a presentation on general surgery and modern advances versus the cost to the NHS and ways to streamline the process without turning to private care.' He nodded in her direction. 'Which, by the way, I enjoyed reading.'

Chloe reached for one of the few remaining cushions on the couch, gripping it tight. 'You... read my research paper?' *And enjoyed it?* She hadn't shown anyone that paper, because she knew they wouldn't see the merits. The people she was up against saw things a little differently. The fact Pete had enjoyed it gave her an oddly warm feeling, but she tried not to give it away to the men in the room. Which she was pretty solid at by now. Till she looked at Logan and caught the admiring smirk he covered with a press of his lips.

Pete shrugged like it was all in a day's work. 'On the helicopter.'

'What else do you know about me? My bra size?'

'You're 34—'

Logan grabbed the cushion just as Chloe threw her arm back to launch it. 'Er, Pete. Can you give us a minute?'

'Yeah, Pete,' Chloe called after his retreating form. 'Why don't you get your spies to have a rummage through my trash while you wait? Track my cycle or something!' The hotel door room closed, and Logan let out a breath. Dropping the cushion between them, he caught her eyeing it and threw it into the corner instead.

'Listen, I know Pete's a lot, but he means well.'

'A lot? That man makes MI5 look inept. We can't do this; no-one will believe it. I'll be even more of a laughing stock than I already am.'

'I don't think you're a laughing stock, wildcat.' His brows knitted together. 'Why wouldn't people believe it? It's not that far-fetched. The photos are out there. Pete can spin a good tale, let me tell you. He works with some of the biggest stars out there, and none of them are whiter than white. I think this could work. We're already here. You said yourself that we need to get control of this. I don't want to tank your job, and I have a lot riding on this. One more misstep and I'm done. Belinda will blackball me.'

'Belinda, as in Belinda from *Doctor Love*? The owner and creator?'

Logan stilled. 'I thought you didn't know the show.'

Shit. 'Like I said, I might have seen the odd headline. The hospital's not a black hole you know, we have television. She's been all over the news the last few days.' She risked a glance at him and regretted it when she saw the intense look he was shooting her. Like he was trying to work her out and failing. 'I take it her husband's shenanigans didn't go well with your... news.'

'Yeah,' he huffed. 'Went down like a lead balloon.' He ran a hand down his jaw, and she was taken back by how similar he looked to the man she saw on her TV screen. She knew that the industry was all make-up and good lighting, but seeing him in the flesh like this? Even with his tired eyes and frown lines, she could still concede that he looked good. Better than good in fact. It was very distracting. Like being in the room with the sun and trying not to get engulfed in its warmth. 'The truth is, wildcat, I kinda need this to work out. My career's on the line too, and I know you never asked for this but we're sort of stuck with each other.'

She reached for the last throw pillow and caught his wince. Hugging it to her, she gave herself a minute to think. The photos were out there. The whole world thought that she, Chloe Henry, the woman who didn't have a life outside of the OR, was dating one of the most recognised men on the face of the earth. Not only dating him, but from the snaps of her being smushed against him in a state of undress, having rather hot-looking sex too. *Funny, none of my Dante fantasies involving public embarrassment.*

The phone by the bed rang. The pair of them stilled.

'Pete already told the hotel to hold all calls,' Logan told her as he went over to look at the screen. 'It's reception.'

He held the phone to his ear but said nothing. Chloe heard her name, saw Logan's frown. He held the phone to his chest, covering the mouthpiece. 'Front desk said that your father's been calling you pretty insistently. He's threatened to come to the hotel if he doesn't speak to you soon.'

Great. Daddy dearest was being pushy, as per. The one

thing she didn't need was the Henry monkeys joining this circus. Their PR team made Pete look tame.

'He's on the line, holding,' Logan added. 'What do you want to do, Chloe?'

'I'll speak to him.'

The last thing she needed was her parents coming to Cornwall. She'd never get rid of them once they descended. Her father would be keynote speaker before the day was out. She couldn't afford for anything else to derail this week. Taking the phone from Logan, she steeled herself.

'Hello, you can put him through. Thank you.'

A couple of clicks came down the line.

'Chloe, what the hell is going on? The news is full of pictures of you, half-naked with some halfwit?'

She jumped, covering the phone with her hand. Logan made an indignant huffing sound from the couch. When she shot him a glance, he mouthed 'Me, a halfwit?' at her. She mouthed 'Sorry' back, and turned away, cheeks flaming.

'Dad...'

'You told us not to come to the conference because you wanted to do this yourself. You could have been in a private hospital by now, running a department, but we allowed you to go your own—'

'Dad, I—'

'...if you are there to just play around with that fella, then you could have warned us, Chloe—'

'Dad! Would you let me talk?' The silence was sudden and disapproving. She never spoke back to him. Ever. 'It's not what you think. Logan is...' Logan is what? *A colossally sexy pain in my posterior? A stranger who saw me naked?* 'Well, he's...'

'He's a joke, that's what he is, my girl. I googled him. The man wouldn't know fidelity if it smacked him in the face. He's not our kind of people.'

'Our kind of people? Dad, he's a successful man. Sure, he's not a doctor, but many people aren't.' There he went again, passing judgement on everyone around him like some kind of god. She was sick of craning her neck to look up at Mount Olympus, seeing her family look down their noses at everyone down below. 'You don't know him, Dad.' *And neither do I, but he's at least trying to be nice about this.*

'I don't need to know him, Chloe. I can glean enough from what the press has to say. What kind of message do you think this shows the board? Cavorting about with an actor?' He said 'actor' with the same level of disgust that one would say 'serial killer'.

'Dad, it's not like that, okay? I got here today, and—'

'I don't care about the specifics,' her father boomed. 'End it. Now.' *End it? He... Dad believes we're together? This might be the most surprising thing to happen today, and that's saying something.* 'This is not the Henry way, and you know better. We will not allow you to shame the name any more, Chloe. It ends now. All of it.'

Chloe flinched at his tone. Every little thing she had done in her life. Every little part of her studying, her childhood. It was all for the show of it. All for the legacy of the damn Henry empire. She wasn't allowed to go drinking with her friends, or even have friends other than the ones deemed good enough. Hell, she'd escaped to Manchester from London to try to get some separation, but it wasn't enough. It would never be enough. When she looked Logan's way, he was staring right back, and she knew he'd heard every word. Had listened to the way her own father had spoken to her and ridiculed him. Neither of them had asked for this. She might not be happy about the situation, but at least Pete and Logan were trying to help find a solution instead of playing the blame game she was so sick of playing. The embers of irritation in the pit of her stomach flared to blue flame.

'Dad, last time I checked my love life was my own affair.'

'Not any more. Not when it's on the front page of every gossip rag, my girl.'

'I'm not your girl, Dad.' She glanced up at Logan as he came to stand by her side. 'I'm a grown woman.'

'Well,' her father retorted, 'maybe you should act like it. Your sister would never do anything like this, she—'

'Oh, golden Liz? Of course she wouldn't! She's too busy trying to be the next zit-popper influencer!' Logan made a strange noise that almost sounded like a snort.

'In her own private clinic! And she doesn't do it naked! I really don't like this tone of yours, Chloe. Talking back? I bet this is his influence. You would never have—'

Logan took the phone right out of her hand. She could still hear her father ranting away as Logan put the phone to his ear.

'Mr Henry, Logan Broderick. I can't say I like the tone you're using with my girlfriend. Chloe is here to work. The press stuff, that's on me. I would appreciate it if you didn't speak to her like that. Even a halfwit like me can take offence, and we both know that Chloe is a very smart woman. We'll speak to you after the conference, which I am sure you won't wish to attend. I do have some friends in the press, I can assure you, and I wouldn't want them to hear about this little conversation. My girlfriend will be in touch when she's ready to speak to you again.'

He slammed the phone down, chest heaving. Chloe didn't speak or move. She just watched Logan run a hand down his jaw. His hands were shaking, his face stony. The change in him was profound. All traces of the annoyingly chirpy man she'd

been thrown together with all day was gone. This guy was...
brooding. Masterful. And hot? Amplified, to the power of ten.
Taking charge of her father like that? Even Dante Love might
have balked at that challenge.

The sigh he released came from the very depths of him. 'I'm
sorry,' he started, turning to face her. 'I just didn't like the way
he was... Oof!'

He barely stayed upright as she barrelled into him,
squeezing him tight.

'Thank you. For doing that. He's... difficult.'

'Difficult is probably the nicest way you could describe
him,' Logan rumbled. She was about to pull away when she felt
his arms close around her, holding her to him. She felt the solid
warmth around her and couldn't help herself. She leaned into
it. Held in a cat-like purr when one hand stroked along the
length of her back, leaving a trail of heat in its wake. 'I'm sorry I
caused this for you, Chloe. I really am. This is not your mess,
and you got dragged into it. I shouldn't have stepped in then,
but you didn't deserve that.'

'I never do. It's just the Henry way.'

'Yeah, well.' Logan didn't sound happy. 'I hate bullies.
Always have. I'll speak to Pete, see what we can do. Maybe I
could still do an interview or something. Clear things up. I'll
take the hit. It won't be pretty, but it will get you out of this.'

'It's too late for that. Pete will fire you.'

'Yeah, well, maybe not.' He didn't sound convinced. 'It was
an accident. He believes that at least. It will probably cost me
the film though.'

'Doctor Love is getting a film?' She'd heard them talking
about it, but it hadn't really registered till now. She hadn't read
anything about it on the fan pages.

'No, er... there was this role in a World War Two epic

coming up. I was being considered for the lead. A soldier trying to survive the war, get back home to his girl. That's sort of why I'm here. To learn my lines and keep a low profile. Ride out the media storm.'

She pulled away, looking up at him. He only released her enough to let her meet his eye, and her stomach flipped over when his hand resumed its comforting stroking. She could see the sadness in his eyes, and she realised for the first time that she wasn't the only one with real dreams to lose.

'You want it, don't you.' His eyes widened at her choice of wording, his hand momentarily stuttering to a stop. 'The film, I mean.'

He smiled ruefully, his eyes softening at the corners. 'I did, but that's not your problem, it's mine.' His gaze dropped to her lips, just for a moment, before sliding back to meet her eye. 'It was kind of nice having a beautiful girlfriend, you know. The public aren't wrong, you are something special.'

She rolled her eyes, smiling despite herself. *He thinks I'm beautiful?* 'I'm sure you've had plenty of those in your time, Broderick.'

'No,' he murmured, his face serious. 'None like you, Doc. A woman like you would never give me the time of day.'

Her heart thudded in her chest at his words. She wondered whether he could feel it. Hear it, since it was pounding so loud in her own ears. He really had no idea of how many women would kill to be in his arms right now. Good women. Most of the nurses she worked with adored him, and they weren't the type to try to hang off his shoulder in clubs. They were smart, accomplished. Heck, if she wasn't so annoyed by him, she would be the first in line. He wasn't what the media made him out to be. He was much more than that. She found herself wanting to tell him that, but he resumed his rhythmic stroking again, and the words died in her throat.

'It's a shame really. I think—'

'Hope you're decent!' Pete strode back into the room, knocking pointlessly as he came bounding in, phone in hand. They sprang apart, Logan's now free hand clenching as he turned to glare at his agent.

'Too soon, Pete, and you're supposed to knock *before* you come in.' His voice was oddly deep, a sharp contrast to the soft almost-whispers of a moment ago.

'Sorry.' Pete didn't look it. 'I just wanted to let you know everything is ready to go, if you are. Doctor Henry, did you make a decision?'

Chloe knew she should take the out. The truth was the truth, after all. It had been a simple room mix-up. People would believe it, or most would. The rest would die down, eventually. She'd still be a laughing stock at the conference. It wouldn't erase the photos, and her father wouldn't let up. He'd find some way to blame her. And Logan would take the brunt. He'd already said he would. She knew his history with the press. The way they'd documented his private life lately. If he had come here to lay low, it had backfired for him spectacularly. He wasn't in charge of his life any more than she was, she realised. They were both puppets, neither in charge of their own strings. She stepped closer to Logan.

'Do you always have this kind of pressure?'

Logan winked at her. Behind his gesture, she could see the tightness around his mouth. The tiredness around his eyes. He reminded her of something she saw in herself, in the mirror. 'Pressure? Nah. Everyone knows I'm just a slutty halfwit.'

Slutty halfwit or not, he'd gone to bat for her with her father. No-one, not her mother or her perfect sister, had ever done that. Any potential boyfriends had run off at the first sign of trouble. Logan hadn't hesitated to stand in her corner. Maybe someone should stand in his. If they both used each other to get what they needed out of this, maybe it would be worth it. If she could stop getting irritated and turned on in his presence, that was. The parts of him that were Dante Love, the softer, protective side, were hot. The other side – the arrogance, the annoying golden retriever energy? That would take work, but it was only for a week. She'd suffered through worse in far less attractive packages. Perhaps having him around for the conference might just make it bearable. Besides, after what she'd seen, she wasn't entirely convinced that the overly cocky bravado wasn't just another act for the masses. She knew a little something about cladding fake armour around herself to face the world and its assumptions.

'I'll do it,' she told Pete. 'For the week at least, till the conference is over. We can tell people the press broke us up or something down the line.'

'Chloe, you don't have to.' Logan ignored Pete's frantic shushing, blocking his view by coming to stand closer. 'It's a lot to ask.'

'I know, but this whole thing is a mess. If we tell the truth, then not everyone will believe it. At least if my colleagues think it was a private moment between a couple, it's better than the alternative.' She bit her lip. 'I'm working in a boys' club environment, Logan. My parents are friends with them all. I don't want to have things handed to me, and I don't want them to treat me like some dolly bird either. Most of these guys have families, people back home. I don't have the biggest personality at work.' She chewed her lip. 'Anywhere, really. Maybe a partner in the limelight might just make them notice me for once. It's the opposite of what I want, but let's face it – I probably wasn't going to win anyway. Maybe this way I can at least get them to listen.'

The clench of his jaw was the only reply he gave. Peter clapped his hands together behind them.

'Excellent! Now we're in agreement, I'll get going. In the meantime, the conference has a mixer event tonight. Get ready, Logan, I checked with the conference organisers, and they were happy to accommodate you.'

He ignored Pete, his eyes firmly on Chloe's.

'You're sure about this? Really? It's not going to be easy.'

'Nope,' she admitted, trying to ignore the way her body reacted to his proximity. 'But we both have things to salvage. I think we have to try.' She folded her arms. She hadn't spoken to her father like that in her whole life. Something about this man brought out a side of her that she couldn't help but love. Maybe spending a little more time with him, even under these circumstances, might just be worth enduring. For their careers, it was worth a shot, right? Those photos did sound a lot better the way Pete was planning to spin them. One week and then they could go back to their own lives. 'Those photos are going to follow both of us around if we pull the plug now. Pete's way, as much as I hate it, makes sense.'

'I knew I liked you.' Pete grinned. They both ignored him.

'I can handle it if you can. One week. We do the conference, and then it's over. I get my promotion, you get your film.'

'And what if we drive each other crazy in the meantime?' he asked, and her heart did that stupid trippy thing again. If she wasn't a doctor, she might have worried.

'Oh, we definitely will, but we both know we don't really have a choice.'

'Well.' Logan shrugged, his face slowly reverting back to its usual happy-go-lucky grin. 'Looks like we have our first date, wildcat.'

She groaned, which only made him chuckle. A week. She could survive his charms and not murder him for a week, right?

'I am so going to regret this, and don't call me wildcat.'

He grinned, laying back on her couch like a conquering king. Pete was already talking into his phone, tapping away on his tablet.

'Whatever you say, Doc. We can work on the pet names later.'

Chloe fired another cushion, laughing when it hit him square in the junk.

5

The crowd gathered around him at the bar was in raptures. It was... bizarre. Whatever he was saying to them, they were all lapping it up. *Perhaps making him go first before her entrance wasn't the best idea after all.* Chloe took another gulp of the champagne she was cradling, praying it would do something to drown the nervous butterflies that were currently doing the samba in the pit of her stomach. She made the mistake of looking back at the crowd, and Logan's eyes locked with hers. *Shit. This is it. Operation Fake Relationship is a go.* If she could manage not to vomit, it would be fine, right?

'Darling!' he half boomed, striding across to her. The crowd parted like the Red Sea, and he was in front of her in a couple of steps.

'Moses,' she muttered, which elicited a frown from him.

'What are you doing over here on your own?' His grin was lopsided and positively devilish as he leaned in. She was about to step back when she felt his hands grasp her hips. His fingers were warm and strong against her black slacks. *Damn it. Sparks.* 'Come and join us.' He dipped his knees, and she couldn't stop the shudder that erupted down her spine as his lips brushed the spot just below her ear. 'Are you really wearing that, Doc?' he whispered. 'You look like an accountant.'

And the shudder died, leaving a rod of indignant steel behind. The irritating persona was out in full force tonight, and it did not float her boat. Except it did, because she still remembered his touch, the way she felt in her arms. The protective way he'd told her father where to go. This week was going to feel like forever.

Smiling for the crowd that was watching them, she leaned up, ignoring the rush of wings in her gut as the smell of him enveloped her senses. He smelled... woodsy, male. It was not what she was expecting. Not that she'd thought about it, but didn't celebs usually smell different? Like, money or something? The scent emanating from him was less runway and more log-cabin hero. Logan smelled like, well, how she'd imagined Wolverine would smell like aside from the suit sweat. It was jarring, to say the least. Sharing a room with him with *that* scent was going to be an experience. Still, given that this was already the week from hell, she could roll with it. The fact her fake boyfriend smelled nice was way down on the list of problems. She shook her head to clear the fog. Readjusted her armour. Met him putdown for putdown, which was seemingly their go-to move when things got awkward.

'And you look like a dick, so at least one of us is on brand, eh?'

'Ouch, Doc. Remind me to teach you some better comebacks, eh? I look fire.'

Chloe made a retching noise at the back of her throat. 'And sound like a tween.'

'Careful,' he murmured, his voice deep and close. 'Your snark is showing, and you're supposed to be mad for me, remember?' Before she could answer, he hooked an arm around her waist and pulled her with him back to the bar.

'Sorry, guys, I wanted to keep this one all to myself for a minute.' She felt his hand squeeze against her hip, the warmth from his palm. Her stupid body leaned into it eagerly. As she kept her gaze, and her smile, carefully trained on looking like this was a normal day, she was shocked to see the faces around her. They were... smiling, enraptured. *So this is what it feels like to be on the arm of a superstar.* Some of the greatest minds of medicine, and they were all positively fawning over Logan. As she sneaked a glance up at him, he locked eyes with her, shot her a cheeky wink. *Such long, dark lashes.* She looked away, focused on a lapel of one of the doctors across from her. He was wearing a little pin on it, and she stared at the emblem till her eyes blurred. 'So.' Logan suddenly announced brightly. 'Let's enjoy the festivities, eh, chaps?'

Festivities was not the word to describe the evening. Being the first night, it was a mixer dinner. Which meant that everyone was basically stuffed into one large ballroom and plied with food and drink. Usually, she would have melted into one of the corners of the room and just got through it; socialising wasn't exactly her favourite thing. Had she been able to leave and go home, she would already have been planning her exit. Impossible, with Mr Charisma on her arm. He was like a flashy compère, so much so that she kept expecting him to flip his jacket inside out, to produce a sequined coat of many colours. He was more Dante Love here than the Logan she'd glimpsed before. She wondered who the real version was; whether or not he knew himself. More to the point, did she? Looking around the room at her peers, had she really ever truly fit in here? At work, sure – she had the nursing staff, and the patients. They were her focus, her reason for all the hard work, getting up in the morning and facing the day. These types of events, however, always made her feel like some kind of imposter, an interloper even. It seemed it didn't matter how much work she put in, or how many qualifications she got, growing up she had always been the one who felt like she didn't pass muster.

They did their bit, chatting their way around the room until her feet ached and her jaw tingled from all the smiling. Eventually, she'd drifted away while Logan held court with a fawning crowd. She'd needed a hot minute to gather herself. Get away from the woodsy scent and clear her head. This week was going to be awful. She had a hard enough time functioning at these things on a normal week. Now, on the arm of Dante Love, she just felt deflated. The old familiar feeling of being a lesser being was smarting, to say the least. Around her family growing up, she was used to it, but this week – she'd wanted things to be different. Was it ridiculous to hope for a chance to show what she was made of? She needed to wow people, get the job and maybe then she could silence the critics. And the critic inside her, the one who whispered in her ear that maybe she wasn't living life for herself at all. Sighing, she plucked another champagne glass from the table she was skulking by and half drained it.

'Hey,' a smooth voice said at the side of her.

'Hi,' she muttered. 'Having fun?'

Logan picked up a glass of champagne, brushing his arm against her shoulder as he came to stand next to her. She was still getting over how tall he was. He looked shorter on TV somehow.

'I am actually, it's not half as bad as I thought it was going to be. Fun, even.'

'Fun,' she scoffed. 'Really.'

'Really.' He turned, fixing her with a piercing look. 'It's interesting. Being around so many real-life doctors. I mean, we have consultants who work on the show, but you guys are out there, doing it every day. It's different.'

'Well, it's certainly that. Often a lot more mundane too, than your show.'

His brow quirked. 'My show, that you said you've never watched?'

Shit. 'Well, I've seen adverts.' She pointedly ignored his knowing grin. 'It's not exactly accurate, I heard. Medically.'

He shrugged. 'Well, like I said, we have consultants, but some of them are not exactly up on the current medicine.' He waggled his eyebrows. 'Plus, if all we were doing was lancing boils every episode then people would soon change the channel. They love the drama, the life-and-death stuff, you know.'

That was true enough. *Doctor Love* was pretty dramatic. It kept her watching every week even when she spent half of it screaming at the screen when they used the wrong jargon for a procedure or broke patient confidentiality to add more brevity to a plotline. Her train of thought stuttered to a stop when his lips dipped close to her ear.

'Besides, the romance is what the fans really watch it for.'

She laughed softly, hoping it would cover the weird little shiver his hot breath had elicited. 'Don't get me started on that. I swear those medical dramas portray us lot as horny little devils, shagging all over the hospital.'

He gasped, a mocking little sarcastic intake of breath.

'You mean they don't?'

She shook her head, rolling her eyes at his melodramatic reply. 'Nope.'

'So you've never...'

The blush was so quick her cheeks were aflame before she

could stop it. 'No! I haven't! Not that it's any of your business, anyway.'

'Well, as your boyfriend—'

'You are not my—'

He put his finger to his lips. 'As your boyfriend, it's only right that we have the ex-talk, right?'

She looked down at her watch, almost spilling the rest of her champagne on the floor.

'Well, we only have a week, so going through yours might be a push.'

She saw his face fall as he looked away. The hard swallow of his throat through his open shirt. Waited for the stab of triumph to hit her. It never came. She didn't know why he pushed her buttons so much. Her filter and guard were both useless around him. Her tongue was loose around him like no other person. It didn't mean she should be so mean, though. She knew what barbs did to a person. Nudging his arm with hers, she waited till he looked back at her.

'Sorry. That was harsh.'

He pursed his lips. 'It's fine. Used to it. It just occurred to me that you might have dated someone here. I know medical professionals spend a lot of time together. Things happen.' He thrust his tongue into his cheek. 'Figured you knew my dating history, or the press's version of it. It might seem off if there's someone here from your past that a boyfriend didn't know about.'

'Good point,' she replied, sheepishly contrite. 'If it's any consolation, my love life would fit on the back of a postage stamp. In capital letters, with a Sharpie.' She saw the moment the light flashed into his eyes again. Regretted snuffing it out in the first place. They were stuck in this together, whether they liked it or not. He had just as much to lose as she did. Professional suicide awaited them both if this didn't work out. 'I am sorry for the little snipes. I get defensive when I feel cornered. I usually go quiet and rant to myself in the mirror when I get home, but around you I just let it rip.'

'Wildcat,' he teased. 'Are you saying I bring out the fire in you?' She snort-laughed, covering it far too late by clamping her mouth shut. 'Wow.' He grinned. 'I really do make you react. What was that?'

'Nothing,' she squeaked, ignoring it entirely. 'You are annoying, but I was out of line.'

'It's okay.' His jaw clenched, the muscle ticking in his cheek. 'It's what everyone thinks about me anyway. This lot too, probably.' A small smile crossed his features, turning him from sullen back to beautiful in an instant. It was her swallowing hard now, pushing the shock of attraction down to the pit of her gut. Imagining it being digested by the acid in her stomach. 'Kinda funny, if you think about it. Of all the hotel rooms to walk into' – he fixed his gaze on hers – 'you had to walk into a man-whore's. Ironic, really, that my agent thinks I'm the solution to your problem, eh?'

Did he really think that about himself? He'd never seemed bothered by the interview questions she'd seen in the past. If anything, he seemed to embrace the role. This was another piece that didn't quite fit in the puzzle that was Logan Broderick. Was the bravado really just that? The way he'd stuck up for her with her dad kept sticking in her brain. This man was someone with value.

'It was *my* room, and I don't know about that,' she countered, drawing in a breath and reaching for his hand. 'I mean, the whole room is half in love with you. That's some pretty good street cred for a certified and proud nerd like me. Come on. Let's do another lap and then escape. Those hors d'oeuvres were tiny. Room service has some pretty nice-sounding burgers on the menu.'

She winked at him, making his lips twitch up at the corners. His fingers wrapped around hers without hesitation, at odds with the confusion on his face. 'What are you doing, Doc?'

She pulled him closer. 'Well, Mr Broderick, I'm showing off my boyfriend.' Nodding over her shoulder, she grinned. 'The cameras over there? They use them for the promos, and since the paparazzi are not allowed in here, we can use them to get you some medical street cred. Belinda and Pete would be happy with that, right? Dante Love in a real medical publication? You in?'

His eyes crinkled at the corners, and she wondered for a moment how his co-stars managed to get their lines out with his face staring back at them.

'Lead the way, Doctor Nerd.'

* * *

'That's so good.'

'I know. Jesus, I can't get enough.' Logan took another huge bite of cheeseburger, moaning at the taste. Chloe shoved a chip in her mouth to cover up her blush at the noise he just made. 'Wow.' He sighed, wiping the relish from the corner of his mouth with a napkin. 'I never get why they serve up such tiny things at events.'

'Because they want you to fill up on booze probably.'

'True. I went to the British Television Awards last year, and the biggest thing they served was bruschetta. I swear, it was the size of a fifty-pence piece. I had to eat about ten of the things before I even got a taste.' He pointed at his half-eaten burger. 'If they served these, I think people would be a lot happier.'

'Yeah, but a doorstep-sized burger isn't exactly portable. Or couture-friendly. Some of those outfits look pretty hard to move around in.'

'Yeah, and half of those people don't eat burgers, trust me. I like that you eat.'

'Oh, I don't usually. At work I tend to only eat salads.' His affronted grimace made her laugh. 'What?'

'A salad? You're a surgeon, right? You need the energy!'

'Well, in my family we were brought up to always be elegant when eating in public.' She paused, replaying her own words. 'Huh. I never really thought about it that way. I guess it just stuck. Wow. I've been drinking the Kool-Aid more than I thought.' *Seeing things through Logan's eyes, it's... eye-opening.*

'I don't know about that, but I do think it's kinda nuts to deprive yourself just to please others. Everyone needs a bit of fun in their lives. And a good burger. I learned a long time ago that you can't please everyone.'

'Yeah, well. Welcome to the Henry family. Everything is about perception to them.'

'But you want to do your own thing, right? Even though you are a doctor too. Did you get a choice in that?'

She twirled a chip between her fingers. 'If I'm honest, not really, but it is what I wanted to do. I just want to help people who really need it, you know? My family are all about the private sector, which is all well and good, but you only have to look at other countries to see that we are so lucky to have the NHS. I see people all the time who would not survive if we privatised the system, and it worries me. I want to make a difference in the system, not work outside of it. My family don't really get that, and they kind of see it as more of a business. It's in my blood, so I never felt like my job was chosen for me as such. I would have become a doctor anyway, but being a surgeon was my choice definitely. I find the human body fascinating, and I love my patients. I gel better with the nurses, but I think that's because they treat me better. They are not as intimidated by the Henry name, for a start. Nurses are no nonsense; they treat you like you treat them.'

'They see the real you. That's important.'

She nodded, feeling a weird kind of kinship with the man in front of her. He kept showing her these glimpses of the man behind the megastar. Parts she wanted to cut open and examine closer. They weren't so worlds apart as she'd once thought.

'So, who sees the real you?' she asked, wanting to peek a little closer to what he'd alluded to during the time they'd spent together.

'Me?' She almost saw the moment he gripped the mask closer to his face, resented it. 'Half the world knows who I am. I've been acting since I was a teenager.'

'Yeah, but is that the real you? I can't seem to get a true read.' *Never a truer word spoken.*

'On what, me?' His eyes zeroed in on hers.

'Yeah. I've been with you a day, and I've seen so many sides of you.'

'Sides of me?' He put his burger down on his plate. 'Today wasn't exactly my best day.'

'I know, but the way you took charge with my father was very different to how you were down in that ballroom.'

'I told you, I don't like bullies.'

'You think my dad bullies me?' Bullying was a strong word. Not one that was usually associated with her family either. They were pushy, sure. Immovable, definitely. But bullies? She wanted to dispute the point, but she thought of how her parents tried to run her life. Pointed out her perceived failings constantly. Even her sister, with the Botox thing the other day.

All well-meaning to her, but it sure didn't make her feel that way. Bullying wasn't a word she'd even considered before now. She bit at her lip, feeling Logan's keen gaze. 'I... You really think that's what he does?'

'You think he doesn't?'

'Well, no. Maybe – I... don't know. It's just his – their way, I guess. My father is used to getting his own way, in all aspects of his life, including his family.' She released the sigh that had built up in her chest since the phone call.

'I gathered that when I spoke to him. He was pretty quiet when I spoke my mind.'

'That's because no-one speaks to him that way. He won't take kindly to how you spoke to him. It's a good thing he won't be here this week.' She let out another sigh, shoving the chip into her mouth. 'For both of us.'

'You should stand up to him more, I think you held your own.'

'That's the thing,' she huffed, sagging back on the couch. 'I never answer back. I've always done what they ask. The only time I've ever gone against them was when I took the job at Manchester General. My mother and father didn't speak to me for a full month.' She couldn't stop the smile that burst out of her. 'It was the best time.'

Logan chuckled. 'See, there's the wildcat.'

'I hate that nickname, for the record.'

'Doc it is then. We should get some sleep. Any idea what the team-building exercise is tomorrow?'

'Not a clue. It just said to wear sportswear. Which means we are about to see a lot of middle-aged men in tracksuits.'

'Nice. Are you sporty?'

'I run sometimes, but usually it's when I need to work off stress. Did you hear anything else from Pete?'

The news had been full of the two of them. Logan's statement had caused some fans to call out the media, which was good, but it also meant that they were still awash with news of their new relationship.

'He emailed a while ago, just to remind us to keep the details of how we fake-met under our hat. You know, to play into the whole private relationship thing. Our insistence of privacy. It will blow over soon, I promise.'

'I hope so. I need my presentation to go well. I'm pretty sure my parents will have me kidnapped and shipped to Harley Street if this doesn't come off.'

'I won't let that happen. I will fix this, Chloe. I know you didn't ask for this chaos.'

'Thanks.' She felt shy all of a sudden. When he called her Chloe in that soft, kind tone, it tore at her armour. He was being so supportive, protective even. It was so new to her and surprisingly endearing. Having Logan Broderick in her corner made her feel a type of way she had never encountered before. She pushed her swirling emotions down, focused on the practicalities. 'Are you going to be okay on the couch? It's a little small.'

Logan was well over six foot tall. There was no way he was going to fit on the tiny couch. They both knew it, but he just nodded and took another bite of his burger.

'Goodnight, Doc. I'll see you in the morning.'

'Night, Logan.' She paused in the archway to the bedroom. 'You know, you're not going to fit on that thing.'

'I know. I'll just sleep on the floor.'

'The floor?'

'Yeah. I'll just pull the cushions off or something. I'd call down for a cot, but they would probably tell the press.'

'What if housekeeping come in and see that we're sleeping separately?' She looked back at the bed. She knew the obvious answer, but the solution blurted out of her mouth before she could process what it meant. 'We should just share the bed; make it look real.'

He stilled before answering. 'You don't have to do that. They won't know.'

Housekeeping might though. They would be cleaning the room this week, and given their jobs, they could easily smell a set-up.

'Well, the porter tipped off the press, so I'm not sure we can trust the staff here. It's not like we're the only people who will have access to the room.'

Logan bit at his lip. 'That's a good point.' He looked towards the bedroom. 'Are you sure?'

Am I sure that sleeping in the same bed as my TV crush is a bad idea? Yep. 'If we do this, I think we should make it look as real as possible. If we get found out now it would be worse, right? It's fine. We're adults, right? It's just sleeping next to each other.'

'If you're sure.' He didn't look convinced, but she just gave him a nod and headed for the bathroom. 'Thanks for this, Doc. I mean it. You're really saving my ass with this.'

'That's what fake girlfriends are for!' she trilled, sagging behind the bathroom door the second she closed it. 'Jesus, this is not happening. Why did you say that. Oh, Logan,' she said, mimicking herself. 'Share a bed with me. It will be fine.' Pulling out the sleepwear from one of the bags she'd left in there, she got to work. 'Of course you packed the most unflattering PJs in the history of the universe, Chlo. Well done.' She grabbed a brush and ran it through her hair, wincing at the little panda bears on her sleep short set. 'You look like a twelve-year-old on a sleepover. Sexy.'

She brushed her teeth and tried to pull herself together. He was just a man. A hot man, sure. A man she'd had the odd

dream over, of course. Lots of women had, and given that half
the time she passed out on the couch watching him on TV, it was
inevitable, right? His voice narrating her dreams was perfectly
normal. There was science behind the phenomenon. Which she
knew, because she'd looked it up. Regardless, she could do this.
Had to do this. It was just sharing a bed. *A bed that would smell
like him.* Part of the ruse, which would be over in a week. *A week
of trying not to accidentally brush against his solid, muscular body in
the night.* After that, she'd be back home with her cat, and this
would be like a weird fever dream. *Yep, if you survive the week
without bursting into horny flames of unfulfilled long-hidden desire.*

'You can do this, Chloe Henry. You're a fricking strong independent woman.'

'You talking to yourself in the mirror, Doc?'

Crap on a cracker. 'No! Just er... singing.'

'Oh... uh... okay. Cool. Well... I'm in bed, it's safe to come
out.'

'O-kay!' she squeaked, pulling a face at herself in the mirror.
'You're an idiot,' she whispered to herself. 'Get your shit
together!'

The bedroom was dark when she entered. 'Hell of a lot of
cussing in your singing, Doc. Cute PJs.'

Saying something snippy back would have been her next
move, but Logan Broderick was in her bed bare chested. The
light from the half-closed window behind the bed illuminated
him like a damn Greek god as he lay there with one arm behind
his head, looking like he didn't have a care in the world. It took
all of her focus to cross the room and pull back the covers
without falling flat on her face or stubbing her toe on the bed
frame.

'I've set an alarm, that okay with you?' His voice was soft, but she couldn't bring herself to look at him as she settled down under the covers.

'That's great, thanks,' she murmured, trying to stop her breathing coming out all... breathy. 'Do you snore?'

'Um...' He sounded far too amused by the question. 'I don't know.'

'You don't know?'

'Nope. Haven't really done this, so I guess no-one ever told me whether I do or not, Doc.'

'You've never had a sleepover?'

Even in the dark, she could see he was trying not to laugh. Probably because she'd just referred to sharing a bed as a sleepover. 'A sleepover? We're not twelve, Doc, despite the fact you're wearing little endangered animals on your PJs. I've never slept overnight with a woman. Not like this. So I don't know if I snore. Do *you* snore?'

'Nope. Not that I know of.' She was feeling stupid for even asking the question in the first place. 'I've not exactly done this before either.' She felt him turn her way and risked a glance. His head was on the pillow right next to her. She caught a whiff of his aftershave. There it was again, that woodsy scent.

'I guess we're both virgins then,' he rumbled back. Her stomach somersaulted at the double entendre, waking up her dormant snark.

'I will throw another pillow.'

He chuckled.

'Sorry. I don't even know why I asked.'

'It's okay. I get it. I can still sleep on the couch if you feel uncomfortable.'

'No, it's fine.' She sighed. 'I don't feel uncomfortable. It's just... weird.'

'I get it. I feel a bit weird too, doing this.'

'Weird is an understatement. We met today and so far you've seen me in the nude, we've had a fight and been outed to the media, pretended to be a couple at a dinner, and now we're essentially living together for a whole week.' She turned to lay on her back, feeling a bubble of mirth ripple through her body. 'Oh God. Saying that out loud' – she giggled – 'it's...' Another giggle burst out of her. 'It's crazy! And you even spoke to my dad and told him off! I mean...' She couldn't speak, and the next minute they were both laughing their heads off.

'You know,' he said when they'd finally stopped chortling. 'You're pretty fun when you're not being uptight.'

'Oh yeah.' She chuckled. 'Well, you're pretty nice when you're not being a jackass.'

'I think there's a compliment in there somewhere.'

'Don't let it go to your big head, Broderick. I still think people will suss us out before the week is out.'

'Maybe.' He nodded, and when she turned his way, he was already watching her. 'But we can try.'

She looked into his brown eyes and saw the vulnerability behind his easy smile.

'Yeah,' she agreed. 'We can try. Goodnight, jackass.'

His teeth shone in the moonlight. It was the most beautiful thing she'd ever seen.

'Night, Doc. Sleep tight.'

Oh, she planned to. Sleeping in the same bed as him all night. She was pretty sure she was going to spend the night coiled like a spring.

6

The sun was already high in the sky when they headed to the beach behind the hotel the next day.

'This is beautiful.' Logan smiled, looking out at the water. 'Honey, it's gorgeous, right?'

'It is.' She grinned as he pulled her closer. They were standing on the edge of a group of tracksuit-clad people, all eyeing the boxes set out on the sand as if they were waiting for a cadaver to jump out. 'Can you quit with the honey stuff? You're making me nauseous,' she said out of the corner of her mouth. Which also helped to quell the scent of him in her nostrils. The man was entirely lickable, and after spending most of the night tossing and turning, her ability to stay professional and maintain the loved-up façade was decidedly blurry.

'What's the matter, Doc, you don't like being called honey? We have to be believable, remember?'

'Believable, sure, but I am here to work, remember? I'm not really a honey kind of girlfriend.'

'Okay, fine. I'll work on the terms of endearment.' He looked around, quirking a brow. 'So, is this what they want you to do for team building? Beach games?' He motioned to the other doctors, who were standing around talking. 'Half of these guys look like they never see sunlight, let alone exercise. You sure you don't want me to be part of this? I could ask?'

'No,' she hissed from the corner of her mouth. 'There's hardly any partners here, it would look weird. You should go back to the hotel, read your script or something.'

'Well, I don't have to—'

'Good morning!' A very chipper man wearing shorts and a polo shirt with the hotel's logo emblazoned on it stepped near the net, holding a microphone. 'I'm Des, the hotel's activity co-ordinator, and I'll be hosting today's survival games!' He waggled a clipboard around. 'Now, if I say your name, you will be on team one and you need to stand in front of the box labelled team one. Teams two, three and four – same thing. Understood?'

The doctors all nodded, shuffling over to the correct boxes when their names were called. Chloe was on team three, and as she stepped across to her team, a familiar voice shouted from behind her.

'Sorry I'm late! Doctor Jonathan Carson, I should be on the list.'

Chloe cursed as she quite literally felt her heckles rise at her work nemesis's approach. Jonathan flashed her a wink as he passed.

'Hey, Doctor Henry, need a towel? I think we might get a little wet today.'

Chloe stared straight ahead, pretending she didn't hear the ripple of laughter surrounding her. She'd been expecting him to come, of course. Doctor Jeffries had mentioned that his little mini me was going to miss the first night, but her heart had still sunk into the sand when she'd heard that nasally voice of his.

'Doctor Carson, you're on team four. Glad you could make it!' Des, of course oblivious to the tension, greeted him enthusiastically and made another tick on his clipboard. Taking his place with his team, Jonathan looked right at her and shot her an over-the-top wink.

'May the best man win,' he called out. Chloe flashed him a tight smile. On the beach a little way back behind Carson, she spotted Logan. He was sitting there in a damn deckchair, looking like he was modelling swimwear in a pair of red shorts. When had he changed out of the tracksuit? She'd told him to go back to the hotel. Johnny kept talking, and she saw Logan's face drop into a scowl. 'And I do mean man, right, fellas?'

The other blokes on his team all chortled, and Chloe felt her heart begin to race. There were only two other women doctors here, and none of them were on her team.

'Do you know him?' the man in front of her asked under his breath, nodding towards Carson.

'Yep, unfortunately. We are going for the same job.'

'Ah, that will do it.' He held out a hand, and she shook it with a sweaty palm. 'Baldoni. Anthony.'

'Chloe Henry.'

'Oh, I know who you are.' She pulled her hand back, and he winced. 'I didn't mean it like that. I think you've had a rough deal. The press had no right to do that to you.'

'Er... thanks.'

'No problem.' He flicked his gaze at the other team, where Johnny was holding court with the other guys. 'Just ignore him. Focus on winning.'

'I'll try.' She smiled. Baldoni thumbed behind him, towards Logan.

'If it's any consolation, your boyfriend looks like he's ready to rip the guy's head off.'

'Oh, no. He—'

The words died as she looked at Logan. He was glaring at Carson, his lips so tight together they were bloodless. 'He's just protective, that's all.' And a great actor. If she didn't know better, she would agree with Baldoni. Logan looked ready to take Carson apart with his bare hands. When his eyes flicked to hers, he raised a questioning brow. She threw him a smile, and he blew her a kiss before pinning his gaze back on Carson. 'It's been a bit of a week,' she told Baldoni truthfully.

'I get it.' Baldoni nodded. 'Him being protective.' He tipped his head towards Carson. 'I'd be pretty annoyed too if someone did that to my other half.'

'You brought your partner too?'

Baldoni laughed. 'Nah, no girlfriend. With our hours? It's pretty hard to find someone who understands. I guess Logan gets it though, so that's got to be good for you guys.'

Logan's eyes were firmly on hers when she looked back. 'I think we're still figuring things out, but thanks.'

'No problem.' Baldoni's stare filtered back to Carson, who was laughing like a donkey at something one of the other doctors had said. 'I don't like bullies, and I hate grandstanders even less.' *There was that word again. Bullies.* Was she really the only one who didn't see that behaviour in her life for what it was?

Des tapped the megaphone to get their attention.

'Now, teams! Your challenge for today is to open the box in front of you and make a working vessel out of the materials. You will have ten minutes to make your vessel, and then when the klaxon goes off, one member of your team will row your vessel to the first red buoy, turn around and head back to the beach. The first team to make it back to the beach with their vessel intact is the winner and will be presented with medals at the dinner tonight.'

'A boat-building competition? Seriously?' Carson scoffed. 'How is that meant to showcase our talents exactly?'

'Oh, I don't know,' Chloe cut in. 'Teamwork, strength, problem-solving? Did you never build Lego as a kid?'

Baldoni laughed, holding out a fist to bump Chloe. 'Good one, Doctor Henry.'

'Yeah. Whatever.' Carson shrugged, looking put out. 'We'll see who's laughing soon.'

'Okay, teams. Remember, this is a team-building day, so careful on the trash talk and good luck! Remember, water safety first! We do have lifeguards at the ready, but let's try not to need them. Get ready to open your boxes. Three, two, one!'

The klaxon went off, and everyone sprang into action. Rolls of duct tape were flying everywhere, pieces of thick cardboard being hauled out. Chloe grabbed a broom handle from the box and a piece of cardboard and started folding it into a shovel shape. Once it held, she grabbed one for the other side of the handle.

'A paddle? Good shout,' Baldoni said. 'I don't think everyone had the right idea.' He nodded towards Carson and his team of alphas, who were making some kind of masthead with theirs. 'We have to smoke that guy out of the water, Henry.'

'Definitely.' One of the other doctors on their team looked her up and down, and Chloe wanted to shrink into the sand. 'What?'

'Nothing. I think you should do the boating. You're the smallest out of all of us.'

'Oh.' She chuckled with relief. 'Yeah, of course I will.'

Des called out, 'Three minutes left!' and they all mucked in. She shot a glance at Logan, and he was still eyeing Carson.

When he caught her looking, he flashed her a toothy grin and a thumbs up.

Baldoni fixed another piece of tape across the front of the makeshift boat, which was essentially a small box with corrugated cardboard fixed to the sides and bottom. 'I think we are as ready as we can be. I hope you have your sea legs.'

She looked across at Carson, who was trying to fit himself into their boat. His legs were practically at either side of his ears, their boat was so small. The mast was cock-eyed, leaning forward like a crappy battering ram.

'Oh, I'm going to paddle my arse off. Go team three!'

They all clapped hands, and when the klaxon went off, she was ready.

'Push!' her team shouted, all giving her a shove into the water. 'Go, Chloe!'

Shoving the makeshift paddle into the sea, she ignored the spray of water and the shouts of everyone around her as she set her eyes on the buoy and went for it. Carson was not going to win this. She would rather drown than endure his gloating.

'And team one is in the lead, closely followed by team three – but here is team four, coming in hot!'

'Yeah, baby! Team Carson is a-coming!'

'Just remember,' Des chipped in, 'this is a team effort! There is no I in team.'

'No, but there's one in dickhead,' she heard a voice yell. *Logan.* 'Keep going, Chloe! Eyes on the prize, baby!'

She was just nearing the buoy when she felt a wave ripple across her boat. She paddled to the left, and just as she passed by the bobbing device, she was smacked to the side.

'Hey!' Carson was there, using both hands as paddles. He was wet through, his boat starting to fall apart at the sides. The look on his face was maniacal as he grabbed for her makeshift oar. 'Jonathan, what the hell!' She glanced back to the shore, but she knew that no-one could see what was going on in the chaos of the water. 'Get off!'

She tried to pull it out of his grasp and almost tipped over. He just laughed harder.

'Hey, whatever it takes to win, Henry! Didn't your daddy ever teach you that?'

'Cheating isn't winning, Carson!' She gave it another yank, but he didn't budge. He was starting to push her boat back, and she felt the water come over the sides.

'Winning is winning, honey. Better get used to coming second place, eh?' He shoved her again, but this time she was ready for it. Anger fuelling her, she gripped the wooden handle as hard as she could and pushed it towards him. The sudden change in direction sent him careening back, and the second he let go of the paddle, she pushed off the buoy and paddled like a woman possessed.

'Yes, baby! That's it! Keep going!' She could see Logan on the shoreline, shouting at the top of his lungs, and it felt good to have someone in her corner. She could hear Carson cursing at the back of her. He sounded like he was close, but she didn't dare look back. If she saw his smug face again, she might be tempted to shove her broom handle somewhere he'd need a proctologist to remove. The other two teams were just rounding the buoy now, and she could feel them at her back as she pushed her bedraggled hair out of her face and concentrated on keeping the boat afloat. Left, right, left, right! She shoved her oar through the water, grunting like a linebacker as she powered through the water. Her boat was starting to sink, but she ignored the tangy salt of the water and the bellowing men behind her and focused on the shoreline. On her teammates, and Logan, who were all cheering her on. She was not going to lose to Carson. Not now, and not ever. Right now, she didn't care if she had to capsize the smarmy pig; she'd happily do it with a smile on her face.

'And team three are killing it!' Des shouted through the megaphone. 'Followed by team two and team one!' *No team four?* Hmm. Maybe she had finished him off! She pushed harder, and the second the bottom of the boat hit the sand, her team pulled her and the bedraggled boat to safety.

'We did it!' she screamed, holding her oar aloft like a conquering hero. 'We won!'

Her team picked up the boat and held it aloft, whooping and hollering. She was about to follow them when her bare foot caught on one of her teammate's legs and she went down. Just as she was bracing for a face full of sand, Logan's arms wound around her.

'You did it! You won!'

She jumped up and wrapped her legs around him effortlessly. She didn't even think about it; she wanted to be there – in his arms. Sharing this triumph with him. She could chalk it up to exuberance later. They were pretending to be a couple, right? The fact that she was getting addicted to feeling Logan wrapped around her was neither here nor there.

'Well done, wildcat!' He was grinning his head off as he dipped to kiss her forehead. His arms wound tight around her, pulling her closer to his hard torso. 'You did so well out there! I swear, I've never seen anything like it!'

An incensed voice cut through the celebrations. Logan gripped her tighter, his face dropping into a murderous frown. 'She cheated! Des, team three should be disqualified!' Carson came out of the water, spluttering and red-faced, dragging what was left of his boat behind him.

'As if,' Baldoni shot back. 'We won fair and square. Your boat is mush!'

'Because she sabotaged me! Did you not see her attacking me?'

'Attacking you? I'll give you attack—' She tried to get down, but Logan's grip were bands of steel around her. 'Logan, let me down.'

'Not a chance, wildcat,' he rumbled, his voice deep and low. 'Don't give him the satisfaction. Look at him.' She turned to see Carson being placated by Des, while the other teams were looking at him like he'd just emerged from the swamp. 'I saw what he did. Grabbing your oar. I swear I wanted to wade in and deck him myself, but you had him.'

'I really did.' She giggled, feeling her anger wash away. 'Did you see him try to drown me?'

'Yeah, and I saw you shove him right into the water. You were amazing. I'm proud of you, Doc.'

'Not a bad fake girlfriend to have, eh?'

'No,' he murmured, and she felt the heat from him warm her sea-soaked body. 'Not bad at all.' He looked at the melee around them. 'Come on, let's get you back to the room and out of those clothes.' Her breath caught in her throat, making his eyes widen in surprise. She barely held in the moan as she pictured being in their room, him stripping off her wet clothing. Holding her in his arms, just like this. 'I... er, I mean, out of those wet clothes. We have the drinks thing tonight, and I'm pretty sure I saw a reporter a minute ago. I don't want them getting photos of you like this.'

'You've got a point.' She smiled, feeling a frisson of disappointment in her gut and pushing it away. 'Let's go, let the rest of them deal with the sore loser.'

7

The loser was still decidedly sore at the dinner. All through the main course Chloe could feel Carson and his team throwing her mucky looks. They'd obviously bought into the sabotage story he'd been spinning at the beach, even if her teammates hadn't. The hotel had arranged for them to be sat on tables in their teams, and her table, along with Logan, was definitely the most upbeat.

'You were pretty awesome out there.' Doctor Patel grinned. 'I've never seen someone so determined to win.'

'That's my girl,' Logan cut in, filling up her wine glass. 'Once she sets her mind to something, the only thing you can do is get out of her way.'

'I still can't believe Doctor Carson pulled that stunt though. He was obviously going to lose; he was a mile off after the buoy.'

'Yeah,' Logan retorted through clenched teeth. 'Some people don't know how to act in these situations. Gets them in trouble.'

Turning back to his steak, he finally unclenched his jaw. It was weird, how tense he was. Even back in the hotel room, he'd been concerned that she was hurt or something. His intensity was pretty cute, and his worrying had managed to tamp down the weird sexual energy she'd felt at the beach. A little, at least. The protective bit was definitely something she was finding sexier as time went on, despite herself. She knew she should feel offended, perhaps, that he was worried that Carson had hurt her out in the water, but the reality was different. Horny different. It had taken a lot for her to be there in that room all wet and bedraggled, with Logan standing there in a pair of shorts showing all kinds of concern for her. Seriously, his fans would pay hard cash for the boyfriend experience she was getting, and knowing that it was all fake didn't cool her off completely. He was so different to what she expected. So Dante and so not in other ways; it was giving her whiplash.

'Let's hope tomorrow's activity is a bit calmer,' she mused, taking a sip of her wine.

'Oh, you bet your ass it will be, wildcat.' He said this only for her, judging by the way he leaned in and spoke with his lips practically on her neck. It took her a full minute to absorb his words, because all she could focus on was the way his hot breath skittered across her skin. 'By the way, I like your tattoo. What I could see of it.'

Holy fuck. She'd forgotten all about that. She was pretty sure he'd seen it before, given that he'd seen most of her body by now. In fact, he'd probably seen more of her than most of the men she'd dated, which wasn't saying much.

'Er... thanks,' she muttered, face aflame as she pulled her Bardot top up over the ink on her shoulder. 'Had it a while.'

'Hmm,' he rumbled, and she felt that rush of breath again. 'Maybe I'll see the whole thing sometime.'

Not. A. Chance. She would take an angle grinder to her flesh before she let him see the truth of her little motif. Although, the thought of baring her skin to his roving eyes, it might even be worth it. Him seeing the truth of her. *Nope. Not even then.* Fake boyfriends didn't get to see their fake girlfriend's tattoos. Their closeness was for their audience only, and she needed to remind herself of that. *He's sexy, and not yours to touch.* She needed another drink. Something to numb the throbbing between her legs. Just as she reached for her glass, the servers came to take their plates, and Des walked out to the small dance floor in front of the tables.

'Good evening, delegates,' he said through the microphone, sounding a little like a boxing announcer complete with rolled r's. 'And well done on the first team-building exercise! Before I bring team three up to collect their medals, I just wanted to run through tomorrow's exercise. As you know, the week is all professional, with lectures and presentations. Thursday is our expo day, for those who are taking part in exhibitions, and Friday we have an optional goodbye lunch before we depart. I am sure that you are all looking forward to giving your presentations, and I know some of you are being put through your paces by prospective employers, so tomorrow we are going to have some fun! Are you with me? Because I have something planned that will definitely get you working together!' He looked straight at Logan. 'And partners are welcome to take part in this one, too. Who here has a partner with them?' A few of the other team members lifted their hands. Logan nudged her, leaning in close. 'That's you, darling.'

Des laughed when he saw the interaction. 'Doctor Henry there, forgetting who she's dating. Have you not read the papers today?'

She felt the awkward smile freeze on her face. Logan's hand covered hers on the table, and she felt his fingers squeeze gently around hers. Carson was sneering openly from his table, and she made a point of focusing a steely glare his way.

'Sorry, Des.' She grinned, feeling the fire being stoked in her belly by the fingers clutching hers. 'I've been too busy crushing the competition to read the gossip rags.'

'That's my girl.' Logan chuckled. She flashed a cheeky smile at him, and his whole face lit up at the sight of it. Bringing her hand to his mouth, he dropped a sultry kiss on the backs of her fingers, one at a time. She watched every touch of his lips to her skin, lost in the look he was giving her. His eyes didn't leave hers, until Baldoni cleared his throat. Logan seemed to snap out of a stupor, and he pulled back. She uncurled her fingers, but he tutted. When she met his eye again, he shook his head and brought their hands down onto his lap as if it was the most natural thing in the world. As Des started speaking again, she tried to focus on the room and not the heat she felt between them. *He's an actor, Chloe. He's playing a part.* He wasn't Dante Love. He was a relative stranger, here hiding from his reputation. Trying not to take her down with him. Sure, he'd been nice, caring – but that was all it was. An agreement, forged out of necessity. A business deal, where they both had mutually assured destruction to avoid. 'Not a love story,' she muttered under her breath. Logan cocked his head, and for a second she worried he'd heard her. She eyed him warily, but he didn't look her way.

The rest of the evening ran smoothly. Dessert and medals dealt with, Chloe was already looking forward to getting out of there and putting a bit of distance between her and Logan. As much distance as she would get still sharing a bed with him. He'd held her hand most of the night, touching her in little ways, kissing her cheek when she returned to her seat with her winning medal around her neck. It was getting too much, trying to focus. She was tired of pretending. Had been tired of it for a long time.

When the servers came armed with coffee, she declined and was halfway out of her seat before Logan had a chance to answer.

'I'm pretty tired,' she announced to the table as a whole. 'Good evening, gentlemen.'

'I'll come with—'

'You have your coffee,' she cut in, not looking at him. 'No rush, I'm just going to go straight to bed.'

Clutching the medal around her neck, she kept her head high as she crossed the room. When she rounded the corner to an empty corridor, she heaved out a deep sigh. She could still feel Logan's touch, smell him on her. It was getting ridiculous, her reaction to his proximity. He was annoying, and cocky. Sometimes she wanted to shove a pillow over his head and suffocate him to death, but at other times she had to stop herself from kissing the holy shit out of him and begging him to tell her all his secrets. He was so complex, such an anomaly that the man needed to be studied for the future of mankind. Everything she felt around him was amplified, louder. She just needed a moment of quiet. A second to silence the parts of her that responded to him. The parts that wanted nothing more than to be the kind of woman that Logan Broderick looked twice at. But, true to form for the week she was having, that silence never came.

'Well, I'll give it to you, Henry. You needed something to get the panel to notice you this week, and you didn't do it by halves.'

Carson was already in her face when she turned to face him. His auburn hair shone under the lights of the corridor, making his eyes look sharklike.

'No coffee for you either, Carson? I thought after the soaking you got today you might need something to warm you up.'

'Oh, I think you are the one getting warmed up. How did you swing it, eh? Logan Broderick is not exactly the book-club type. Where did you meet him?'

'I don't think that's any of your business, and we are not here to discuss my love life.'

'Love life? I didn't think you even had a life at all, never mind dating some TV star.' His eyes narrowed as his sneer broadened. 'Did Daddy rent him for you or something? Is that it?'

'Fuck off, Jonathan. I don't need to cheat to beat you, I think we proved that today.'

His jaw flexed as he took a step closer, using his frame to tower over her. She didn't give him the satisfaction of moving an inch.

'You won't get the job, princess. Just because you can paddle a stupid boat means nothing. Jeffries wants me to take over, and I won't lose again.' He flicked the medal around her neck with his finger. 'Go home, before you embarrass yourself any further. You're not up to the job. Do yourself a favour.' He flicked it again, and she pulled it out of his reach. 'Bow out.'

'Touch her again. I dare you.'

Carson whirled around. Logan's fists were clenched at his sides, his anger evident. The animosity was rolling off him, his gaze fixed on Carson.

'Logan! We were just discussing our little competition.'

'You weren't discussing anything. Put your hands on her again and I'll break them off.'

'Woah!' Carson raised his hands, the colour draining from

his face a little as he tried to laugh it off. 'No need for threats. Chloe and I are old friends. Right, Chloe?'

'If I see you corner Doctor Henry again like that, you won't like what happens, Carson.' Logan strode over, and Chloe watched in wonder as Jonathan Carson shrank back against the corridor wall. Logan didn't acknowledge him but simply took her hand in his and dipped his head to hers.

'I came to walk you back to the room. You ready?'

Feeling the tension in his body, she nodded, letting him lead her to the lifts. Logan jabbed the button for their floor too hard, pulling her against him the second the doors closed.

'Are you okay?'

His voice was softer now, the Logan she recognised. His arms folded around her and she could feel the coiled anger in them.

'Yes, I'm fine. Carson's just a—'

'I don't want to talk about him. Not right now. I saw him standing over you, touching you. He's lucky I didn't pop him.'

'I'm fine.'

'Not the point.'

'I can look after myself, you know.' She felt him still and regretted her words the second his arms dropped to his sides. *Fake* was playing on repeat in her head, and she let her words fly. She needed to stand on her own. He was in her corner now, but next week? He'd be gone, and she would be right back here, having to defend herself against the Carsons of the world. 'I don't need a guardian. I'm not a princess.'

'Never said you were.'

'You didn't have to, everyone thinks it. That I need someone by my side to face the world, but the truth is the opposite. I just want to be left alone, Logan. I just want to live my life, okay?'

'Fine,' he huffed, turning away to face the doors. 'Sorry I

overstepped. I just... I don't know. I didn't like the way he was towering over you.'

There he went again, being all sexy and protective. Heaving out a sigh, she focused on the task in hand.

'Let's just get to the room, okay? We have the team-building thing tomorrow, and that's going to be bad enough. Carson is going to want blood now.'

'As long as it's not yours, he can do what he wants. Guys like that don't bother me, wildcat.'

She didn't say anything back. She had just seen another layer of Logan, another layer that she liked. The touch-her-and-die thing was another level of *take me now* for her. This man was unlocking kinks she didn't know she had. And she didn't have the first clue what to do about it. She didn't need anyone; she was truthful on that count. The problem was that over the last few days, she'd gotten a glimpse of what having someone in your corner felt like even if it was all fake. Just like her parents' concern, just like the way her sister sniped at every part of her life and told her it was for her own good. He wouldn't be here if this was real. It wouldn't be real, because Logan Broderick would never have crossed paths with her in real life. They had been thrown together, but it was all for show. She had no right to be mad at him for defending her, but she was anyway – because when he had warned Carson to stay away from her, just for a second she had wished it was all real. That he was hers, and he did care about how people spoke to her. The way his voice had held so much anger at the thought of someone touching her, it had sent her pulse skittering and her heart racing. She might be a feminist, but the whole 'you're mine' thing she read in novels and watched Logan's character Dante on TV was perfection. Belonging to someone like that, being seen? It was everything she wanted for herself. Career aside, being cherished like that, cheered for? It would be hard to walk away from the charade of them, that was for sure. So she decided to do what she always did. Focus on the job, and getting that department headship. When all this was done, he would leave her life to go back to his career, and she would have what she always wanted. The job, her parents' approval, or at least their grudging acceptance that she had control of her life. And when the loneliness came calling, she could watch *Doctor Love* and remember what it felt like to have a little piece of Logan Broderick in her life, no matter how fake or fleeting it was.

* * *

'Why do you want this?'

Chloe started at his voice. She was laid under the covers, but sleep was a way off. Her social battery was wrung out, and the pretence of being all smiley and in love was starting to wear thin. By now, she'd be in bed at home, watching true crime dramas and trying to wind down for the next shift. Instead, she was going to be spending another night with a veritable sex god after another night of enforced socialising and arguing with a man who had done nothing but defend her. Laid next to a man that she was often irritated by and also seemingly obsessed with working out. It was unlike anything she'd experienced before. He was like a rare disease, one that was begging to be diagnosed but kept throwing out more symptoms. She'd spent only days with him, and it felt like she'd been here forever. Like he'd been on her mind, forever. When he was around, she wanted to study him. It was intensely annoying, frustrating, intriguing. Logan Broderick was the first person she'd met who she couldn't get a read on. The one thing she couldn't cram into a neat little box, and given that she was publicly linked to him, that was irksome, to say the least.

'Doc? Did you hear me?'

'Yes, sorry. Want what?'

'This, the conference thing. The job.'

Chloe shrugged. 'You mean head of the department? Well, it's my next step.'

'To what?'

'My career.'

'Right.'

'It's what I've been wanting forever. I need it.'

'You need it.'

'Yes.' Turning to face him, she bit her lip. He was laying with one arm behind his head again. He looked so sexy laid back like that. She was sporting her panda PJs again, trying not to accidentally brush her bare legs against his. The body heat from him last night had felt like a furnace. Even just in his boxers, it had been like lying next to a radiator. 'I've been working for it a long time.'

'Right.' He drew out the word, shaking his head as he stared back.

'What do you mean, right? Why do you keep saying right?'

He shrugged and it drove her crazy. 'Right, as in, I understand. I think. I mean, I get your way of thinking, but why do *you* want it?'

'Well, who doesn't want a promotion? That's the way careers work. You pick one, work hard at it, climb the ladder as high as you can. What about you?'

There it was again. That eye crinkle. She ignored it.

'What about me?' She didn't miss the surprise in his tone. For a man in the spotlight, he sounded like he wasn't asked too many questions.

'Well, it sounds like you can't be Doctor Love for much longer. Even if we pull this stupid charade off, keep it going long enough for what we both need, what then for you? Those programmes don't last forever. People leave. What's your next step?'

'I have the war movie. I get a lot of scripts, but this one was the first one that really spoke to me. I think I could do a good job. I don't plan on leaving Dante behind, given the chance, but you're right. I can't do that forever. Actors tend to get a little typecast if they don't branch out. I always figured I would do more movies. I mean, I've done some lower-budget ones when I was younger, but nothing like this.'

'So if you really want it? Why did you mess up, with the media? The bars, the women. I know you weren't seeing them, but why did you take the risk, knowing how they write about you?' It didn't make sense to her now. She'd judged him like a lot of people had, but the man in her bed wasn't matching up with the articles she'd pored over in the past. There had to be a reason. Something to make everything click into place in her head. She knew first-hand how people hid their true feelings behind a persona. 'Sorry, that sounded judgy.'

'No,' he murmured. 'I get it. Since we're doing this, I guess I owe you the truth. The press, they have their reasons to keep reporting on me. I don't need to mess up for them to spin stories, if I'm honest. They're used to me failing. A while back, when I was first cast in the show, I had some stuff going on. I didn't handle things the right way. I was a bit naïve, in some ways. I wanted to keep my personal life quiet, but I was struggling. I went from being a normal young kid to a star overnight. Lost those I was used to having around. I spent a lot of time on my own, and then all of a sudden people wanted to know me. I got invited places, and so I went. Partied some. And then things got worse behind the scenes, so I partied some more. I didn't know the truth of people back then.'

'The truth?'

He sighed, his leg brushing against hers. She squeezed her own together to stop the thrill it elicited. When she glanced his way, his gaze was already pinned to hers.

'People think that because I'm a pretty boy, and I partied when the show first came out, that I am that person. The parts of Dante, the softer side, the one that cares for people, that's more me than the arrogant git they show in the press. Don't get me wrong, he's in there too.'

'I met him the first day,' she teased, wanting to see that smile of his. Erase the sadness.

'You sure did.' His lips twitched. 'I didn't know you then, Chloe. I can be a defensive arsehole when I want to be. I guess I'm sick of trying to get people to see the real me. The die was cast when I was coming up in the industry, when my personal life was in tatters, and they never bothered to recast another villain. Those girls I get photographed with; half the time they are just people out on the same night. Others are women trying to get with a movie star. I don't want that life.'

'And then you got landed with a fake girlfriend for a week. Your plan really worked out well, eh?'

He chuckled, shaking his head. 'Getting a woman like you to look at me in the real world wouldn't be a thing, trust me.'

'Oh, come on, that's bull crap right there.' *I'm looking, believe me.*

'It's not, I swear to God.'

'Logan, half the women at my work have the hots for Dante Love.'

'Yeah, Dante Love. A fictional man written by a woman. He's a man who always does the right thing. He's loyal, protective, in love with a woman he can't have but always lives for. Of course they all love him. He's a great guy. The man doesn't know how to fail.'

'All people fail, doesn't mean they don't deserve to be loved by someone.'

'Tell that to the press, please.'

'Well, after this maybe you could find someone who will see the real you.'

'Yeah?' He didn't look convinced. 'We'll just have to see. I'm kind of used to being on my own at this point. I have to say, it's kind of nice having someone. Even if she does get mad at me pretty much all the time.' She didn't miss the hurt look on his face and the urge she felt to wipe it away. He'd done nothing but look out for her, but she'd lived up to her nickname. Had clawed him a few times.

'I am sorry for that. Jonathan Carson is just someone who brings out the worst in me. He seems to know my insecurities, and going against him for the job? It's been a lot. I think he just reminds me of everything I don't like about being a doctor, you know. If I ever end up like him, I know I've lost my way. I can't lose this job, especially not to him.'

'Do you think that comes from you, or because of how your parents brought you up? I mean, even if you don't get the job, you will still be a doctor. I know politics is at play with the promotion. I don't think it's a reflection on you, or your work.'

'Failure's not really an option. It was kind of a dirty word growing up. Expectation was everything to my parents.' She sighed, staring up at the light from the window as it fell across the ceiling. 'I wanted to be a doctor for me, not for them. I love working at the hospital, I just want it to be a better place. If Carson gets the job, I will be leaving. I just don't want to get pushed around anymore.'

He didn't reply for so long that Chloe thought he'd dropped off to sleep. His reply shocked her when it came.

'Sounds awful. Having so much put on your shoulders with your job, I get, but expectation? I don't think anyone even thought of that word when it came to me. It's kind of hard to be considered a failure before I even open my mouth, but I guess I'm used to it. People don't ask me questions, they don't think about who the real me is. They just believe whatever the press tells them. No-one has really believed in me like you believe in yourself.'

Her gut lurched at his words. This was the opposite of cocky. He was so down on himself, it made her heart ache for him. The urge to wrap him in her arms was all-consuming, but right now, in bed? It might just tip her control over the edge, and that wouldn't be good for either of them. He'd never outright said that he felt this, this thing between them. Trying to merge reality with fantasy was a dangerous game, and it was not the time. He needed a friend. Someone on his side. She could be that for him and push down the rest. Reach for him without touching. Make him see that even after this week, he wasn't alone.

'That can't be true, surely. Your agent has stuck with you, right? I know he was mad, but I get the impression he wants the best for you. There must be other people in your life.'

'Not really. I know it looks like I'm out there, living it large, but I just end up going out half the time because the alternative is sitting in my apartment on my own.'

She didn't tell him that her life was all work and being alone in her place too. He was opening up, and she wanted to hear more. 'What about outside of showbusiness though? I know you hang out with people in your industry, but you had people before your career, right?'

'Not really. My mum was probably the last person who knew the real Logan. My childhood was pretty weird. I was auditioning all through school, so I never did the usual growing-up stuff, you know. It was a pretty weird time. For me, childhood was pretty rough.' She wondered how a big star like him had that view of his childhood. Why the disappointment in his voice had made her gut pitch down to the bottom of the bed.

'Are you close to your mum?'

'I was. Very.' No hesitation. She could hear the smile in his voice, the audible swallow in the pit of his throat. 'She passed away a few years back. MS. She was pretty great. My biggest fan.' Another piece of him clicked into place. When he said he'd lost people, he meant lost in a real, final way.

'I'm sorry. MS is really tough.'

'Yeah, it sucked. I was able to get her the best care, but it was still hard, you know. It was just the two of us, so I did what I could. I still miss her.' He cleared his throat. 'I take it you're not so close with your parents. Has it always been like that?'

Chloe sighed, straightening the edge of the duvet for something to do. *Or not do.* The urge to pull him to her was palpable. 'Oh, I avoid them as much as possible. Family dinners are like a bad WASP sitcom, complete with caterers ducking for cover. Add in the competitive doctor edge, and it's forks and knives drawn at dawn. I tend to pick up shifts whenever there's a family event.'

'Ouch.' The direction of his voice had changed, as if he'd rolled over to face her. She didn't dare look. She'd gotten another glimpse of bare chest when she'd jumped under the covers, and she didn't trust herself not to gawp if she looked at him again. He might come across as a bit of a poser sometimes, but she was still a hot-blooded woman. One who hadn't seen a bare chest that wasn't attached to a patient in quite some time.

Logan Broderick, in her bed, opening up about things no-one knew? That was like catnip to her. She was practically purring for this complicated, beautiful man. Right now, in this moment, she wanted to do a damn press interview and tell them all to back the hell off. 'I always wanted more of a family, but I guess every person has their own little things to deal with. Are they both doctors?'

'Yep. My sister Liz too, although she specialises in dermatology. If she didn't have a private clinic on Harley Street and her own YouTube channel with a few million followers, she'd be considered on a par with the caterers in the hierarchy, I guess. It's a pretty tough crowd.'

'Right,' he drawled. 'And where do you come on the scale?'

The bottom. Looking up at the rest of them, up there in the clouds. Not wanting to get there, but being punished for being happy right where I am. 'Well, as you know, I work for the NHS. They are all in private practice. And I am a general surgeon, so not having a speciality, as they see it, doesn't go down well either. My dad has his own ideas of medicine, and my mum... well, she was raised the same way.'

'Lucky they found each other then.'

She snorted, despite herself. 'I think the two of them getting together was more like two companies merging than love at first sight.'

He stayed silent, and she felt herself flush at her admission. She sounded... bitter. 'I do love them, of course.'

'I never thought you didn't. I think parents have their own particular ways of driving you crazy, no matter what they do to try to raise you right.'

He wasn't wrong there. She wanted to ask about his father. He hadn't mentioned him, but if that was for a reason, she felt like she didn't have the right to ask him about it. Fake relationship or not, she sure as hell didn't want him to know every dark corner of her life. She didn't like looking into them herself. He'd already seen behind the Henry curtain, and it wasn't pretty.

'So Carson,' he asked, his voice quieter now. Contemplative. 'Any personal history there I need to know about? You know... for the whole fake-dating thing. You seem to have a bit of history.'

'A rivalry is more the word. Obviously he's going for the head of department job I want. The current head of department thinks he's going to go places, but in reality, he just preens around the place. I heard talk that he's got contacts in pharma, so it's a safe bet if he gets in, he will be wanting to give some of his buddies contracts that the hospital probably can't afford. My parents would never get that. They...' She stopped herself from saying more. She was already babbling, and the guilt of speaking against her parents was swelling her tongue in her mouth. 'It just can't happen. I want the job so that I can make things better, for everyone. If he wins, the whole department will suffer. I love my nursing staff. My scrub nurses are like the SAS. It's a crack team. We all love working together. We respect each other. He just doesn't get that.'

His voice was gentle, almost a whisper in the night. 'I think I understand. You want this job for yourself, and not for your family or the status. You want to protect your team. It's your next step; you believe in it even if those around you don't.'

The blossom of warmth in her chest was shocking when it came. She had to swallow to get her suddenly dry mouth to form words.

'Yes, I do. You nailed it. That's the problem, though, sadly. My opinion doesn't seem to carry any weight.'

He sighed, a deep guttural sound. 'I see now.'

'See what?'

'Why you are like you are. Prickly.'

'Prickly? Listen, I—'

'Prickly's not always a bad thing, Doc. It means you have barbs. Everyone gets that way when they want to protect what they care about. People tend to see the version of you that they want to see, no matter what you do.'

Snuggled under the covers, she let her smile fly. 'Either you're pretty smart, or that's from a movie.'

His chuckle was low and easily given. 'Nope, that's all me.' He paused. 'Was that a compliment, wildcat?'

Stifling a giggle, she turned to her side. 'Goodnight, Logan.' In the dark, she let the smile she'd been holding back break out. They'd weathered another storm today, and sleeping at the side of him tonight didn't feel quite so fraught. They'd opened up to each other, and not judged the other for their admissions. Logan Broderick was a nice guy, with feelings and morals. The type of guy a woman would definitely date. 'And knock off the wildcat,' she said, smirking.

He huffed out a laugh. 'You love it really. Night, Doc. Sleep tight.'

8

'Jesus Christ, how is this supposed to be fun? What does paintballing have to do with medicine? We're pinned by that douchebag on team one!' The shots were flying all around them, a rainbow of lethal colour splattered on every surface.

They were both hunkered down behind a fence, listening to the other teams pick each other off. A high-pitched yelp came from somewhere in the trees behind them, followed up by a triumphant holler.

'I'm pretty sure that was Mrs Patel, she's pretty badass! I'm glad she's on our team.' Logan laughed as he popped his head out to check. 'Yep. She took him out, we can move.'

They'd rejigged the teams to accommodate the other spouses and partners, so now they were five teams of five. Baldoni was on team five now and before the game had started, he'd taken them aside and told them to take Carson out the first chance they got. Logan had shaken his hand with an 'amen, brother' and whisked Chloe away the second the whistle had blown. It was a full-on melee, Des telling them excitedly that the team that survived the longest would be the victors. After that, it had rapidly descended into *The Hunger Games*. A few miles from the hotel, the thick woodland felt a world away from Cornwall. She was about to ask Logan what their plan was when he grabbed her hand and took off running.

'Where are we going?'

'The high point, over there. I saw a structure up in the trees. If we hole up there, we can pick them off as they come past.'

'Pick them off?' she stuttered, trying to keep on her feet as he ran through the undergrowth at speed. 'Logan, slow down!' Her foot hit a tree root sticking out of the ground, and she went down. Her paintball gun, on a strap around her neck, flew up and smacked her in the face.

'Chloe! Are you okay?' He was by her side the second she hit the ground, pulling her gun strap off and throwing it around his own neck. 'Shit, I'm sorry.' Lying on the forest floor, covered in mud and twigs, she looked up at his concerned helmet-clad face and started to laugh. The flash of concern on his handsome features when he flicked up his helmet turned to confusion. 'Chlo, what's happening right now? Do you have a concussion or something?'

'No, you jackass! I just tripped! Did you have to do your GI Joe bit?' He ran his hands up and down her limbs till she swatted him away. 'What are you doing?'

'Checking for breaks,' he said, starting to pull her helmet off. 'Stay still, let me check your head.'

'Logan, I'm fine. Stop fussing.' There was a primal cry of aggression somewhere in the trees behind them, and she went to jump up, pulling her helmet back on and shoving his back down. 'Let's get to the— Hey!'

'Shush.' Shoving his hands under her legs, he hoisted her into his arms and dipped down low. 'I've got you. Stop screaming or they'll pick us off right here.' She had no choice but to throw her arms around him as he took off for the outpost that was essentially a treehouse in the thick of the trees. 'How you feeling? You dizzy?'

'Kinda.'

His step halted as he looked down at her.

'You're throwing me around here.'

'Sorry,' he mumbled, gripping her tighter to him. 'I should never have pulled you like that. Just hang on, okay? Nearly there.'

'I can walk, you know.'

'Well, you fell pretty hard. I thought you'd knocked yourself out.'

'Nope, the helmet took the brunt of it. I think I'll have a bruise or two, but I'm good. To walk.'

He kept running, dodging trees like some kind of stealth ninja. The man wasn't even breaking a sweat. She was feeling all kinds of things right now. Indignation that he was treating her like some porcelain-doll princess and feeling rather swoony because his alpha protector mode had well and truly been activated. Being carried through the woods by Logan? That was a memory to file away for future reference. *Fake*, her rational brain cut in. *Fake relationship, remember?*

'Seriously. I can walk,' she asserted again. 'Like now, Logan. I can walk now.' He didn't even pause in his movements.

'We're almost there. Just watch our six.'

'Six what?'

'Six,' he huffed. 'Our backs, you know. For enemy fire.' When she turned her head and crooked a brow he couldn't see, he blushed all the same. 'Shut up. It's a thing, in battle. I've been learning my script; you pick things up.' He stopped in front of a ladder carved into a thick tree trunk. 'Are you good to climb? I've got your gun.'

'I'm not helpless, you know.' *Slightly dazed about being in your arms again, however, definitely.* Scrambling out of his grasp, she hit the ladder like a rat up a drainpipe, shimmying up as fast as she could.

'Wow,' she heard Logan mutter as he came up behind her. She looked down to catch him looking away.

'What?'

'Nothing. That uniform... it... fits you well.' He cleared his throat as they both scrabbled to the top. Taking the gun from around his neck, she smirked at him.

'Were you checking out my ass, Broderick?'

'Well, I could hardly look anywhere else. I didn't want you to fall out of the tree and take us both out. You have the balance skills of a drunken monkey.'

'And there he is,' she huffed, lowering the scope of her gun into one of the designated shooting spots.

'There who is?'

'Cocky Logan.' She spotted a body poking out from the tree and lined up a shot. The second it moved enough for her to see the number on the back of their uniform, she fired. 'Got one!'

'Arrghh!' came from down below, and Doctor Evanovich limped off towards the main tent, his head swivelling to scan the trees.

'Get down,' she hissed, lunging at Logan and taking him down as he was pulling his helmet off. 'I took out Evanovich, but he's looking for the shooter.'

Scanning the trees through the wooden slats, she held her breath as the rush of the game shot through her.

'I think we're in the clear,' she whispered, right before realising that she'd jumped right on him. His arms were around her waist, his fingers flexed tight around the soft skin of her hips. Her arms were splayed on his chest, and even through the uniform she could feel his taut muscles, the way their bodies were flush against each other. His huge brown eyes stared right into hers as he lay beneath her. 'Sorry. I think I'm crushing you.'

'Nah,' he breathed. 'Takes a lot to crush me. Just let me...' His fingers slid her helmet straps apart as he took the helmet from her head. Brushing a couple of stray strands of hair behind her ear, he ran his thumb along her cheek. 'Better. What did you mean before, the cocky comment?'

She tried to ignore the drugging effect his thumb was leaving on her skin. 'Just that I never know which Logan you're going to be. I can't quite work you out.'

'I think you can, wildcat.'

'Quit with the wildcat.'

His thumb moved down, rubbing a slow line across her bottom lip. Her whole body quivered, and she could tell he noticed. She was fast becoming an addict for his touch.

'I'll quit when you stop liking me saying it.'

'Who says I like it?'

'You do. When your pulse quickens in your throat, right here.' His fingers moved to caress her neck, his movements slow and sensual. 'When you try not to smile every time I say it. The truth is that you can read me better than most people, same as I can tell that you secretly like me.' She went to move, his words making her skittish, but the hand on her hip tightened. 'You've called me out on more of my bullshit in three days than most people have my whole life. You surprise the hell out of me.'

'I highly doubt that. I bet you've met some pretty impressive people in your time.'

He shook his head, bopping her on the nose with his index finger.

'Trust me, you blew them all out of the water. I get this

feeling around you, like I want to help or something. Like you might just need someone like me.'

'I told you—'

'You take care of yourself, I know. I don't mean it that way, Chloe.' He shrugged, his smile turning rueful. 'I don't know what I mean. You have me all turned around.'

The feeling's mutual, she wanted to tell him, but what would be the point? This was never going to work. It could never be anything. She said it anyway, fuelled by his fingers on her skin.

'If it's any consolation, you do that to me too.'

'I do?' He looked surprised, which gave her another thrill. 'In what way?'

'The weirdest ways. I know I'm prickly, but I do have a heart, Logan.' *One that goes pitter patter around you.*

'So you like me?'

'I wouldn't go that far.' His grin was devilish, and the smile she'd been hiding sprang free. 'Yes, I like you.' *Control, Chloe? Remember?* 'I just think the lines are blurring, you know. We're both on our own here, in this big secret. It's... confusing.'

'Confusing wouldn't be the word I'd use.' His breath was coming out in little pants. An echo of hers.

'What word would you use?'

PHUT PHUT PHUT

Red splats of paint hit the trunk and the boards all around them. Logan rolled like a commando, pushing Chloe underneath him and shoving her helmet back on.

'I know you're up there!' Carson sang out from below. 'I've got them! Over here!'

Logan rolled, pushing his gun nuzzle through one of the openings, scowling at what he saw. 'I really hate that guy.' He reached for his helmet, the scowl on his face downright feral.

'Can we get out of here?' Chloe took up position on her belly next to him, readying her gun.

'Nope. That ladder is the only way up or down. He must have been looking for us this whole time.'

'Doctor Henry! Why don't you come down and make it easier?'

Logan counted under his breath. 'Baldoni's not there, but there's three left on Carson's team and two from team five. Fuckers must have allied up.'

'Jesus, this really is *The Hunger Games*.'

'Yeah, I could really go for a tracker jacker nest right about now.' They giggled, shushing each other and laughing again. 'I love your laugh,' he rumbled. 'You should do it more often.'

She met his eye, and there it was again. That smoulder between them, something that made everything okay when they were like this, together. They were in a damn fox hole and she was having so much fun she didn't even care about Carson being a colossal dickhead below, or the job, or anything else. The world had seen her half nude with this man, but the way he looked at her? Even through a helmet, she knew his eyes were locked on hers. That was when she truly felt naked. Like she wanted to bare herself to him, because he took everything she gave him in his stride.

'Hey.' She grinned, a plan forming. 'How many bullets have you got left?'

Carson was patrolling the perimeter like a wild bear searching for a picnic when he heard a noise in the tree behind him.

'What was that?' one of his teammates called out. Carson took off towards the noise, the others following like a band of lost boys. 'There's something up there in the tree!'

'What the hell is that?' Lifting his gun, Carson swatted at

the pink fabric hanging from one of the lower branches. 'Is that...' He hooked it on the handle of his gun, lowering it to the ground. One of the doctors whistled behind him. 'A... bra?'

Yanking the satin garment from his weapon, he held it in his hands. 'There's writing on it.' The others gathered around, chuckling as he turned it over. 'What the hell.' One word was written in black on each cup. *Behind. You.*

Logan jumped down the last rung of the ladder as they started to turn, taking out two of them before they got a chance to lift their weapons. Running at full pelt, he barrelled into Carson, knocking him to the ground as Chloe popped up from their hiding place and shot another one straight in the butt.

'Get him!' Carson bellowed as his remaining teammate lifted the gun and aimed it right at Chloe. She was quicker on the draw, and he howled as a blue paintball barrelled straight into his leg. Logan had got the better of Carson, who was now grunting under his weight, his face a mar of mud and wet leaves.

'I think that belongs to my girlfriend,' he growled, ripping the bra out of his hand and aiming the gun at Carson's chest. 'Get up.'

'Fuck off,' he grunted, but Logan just laughed.

'Fine, but close range to the chest will hurt a lot more than surrender.'

'Surrender? Never!'

Chloe's boots came into view as she stood over the two men.

'Last chance, Carson. On your feet, soldier, or it's one in the chest. Any more buddies in the trees?'

'No.' He scowled, spitting mud out of his mouth. 'We were the only ones left.'

'Good.' Logan grinned, standing to offer Carson a hand. 'We

can walk you back to camp if you like. I'm sure they have a white flag somewhere.'

Shooting them both a dirty look, Carson sagged into the mud. 'Fine. Let's just get this over with.'

Chloe tugged the bra from Logan's grasp. 'Watch my six, baby?'

Logan beamed back at her, tapping his gun nozzle against hers. 'My pleasure, sweet cheeks.'

'Oh God,' Carson groaned. 'Spare me the cutesy couple crap. I might just vomi—Oww! Jesus!'

A bright blue splat of paint spread across his left butt cheek as he dropped like a stone to the floor, whimpering like a toddler. Chloe whipped her head around to Logan, who winked back.

'Oops. Maybe he should have been watching his, eh?'

9

Logan Broderick – off the market?

Logan Broderick, TV star and bachelor playboy, has issued a statement through his agency this weekend following Friday's hotel room scoop.

Sources close to the mystery woman, Chloe Henry, who resides in Manchester and is a general surgeon, all declined to comment about her relationship status. Logan Broderick, 31, released a statement damning the media for interrupting the private moment of reconciliation with Miss Henry, asking the media to respect his love interest's privacy and not to interfere with her professional career. Hotel sources also declined to comment, stating that guests' privacy is paramount and that all press were banned from the premises until further notice.

Logan's agent, Peter Simpkin, also declined to comment, asking that Logan's love life be left private for the sake of his relationship.

'Logan is focusing on his relationship this week,

choosing to spend time away from his busy work schedule to work on a future film role and support his partner.'

Could this really be it? Has a real-life doctor finally been the one to tame the heart throb lothario? *Inside Scoop* will be bringing you the scoop on this romantic twist!

Monday morning flashed by in a carousel of guest speakers, glossy presentation folders and far too much coffee. Having to get dressed quietly in the bathroom as if she was about to do the walk of shame from a bad one-night stand, Chloe had slipped out of the room, leaving Logan snoring softly in their bed that morning. After the jubilance of the paintball victory, the participants had all chosen an early night after dinner, and she and Logan had spent the night laughing about the day's events and definitely not talking about the treehouse confession session. But something had shifted between them. There was a closeness there, and she needed to focus and snap out of it. Waking up in his arms this morning didn't help matters much either. During the course of the night the two of them had seemingly shifted closer to the other, and when she woke before her alarm, the warmth of his big body spooning her had felt too nice. It was so weird, being comfortable with a man she'd watched on the screen for so long. Living with the real Logan Broderick was fast becoming her new favourite pastime, and she needed to snap back into the professional aloof Chloe Henry before she said something to embarrass herself and make this whole thing ten times worse. They were from different worlds, and she needed to remember that after this week that was where they would be returning. It was just such a shame that she found him so damn cute.

The sight of all his toiletries lined up on the glass shelf had made her laugh so hard earlier she felt sure he would have woken up with the noise. She had moisturiser, shower gel, a toothbrush and paste. A tiny little make-up bag in one corner. The rest of the shelf's contents were all his. Hair pomade, aftershave, deodorant, the lot. She even spotted a Day-Glo green pot of face mask that looked like it cost more than a defibrillator. The wardrobe was the same. He'd filled most of it, for a start. The eye-wateringly expensive labels on his couture clothing made her capsule wardrobe of pant suits and blouses look like the discount rack in a charity shop.

In the break between lectures, she was braving another one of the bitter coffees the hotel offered, and she made the mistake of looking at her phone. Instantly, she wished she hadn't.

She didn't have social media as such, always seeing it as a way of staying ultra professional and separate from her parents and media-loving sister, but that didn't stop people from finding her.

'Seven hundred and eighty-six emails! What the hell?'

She scrolled down, and down, and down. They were neverending. Email addresses from television companies, journalists, and a whole bunch of other people she'd never heard of. Some she had too. Shuddering, she opened one from her old college date, Kevin, who was now an accountant in London. And married with kids, last she'd heard. Apparently he'd seen the news, and his wife had been bragging that she was now married to the ex of a huge movie star. Shuddering, she deleted it without replying. One thing she absolutely didn't need right now was the memory of his fish-lipped kiss and the awkward evening she'd spent swatting away his grasping little hands. She hoped, for his wife's sake, that given he wasn't any better in the tact department that at least he'd become a better kisser.

'That bad, eh?' Doctor Baldoni took the seat next to her, wincing at his own mouthful of coffee.

'What? Er, no. Just emails, you know. It's safe to say that people are in the know about who I'm going out with.'

'Worth it though, eh? You guys are pretty happy.'

'You think so?'

Baldoni quirked a brow. 'Er, yeah. Don't you?'

'Well, yeah! Of course. I mean, it's just a lot, you know. It's still new, and with the conference and everything, I can't seem to see beyond the presentation, if I'm honest.'

'You'll be fine. For what it's worth, I think you'll get the job.'

'Are you not one of the candidates?'

'Sure, but I think you'll get it. Everyone is talking about you and Carson being the top two.'

'Sorry.'

'Don't be.' He grinned. 'Just remember me if a job comes up. I have family in London, it's where I need to be, but the wages just aren't enough with the cost of living and the damn student debt. I need to save for another year or so before I make the move. Manchester General would be a good fit, but if Carson wins, I will definitely be looking elsewhere.'

'Not keen on working under him, huh?'

He swigged at his coffee, pulling a face. 'The guy's an idiot. Everyone here thinks so.'

'They do?' This was news to her. Did people here see through the bullshit? Was that too much to hope for, when all the evidence at work was to the contrary?

'Have you not noticed? Not everyone is here for the job, but Carson hasn't stopped talking about it since he got here. You have to get the job; the NHS doesn't need glory hounds like him.'

'How do you know I'm not the same? I know you've heard about my family.'

'I have, but Logan talked about you wanting something different.'

Logan had told him? He'd talked about her when she wasn't there? Was that part of the act? She thought back to the tree-house, his words of admission. It sparked a frisson of hope in her chest, and she rubbed at it to chase it off. *He's playing his part, Chlo. Not proposing.*

'Your vision sounds much more in line with how a lot of us think in the NHS.'

'He... talked to you about that? My vision for the department?'

'He's always talking about you, Chloe. The man has it bad.' He checked his watch, missing Chloe's shock. 'Next lecture is in ten. See you in there? By the way, did you see how Carson is sitting today? Hilarious. The guy asked for an inflatable doughnut from the front desk. He's sitting like a haemorrhoid patient.'

Chloe had a flashback of Logan shooting him in the butt cheek the day before and stifled a giggle. 'Couldn't happen to a nicer guy. I'm coming, and thanks. I swear, if I get the job, I'll do what I can on the job front. If they listen to me at the presentation, of course.'

'Have faith.' He winked. 'Worst-case scenario, Logan can shoot him again.'

She turned back to her phone and deleted all of the noise. People were behind her. They wanted her to win, not because of the Henry name. Not because of her connections. They liked her, trusted her. Trusted Logan when he told them about her. She had a champion here, a man she was starting to really like. After one damn weekend, she was crushing harder and harder for Logan Broderick the more she was around him. In three days, he'd done more for her than anyone. She just hoped that after all of this, the media would leave him alone and let him get what he wanted. Maybe she could help, once things died down. Tell people how good he was. Make people listen.

One thing was for sure, after all this had ended, she would never look at Dante Love the same way again. She just hoped that when they parted ways, she could live with only seeing him from afar.

10

'How's it going? I saw the pictures.' Pete sounded decidedly chipper. It was unnerving.

'Already? How? You got a subscription to *Medical Monthly* or something?'

'What? No, doofus. A couple of the doctors have Instagram though. You not seen the tags?'

Logan pulled his phone away from his ear. As usual, his notifications were there in bulk, waiting to be acknowledged.

'Er, no. I didn't get a chance over the weekend.' He'd left his phone in their room most of the time. He usually had it glued to his hand. *Huh. I hadn't missed it either.*

He'd been too distracted trying to work his fake girlfriend out. After the weekend, the treehouse, the late-night chats? He was hooked on the sexy doctor that he was holed up with. She made him feel seen, worthy even. She called him out on his bravado, saw straight through him. Then there was this morning. He'd heard her alarm; had felt the moment her body awoke, the second she'd registered that his limbs were wrapped around hers. She'd felt so good in his embrace that even when he'd become aware of it, he couldn't pull himself away. But she had. His body had felt hers freeze and pull away, and he'd hated it. Despised the fact that a woman like that would run from the bed the second she realised it was him holding her. The irony of getting any woman he wanted for years and not being able to get the first woman he actually wanted was not an easy feeling. She wasn't his. It was like the rest of his life. Fake. An act. Something for the media to pick over and analyse. He could never have Chloe Henry for his own. They would never allow it. Everything she had worked for, everything her family wanted for her, would be tarnished. She was trying to get out of other people's control, and here he was – loving the time that they were spending together, all the while knowing that this wasn't what she wanted. It was making him grumpy, to say the least. They had less than five days left in this little bubble, and it would never be enough. She fancied him, he could tell that much. It was the rest that he needed to work on. He needed more time to figure this out. To work out how he could get Doctor Chloe Henry to look at him as a worthy contender for her heart. Because the more time he spent with her, the more he wanted to be around her. He liked the Logan he was when he was with her. With her at his side, he felt more like him than he ever had. He was more than just a prop in some storyline. He was a companion, a damn cheerleader. Hell, he'd don a ra-ra skirt and shake his pom-poms, just for one of her hard-won smiles.

Pete's voice dragged him from his thoughts of Chloe. 'What do you mean, you haven't looked yet? You check your Google alerts daily.'

'Yeah, well, I've been busy. We had a whole team-building weekend, and drinks, dinners. You know the schedule, but I'm reading the script. Chloe's been in lectures all day, I've been working. That's what you wanted, right? Me to gen up on the script for the movie? I even got a little combat practice. Chloe and I dominated the paintballing yesterday. You should have seen her, Pete. She was a total badass.' *I will never look at a pink bra again without seeing her in that treehouse, wiggling it out from under her uniform.* She was so sexy, and smart. He'd had to seriously resist his Tarzan urges. Seeing her use her underwear as a distraction had him wanting to beat his chest and swing her away to his place on the nearest vine.

Pete didn't say anything at first, which was weird. There was an audible pause on the line followed by a surprised little 'huh' sound. 'Oh, okay. Yeah. Good. I'm glad you're finally listening. How's Miss Henry holding up?'

'Doctor Henry, and she's fine. Stressed about the presentation.' At least, he hoped that was the only reason she'd hot-footed it out without saying goodbye that morning. 'She's irritated by the attention I bring, I think.'

'Well, that's a first for a woman you're dating.'

'Fake-dating,' he reminded him, feeling wretched at making the distinction when he didn't quite feel it in his gut. 'Besides, she's not that type.' *Worse luck, because she's definitely mine. Mine.*

'Your usual type? Good. Makes it easier all round. We need to keep this nice and easy, keep her onside. Even when we trigger the fake break-up, the media attention will still be a lot, for both of you. All eyes are on you. Where is she, by the way?'

Logan took a minute to answer, the word 'break-up' icing his veins. He didn't want to break up with his wildcat. Fake or not, he was in this. Wanted to be in her life. Bitter that the man he was meant that couldn't happen.

'In the shower,' he managed to croak out, his gaze falling on the closed door. Knowing that she was in there, naked, was doing all kinds of things to his resolve to be the good guy and walk away at the end of this week. 'Getting ready for tonight.'

'Okay, good,' Pete said. 'Just remember what I said, okay?'

'Yeah, yeah. Play nice, keep it in my pants. It's not like that with her, Pete. It's—' He heard the bathroom door open behind him, and when he turned, the rest of the sentence died in his throat. Chloe came walking out of the steam like a damn maiden of the mist, her hair wrapped in a towel and one of the hotel's fluffy robes tied tight around her body. She raised her eyes in surprise when their eyes locked. Logan turned away before his traitorous cheeks gave him away. Or the stir in the slacks he felt at the sight of her. 'Peter, I need to go.'

'Wait – I need you to ask her something. I've had a couple of journalists get in touch about—'

'No,' he cut in. 'Tell them I'm on a break.'

'I did, but they're not just interested in you, Logan, and if we don't give a couple of exclusives, the hotel won't be able to cope with the locusts when they descend. I'm keeping them at bay from the conference, but unless they get a titbit or two...'

'Fine,' Logan huffed, still not able to take his eyes off the woman in front of him. She stood in the doorway, frozen, staring right back with those wide eyes. 'I'll ask her, but I'm making no promises.'

'Fine.' Peter's tone sounded like he'd already won. Which he probably had, given the fact that Logan wanted the press well away from the hotel this week. He'd seen Chloe when she got back from the lectures, the way she'd grown more subdued as the day went on. He knew something was bothering her, and he'd bet his TV Choice award that this whole scenario was the problem. The last thing either of them needed were more scrutinising eyes on them and their fake relationship. It had enough holes in it already. If that lot started, Swiss cheese would look solid compared. Too much was at stake. Especially now he'd decided that a week was not nearly enough with her. If this was all he was going to get, he was going to make sure he was there for her, like she had been for him. She could have gone to the press, told the truth and got on with her life. The fact was, she'd chosen to protect him, and now protecting her was going to be the role of his lifetime. For as long as she would let him, he would be there. 'Call me tonight, I'll need to answer them asap.'

'Okay.' Chloe was at the wardrobe now, pulling out various grey and black pantsuit combos and holding them against herself in the mirror. 'Oh and Pete, I need a favour. Call Verity, would you? Ask her for the full works.'

'Logan, you brought enough luggage to clothe a village for a mo—'

'Not for me. We'll need day and night.' His gaze fell on a pair of plain well-worn black pumps left on the floor. He leaned down to pick one up. 'Shoes too. Size six.'

'Six, got it. Anything else?'

'Nope. Ask her to put a rush on it. We have a casino-themed night tonight.'

'Tonight? It's gone three, Logan.'

'I did say it was a rush. All part of the plan.'

'Fine, I'll call her now. Keep up the script reads. We'll need to be ready when all this is over.'

Logan bit the inside of his cheek as he watched his fake girl-friend move about the room, all the while pretending he wasn't there. She was going to pitch a fit when the clothes arrived. Hopefully Verity would avoid the spiky heels, save his nether regions from the danger of Chloe's incensed wrath. He knew enough about her to figure she wouldn't be anything like the other women he'd dated who had been bestowed with the Verity treatment. 'I'm on it.'

When he put the phone on the bed, he felt her eyes on him. 'Hear me out,' he began.

She shut the wardrobe door with a little more force than needed.

'You could start with why you just told your agent my shoe size, and who and what is a Verity?'

He ruffled the hair on the back of his head. 'She's my stylist. I use her from time to time.'

Looking down at the rather stiff grey dress in her hands, she pursed her lips. 'Right, so let me guess. You want to make me look different... to this.' She held the dress afloat.

'Don't take this the wrong way, wildcat. I think you're cute, but you do dress like a librarian. A conservative one at that. Did you see how many women there were last night?'

She opened her mouth but huffily closed it again.

'Exactly. You are in a place where men rule the roost and women are thought less of. Even when they are either doing the same job or are infinitely superior. They already look down on you, but you let them by making yourself less. You don't have to dress like some stuffy suit.'

'A librarian, really?' She looked at the dress in her hands as if it was the first time she was seeing it. 'I... I guess you have a point. Still, I don't want to change for this. I want to be me. That's the whole point of this, Logan. I know you don't get it, but—'

'I do get it, believe me. No-one wants to be what they are not' – he tapped his chest – 'inside, but the thing is, Chloe, they won't care what's on the inside. Sometimes what you look like, how you present yourself to the world, makes them take notice. Clothes are just another tool to get what you want, believe me.'

'Yeah, of a fake persona.'

He shook his head. 'No, it will still be you. It just means that they will be looking and listening for once when you have something to say. You should never make yourself smaller to fit into their world. Trust me. I don't want to change you, Doc. I want you to win. So if I can get Verity here, will you at least see her?'

'Okay, I'll speak to her. What else did Pete want? I heard you say you'd ask me something.'

He watched her standing there, so trusting. So wary. The contradictions within her warring for control, and all he wanted to do was walk across the room and take her into his arms. What was this feeling? When he was around her, he wanted nothing more than to keep her safe. To be a damn shield for her. He'd never felt like this. He wanted her to smile at him again. Laugh with him. The press had taken a lot from him over the years. He'd given away pieces of himself, willingly and unwittingly. *They can't have her.*

'Nothing.' He smiled easily, folding his hands across his chest to stop him from reaching for her. Pete wanted to use her to feed into their story with the press, but he wasn't going to risk anything that would upset her. He wasn't about to feed her to a pack of jackals. She was his, for now at least. And he protected what he cared about. He also had a feeling that she would do it, if he asked. Which was all the more reason to tell a little white lie now. 'He wanted to ask if there was anything you needed from him, that's all.'

'Oh.' He got the smile, and it felt ill gained. 'No, I'm good. Tell him thanks, though.'

'Will do. I'll leave you to it, okay? I'm going to hit the hotel gym.' *To work off the sexual tension currently roiling through me before we get under the covers again.* If he didn't work off this energy, he might just slip up and scare her off for good.

She turned to the wardrobe, flicking through her hangers.

Utterly beautiful and unaware of his vehement feelings caused by her presence. 'I'll see you tonight though, right? For the themed night? Will you be back in time to see Verity?'

He brushed his lips against her cheek as he headed for the door. It was all he would allow himself to take. A cold shower was definitely going to be top on his workout routine. 'I won't be long. Wouldn't miss it for the world.'

* * *

Verity was nothing like Chloe expected. She was fully expecting a flamboyant young fashionista to get out of the helicopter that descended less than three hours later, but Verity looked more like Judy Dench. She didn't wait to be admitted into the hotel room; the second Chloe opened the door she strode in, followed by a bellhop who looked like he'd been running a marathon. He was sweating through his waistcoat as he carried half a dozen bags in and returned with a rack of clothing bags all hanging from the rail. When she turned to look at Chloe, her face fell.

'You're her?'

Chloe looked behind her at Logan, who was sitting reading his script on the sofa. Freshly showered, he looked even better than normal. At home, sitting there with bare feet, reading. Every thinking woman's fantasy. He grinned at them both.

'Yep, this is Doctor Chloe Henry. My girlfriend.' Coming to stand at her side, he put his arm around her. Chloe shrugged it off. Verity's eyes narrowed, and then she broke out into a huge grin.

'Well.' She smiled. 'Looks like you finally met your match, Logan. I'm surprised she even gave you the time of day. What are you a doctor of?'

'Medicine,' Chloe stuttered. Verity was now walking around them both, inspecting, and she felt like a prize horse at a stud farm. 'General surgery.'

'A surgeon, and a doctor?'

'Yes.'

'And you chose to date this clod? Can I ask why?'

'What do you mean, why? I'm a catch.' Logan folded his arms like a petulant child.

'Sure, sure,' Verity scoffed. 'If you like that chiselled pretty boy sort of thing. How did you get this woman to go out with you?'

Logan's lips quirked. 'I saw her naked.' Chloe slapped him on the arm. He took a step back, rubbing at his arm. 'Kidding! I wooed her, of course.'

'You did not,' Chloe huffed. 'Peter did that.'

Verity laughed. 'Ah, Peter. I get it now. Well, if he arranged this then I'm sure that there's some sort of PR stunt involved. Are you a consultant on the show?'

'No,' Chloe replied, just as Verity whipped out a tape measure from a pocket in her jacket and started measuring her arms. Verity was obviously a rare human, who didn't read the press. 'Do you work on the show?'

Verity laughed again, as if the idea was absurd. 'Oh God no, I run my own company, darling. Never wanted to tie myself down to one show like that. Besides, there is only so much you can do with scrubs and those godawful clog things, isn't there?'

Chloe smiled. She liked this woman. 'Very true.' Verity continued to measure various parts of her, taking notes in a little book. She lifted Chloe's arms this way and that, the occasional 'hmm' and 'wonderful' coming from her from time to time as she worked. Logan, she noticed, had disappeared off somewhere. Which was a good thing, since she was still pretty mad at him for organising this in the first place. Her little huffs as she thought of her faux beau didn't go unnoticed.

'Driving you around the bend already, is he?' Seeing Chloe's 'trapped in the headlights' look, Verity laughed. 'Don't worry, I won't say anything, but I have been dressing his dates for a while now. I see the signs.'

'Oh.' Chloe winced. 'Lovely.' *Way to remind me that I'm not special, Verity. Reality check well and truly received and understood.*

Verity's arched brow said it all. 'Usually it's his agent who books me. This is the first time Logan's bothered to request me himself. And definitely the first time he's introduced someone as his girlfriend. I thought the journalists had finally lost the plot but colour me surprised that it's true. Peter not here?'

The first time? She tucked away that little nugget to over-think later. Verity knew the smoke and mirrors that surrounded Logan, courtesy of Pete, but she believed that this relationship was more too. And Logan had made her think that, which was probably the most surprising part.

She realised Verity was looking at her expectantly and pulled her focus back to the conversation. 'No, but I doubt Peter knew my wardrobe needs. I've only met him once, and that was quite enough.'

Verity waved a hand. 'Peter Simpkin is like the bloody all-seeing eye. He misses nothing. Usually, I get a brief with the measurements, but this time was different. This came from Logan, not him.' She came to stand in front of Chloe. 'I think he might actually care.' The snort that came from Chloe was a surprise to them both. 'You don't think so?'

'I know so,' she blurted out. 'Well, I mean... I... just think that I'm a bit different to his usual... tastes. That's what this is all about.' She waved a weary hand at the rack. 'And no doubt why you're here. I'm sure Peter will have approved it. From what I've seen of him, he knows what he's doing when it comes to Logan.'

Verity walked over to the rail, zipping open a bag. 'Oh, honey, I don't think there's a person on the planet who knows what he's doing when it comes to Logan Broderick. I don't think anyone even knows what's going on in that boy's head. Maybe,' she said, coming to show her the bag, 'not even he himself. Now, for tonight, I think this one might just be the ticket.'

Chloe couldn't believe what she was seeing. Pulling the fabric through her fingers where it peeped out of the bag, she marvelled at the buttery texture of the material. Verity pulled the dress out, letting the fabric drape to the floor.

'This will be comfortable, wearable with flats or heels. I know you doctors live in those hideous croc shoes, but I have brought some low heels if you fancy trying them out. With your height, they would really make your legs pop in this.' She ran her finger along the thin spaghetti straps. 'Strapless bra too.' She peered down at Chloe's chest for a moment, nodding. 'I knew I was right about the size. I have just the pretty little set.'

'Set?' Chloe would have covered her boobs, even complained about the woman 'sizing her up', but she was so taken with the dress she couldn't think of anything else. Suddenly, she felt stupid for not thinking more about clothes before now. It bothered her that Logan had looked at her and found her lacking, plain. It bothered her even more that she cared what he thought. He or anyone. She'd sworn when she was very young to take her own path and never to live her life for anyone else. Well, as much as she could. Clothing had always been a source of quiet rebellion. They'd wanted her to shine, so she in turn took revenge by dressing to blend in the background. Holding the dress between her fingertips, feeling the silky gold material, she wondered whether this had been the key the whole time. Logan was right about how others saw her, but maybe, if she did it here, wore this dress tonight on her own terms, because she wanted to, then she could make them see *her*. Logan had given her the choice, an opportunity. If she did this, she could still be her. Perhaps people would take notice of her – even if it was just because of a damn dress. And – oh, what the hell was that?

'You mean that? That's an underwear set?' Verity was holding up what looked like lacy dental floss and a bra with scaffolding Chloe had only ever seen on patients who came into the ER after having a sex mishap that sent them to the hospital. 'No. Not a chance.'

Verity tutted, plucking the dress off the hanger and laying it on the bed. 'Sorry to be blunt, but your usual granny panties are going to show through this dress. The material is very fitted, so it's a package deal. How are you planning to do your hair?'

Chloe's hand reached up automatically to grab at her messy bun. 'Well, I don't know.' Verity was pulling things out of various boxes and, putting some shoes on the bed, she brandished an ornate gold clip.

'Well, I don't want to overstep, but girl – with your bone structure, we could do a lot more.'

Chloe turned to look in the mirror, pulling her hair free of its tie. 'You really think so?'

'I know so. Logan is a lucky man. Let's show him just how much. What do you say?'

And that was the moment Doctor Chloe Henry decided that if she was going to do this, she was going to be all in. Even if she only had Logan for a week, she was going to damn well make sure he remembered her.

11

LOGAN

V, where did you take my girlfriend off to? Just came back to the room and she's not there.

VERITY

The hotel comped me a private room for a while. Didn't want you seeing her before tonight, did we?

LOGAN

Fair enough. There are enough clothes in here for a month.

VERITY

Well, I got a bit carried away to be honest. I'll send you the bill. Nice woman you have there. Different from the other dates I've dressed.

LOGAN

She's definitely different. Is she okay?

VERITY

Wow, anyone would think you really care about her, Logan. You know what you're doing here? She's not someone to mess around.

LOGAN

I have no intention of hurting her. She's my girlfriend; that means something.

VERITY

Good. Just don't stuff this one up, kid. There's not many out there like her.

Logan huffed out a laugh. Verity was spot on, as per. Chloe Henry was definitely unique. He fired off a message to Peter, telling him that the no press thing still stood. He knew Pete would be unimpressed, so he distracted him with some thoughts he had on the script he'd been immersed in most of the day. The role was meaty, an utter departure from Dante Love. He was still a man pining for love; the man he would hopefully be playing was tortured, alpha down to the marrow of his bones, and Logan had never wanted a job so much in his life. Hell, he was practically living the whole pining man bit, wasn't he? He wanted this role, this woman. Everything was to play for now. He could show Chloe how serious he was about his career. The role would be the making of his next step. One that a doctor girlfriend would be impressed by, given that she didn't seem to care much about Dante Love. He wanted her to see him as the man who could do it all. It would show his softer side, the parts of him that Chloe had seen since the beginning. This film was it. His next step. If he could get this right, it would prove his mettle to fans and critics alike. *Pretty boy no more.* Maybe then they wouldn't care whether he'd dated or partied or not in the past. He could shed the media taint, be worthy. Someone a woman like her would be proud to have on her arm.

Pocketing his phone, he leaned back against the bar and took in the scene. The huge, imposing wooden double doors were open to the expanse of corridor beyond, the walls all festooned in casino adornments. Tables were set up around the room, croupiers in purple waistcoats ready to deal with the charitable lot that were laughing and chatting around the room. He checked his watch. *She's late.* Her boss Doctor Jeffries was already here, holding court with his smug little mini me. The pair of them were so alike, they sported the same fake laughter. *Time to big up my lady, I think.* He strode over, hooking himself a whisky from a passing waiter. The conversation lulled to a stop when people noticed him.

'Evening, doctors,' he greeted them, his voice full of warmth. 'Ready to lose some money?'

Doctor Carson answered first. 'Ah, well, if we do, it's all for a good cause.' He waved his glass in his direction, a broad shit-eating grin plastered across his face. 'You ready to spend some of that TV money, Logan? Or do you have to wait for Doctor Henry to arrive before you can have any fun?' He patted his chest. 'Oh, sorry. Actually, the fun usually stops when she's around, I forgot.'

Logan smiled back, a toothy, wolfy grin. *Fuck this guy. No wonder Doc was willing to go through all this, with him as competition.* He'd never wanted to pummel a guy so badly in his life, and he'd met his fair share of jerks over the years.

'Oh, Chloe can hold her own. She's a formidable woman, Johnny Boy. As you well know. How's your ass, by the way? Feeling better, I hope.' He patted him on the shoulder, hard enough to make him wince. 'I wouldn't count your chips until they're cashed if I were you.' Jonathan's eyes flashed with irritation, and Logan had to stop himself from outright laughing in the guy's face. The laughter never came either way, because he didn't have breath left to do anything. That was the moment Chloe walked in.

Glided, Logan corrected himself internally. Doctor Chloe

Henry *glided* in like a golden fricking goddess. Logan had seen some sights on the red carpet over the years, but the woman who was walking on the hotel carpet, right towards them, blew them all out of the water.

'You are screwed, Logan,' he muttered under his breath once he could draw enough to speak.

'Christ,' Jonathan breathed behind him. 'Is that... Chloe?'

'You're damn right it is.' Logan smiled as she approached them, her eyes focused solely on his. 'And it's Doctor Henry to you.'

He couldn't help it. He had to look. Tearing his gaze away from her face, he started at her heels and trailed up. Her legs looked so much longer as she strode across the room. Fucking edible, she was. The gold silky dress clung to, well, everything she had and showed it off. Like the dress had been made for her. He owed Verity a truck load of fruit baskets or something for this. He knew Chloe had a nice body, anybody could see that, but wearing this? She looked like a woman who deserved the world and everything in it. His gaze travelled up every single curve, dancing across the fitted bodice which showed off her creamy skin and elegant neck, till it landed back on her beautiful green eyes. They widened as she looked up, locking onto his appreciative stare, her face flushing. *Wait? Was she checking me out, too?*

'Good evening, gentlemen.' Her lipstick made her lips fuller, brighter. It was still her but magnified somehow. Brightened. *It's not the dress*, he thought to himself. *It's still her. The real her. Confident. Sexy.* 'Sorry I'm late.' Her smile dimmed when she looked back to Logan. He'd not moved, his back to the others as he stood rooted to the spot. Furrowing her brow, she turned him to face them, slipping her hand into his and giving him a little squeeze. It woke him up, but only just. Seeing her like this had only made the week feel even shorter. He had to see her after this. *Somehow.*

Looking at her, he grinned, letting his teeth show. Now he knew she responded to him physically for sure, and it wasn't just a proximity thing, he was damn well going to use what was given to him and charm the crap out of her. He spent half his career being the swoony love god, and by God did he summon him now.

'You were worth the wait, Doc.' Glancing at the little band of men before them, he could see they were still in a stupor. Jonathan looked a little green himself. *Good.* He chuckled in his head. 'What do you say? You ready to gamble?'

Her smile said it all. 'Bring it on, superstar.'

They cleaned up, in more ways than one. Chloe might have come across as a shy nerd, but she was one hell of a shark when it came to gambling. It was oddly erotic, watching her clean up. Another kink unlocked in his vault of Chloe Henry. When she took another consultant down with a killer hand, the whole table erupted.

'Well done, baby!' Logan cheered. 'Bad luck, mate,' he said to the loser, tapping him on the shoulder as he held out his hand for Chloe. She laughed, her hand warm in his as she rose to come to his side. 'I think that calls for another drink.'

As he led her to the bar, she was already shaking her head. 'Not for me, I'm not much of a drinker.'

'Well, if there was ever a time to start, it's here.' He nodded to the few tables scattered near the bar, where a number of people were already discussing surgery loudly and arguing about good outcomes. 'Do your lot not know how to let loose?'

Chloe thought for a moment. 'They fight against death; they know what causes it. It makes people wary.'

'Wary?'

'Well, heart surgeons would rather go for a run than eat bacon, for example.'

Logan chuckled. 'Yeah, but life is better with both, don't you think? We're all going to die in the end anyway, right?'

'True, but we're not film stars, we're people. Your lot tend to overindulge in most things. Kind of why we're here in the first place,' she added with a wicked gleam in her eye. *Oh, game on, darling.*

'Touche, but—'

The man at the bar in front of them stumbled as he stepped back, knocking into Chloe. Logan grabbed her instinctively, blocking her from the man with one arm while pulling her close with the other. 'Watch it,' he growled at the man, who apologised and shuffled off meekly. When he turned to check on Chloe, her face was close. Too close. Not close enough.

He could smell her perfume, see the way her pupils dilated when she realised how much of her was pressed against him. His arm cradled protectively around her back, palm splayed against the warmth he could feel through her dress.

'Thanks,' she said, her voice low, breathy. 'I'm okay.'

Neither of them moved. They stayed locked together, the noise of the room a dull rumble in his ears as his eyes fell to her lips.

'You sure?' he asked, his own voice sounding foreign. She placed her hands on his chest, and his eyes half closed from the contact. But then she pushed gently, and his hands released her.

Clearing her throat, she looked at the floor. 'I... er, will have that drink.'

Recovering, he nodded, moving his hand to the small of her back and leading her with him. His fingers tingled, as if willing him to keep contact. The spark he'd felt when he'd touched her was still zinging through his whole body. *Pull yourself together, Logan.* He risked a glance her way and saw the confusion on her face. He'd put that there. He was desperate to know what it meant. For them, for all of this. He didn't want to drag her into his mess, but he'd been a disaster before her. He needed to do this right, make sure it was going to be good for the both of them. She had enough people pulling the strings of her existence, and he'd bulldozed her life enough without complicating it further. He needed to be sure that she could take it, being with him. That it was even something she wanted. Because in only days, he already knew she was it for him. A week, a month, would never be enough. It was bad enough having to share a bed every night. He spent half the night reminding himself that curling his body around hers was not allowed, as much as he wanted to feel her against him. She made one hell of a little spoon. He'd woken up many times in the middle of the night with a body part of hers touching his. The erections were getting painful, and harder to hide. He'd had to jack off in the bathroom a few times when she was out, just to release the pressure enough not to do something stupid. Ever since he'd woken with her in his arms, he'd been a goner. *This is not like you, Logan. You don't fall.*

'Coming right up,' he managed to croak out. 'Champagne? Celebrate our wins?' He ordered from the barman without waiting for her to reply, giving himself a minute. Glancing at her, he could see she was doing the same thing. Something about the way she licked her parched lips, the way her cheeks were flushed, thrilled him. *So she does feel this.* It wasn't just him being a proximity-based freak show. She reacted to him. When was the last time he'd made a woman react like that off screen just by touching her so innocently? When had a woman made *him* feel like that, ever? He stopped his thoughts as best he could, reverting to small talk. Having a fake girlfriend was scrambling his brain. *It's not real, Logan. She's not yours. You don't – can't – have relationships. Not real ones, at least. Not ones worth keeping. Stick to the small talk. This boner shall pass.* 'Where did you learn to gamble like that?'

She shrugged, taking a flute when the barman placed two on the bar with a nod. *Did her hand just shake?* 'I worked a bar job while I was studying. More of a pool hall, really. Some of the regulars taught me when it was quiet.'

'Bet they soon wished they hadn't.'

She flashed him a cheeky grin. 'Sure did. Paid my way through school though.' She gripped her glass a little tighter. 'Better than relying on my parents for everything.' Nodding back to the tables, she grinned. 'Plus, tonight's for charity, so everyone benefits. Where did you learn?'

'Me? Oh, I did a movie based on a card counter.' When her brows furrowed, he laughed. 'Early days. TV movie.'

'Oh.' She took a sip. 'Didn't see that one.'

He squinted at her, and her blush gave her away. 'Thought you didn't watch any of my stuff?'

Chewing the side of her lip, she almost made him forget his question. 'I have Google.'

'Really,' he teased.

'Shut up.' She laughed before catching sight of something over his shoulder. 'Heads up. One of the interview panel.'

'Doctor Henry, nice work. I think your film-star boyfriend might have shown you a few tricks on how the other half live.'

Logan drew his arm around her waist, pulling her closer. He recognised him as one of the suits that was laughing along with Jonathan and the rest earlier.

'Trust me, my girl can hold her own. I'm the one learning.

Logan Broderick.' He held his hand out, just enough to make the guy lean in to take it. 'And you are?'

'Doctor Kowalski,' he said with a firm grip. 'I'm pleased to meet a fellow doctor.' His eyes flashed with mirth. Logan squeezed a little harder, and he pulled his hand back. Logan let his smirk fly, but it soon fell when Doctor Kowalski turned to Chloe. 'Having a good night, Chloe?'

'I am, Dean. Thank you. We worked together for a while, when I was on placement,' she told Logan.

'Brightest student I ever had. My first year of being qualified and she almost blew me out of the water.' He flashed a smile at her, making Logan's teeth clench. He was a good-looking bloke, all blonde quaffed hair and blue eyes. Not much older than Chloe, he figured. *Nice enough, but there's something about him.*

'Almost,' Chloe countered. 'I had a lot to learn back then.'

'Yeah, but you're all grown up now.'

Yeah, I definitely don't like this guy. His grip tightened on Chloe; he couldn't help himself. This fake boyfriend thing was definitely getting to him.

'That I am, and ready for the next step. I don't intend to play any games with that.'

'No,' Dean said, his gaze flickering down her body. Logan's whole core tensed. 'I don't suppose you do. I wish you all the best with it.' Turning slightly to look at Logan, he added, 'You have some competition.'

Smarmy fucker. Logan seethed. Was everyone in this place either a jerk or a letch? Something snapped in him, something whispering 'shut him up'. Looking down at Chloe, he saw the surprise in her eyes as he bent his head and pushed his lips against hers.

What are you doing? That thought rang in his head as skin met skin, and then he felt it. Her hand on his chest, gripping his shirt. *Shit*. It was a mistake. A stupid impetuous move fuelled by something he couldn't put a name to. He felt her grasp tighten, waited for her to push him off. They hadn't discussed this... part of the agreement. She wasn't some leading lady in a part he was playing. The lines were blurring. *Had he crossed it?* He'd never kissed a woman before without knowing damn sure beforehand that she wanted him to.

His mind stopped whirring when she pulled him closer, moved her lips against his. It felt... *Jesus, it feels good*. He could taste the champagne on her soft lips as her other hand came up and grasped his cheek. When she opened her mouth to his, he was lost. Dean didn't exist. Hell, the whole world ceased to be. He tightened his arm, pulling her flush against him. Let loose the throaty growl that erupted in his chest when her fingers plundered through his hair. He'd had a dozen screen kisses, but this... this was something else. He slipped his tongue into her mouth, and she met it. They kissed the holy hell out of each other, their tongues mingling, breaths fast, hot—

Dean cleared his throat from a universe away. He felt Chloe tense in his arms, but he kissed her once more before he broke contact. Pulling her to his side, he linked his fingers through hers.

'Sorry,' Logan said in a tone that implied he was anything but. 'What were you saying again?'

* * *

The lift doors closed with a ding, and the two of them were finally alone. Chloe hadn't said much the rest of the evening, but he'd kept her hand in his as they talked to the other guests. Weaving around the room, Logan had let her take the lead. He was still reeling from their kiss, and as he pressed the button for their floor, he found himself wanting to know what she thought about it. He wondered whether it had rocked her world. It sure had his, and he didn't know what the hell to do about it. When the lift started moving, she finally dropped his hand. He looked down at it, feeling too light for a moment. She was focused on the lift doors, not looking his way. The gold of her dress reflected against the silver steel all around them.

'Are you okay?'

Jolting out of her stupor, she met his eye. 'Yes, it was a good night, all in all.'

'I definitely think they noticed you. You were brilliant.'

'Well, I don't know about that.' She laughed. 'I will still have my work cut out at the presentation. This whole thing is basically the interview. It's a lot.'

'You'll do it,' Logan said as the lift came to a stop. 'Have faith in yourself, Doc.' He stepped out, but she didn't follow him. She was rubbing at her foot, her heel hanging askew.

'Sorry. These things are killing me. Never thought I'd miss my crocs.'

The lift doors started to close, but Logan stuck his hand up to stop them. Striding over to her, he picked her up off her feet.

'Logan! What are you doing?'

'Carrying my woman to bed,' he replied, heading to their room while she squirmed in his grasp. Her heel fell off and he bent to pick it up.

'You're going to drop me!' she squeaked as he retrieved the dropped shoe.

'Never,' he rumbled, lifting her higher just to make her grip him tighter. 'I've got you. You're safe with me.'

She tutted, relenting and throwing her arms around his neck. 'What is this, your caveman routine?'

'I think we've already established that I can be chivalrous

when I want to be.' He got to their door and watched her pull the key card out of her purse. 'Your feet hurt; I could help.'

When she pushed open the door, he kicked it with his foot and walked right over to the bed. Since that kiss, he was emboldened. Hopeful. And so, so horny for the woman who smelled so good, felt so good in his arms. He wanted to keep her forever. And do a ton of dirty things with her that he'd thought of non-stop since the moment he met her. *Slow down, Logan. Long game, remember?*

'I can... er... walk now.'

He ignored her, placing her gently on the bed and kneeling down. He could still do this, at least. Show his care for her. Be the guy she wanted around. In whatever capacity she would allow.

'You still have a shoe on.' Reaching for her ankle, he took off the remaining heel, dropping it to the floor. 'There, all better?'

The silence in the room grew loud as she looked down at where he still held her in place. His touch was warm against her bare skin. She wanted to pull her foot away, shut this down, but something stopped her. Since that kiss, she was having a hard time compartmentalising. This felt so real, and she wanted it to continue. Badly, even when she knew it couldn't. Right now, in their room, she was finding it hard to keep a level head. That kiss had changed her forever. She would never not blush when she saw Dante Love again on her TV.

'So does it?' he asked, his voice deeper now. 'Feel better?' Before she could answer, he ran his thumb along the sole. Her foot arched in response, and she saw his lips twitch. She went to pull away, and his other hand came to meet the other. 'Ticklish, Doc?'

He ran two fingers along her arch, holding her foot tight. 'Maybe, a little.' He massaged it, his touch firmer. Unbidden, a little groan of relief escaped her. They locked eyes, and she could see his chest rising rapidly. She would have teased him, but her own heart was thumping in her chest like a trapped bird. Something had altered between them since that kiss. Before then. It was in the room, with them, and now they were here together till the morning. She didn't know where to put herself, so she did what she normally did. She ignored it.

'I'm not used to wearing heels.' She pulled her foot away, and this time he let it go. 'Thanks for the lift,' she joked. 'I'm going to get changed for bed. It's been a long day.'

When she stood, he stood with her. 'Chloe,' he said as she turned towards the bathroom.

She felt his hand on her arm, running his fingers down it as he moved closer. Those familiar sparks hopped back and forth between them. She had to remind herself to breathe. One movement would be all it took for her to lose her senses entirely. Reach for him like she desperately wanted to. But this was fake, right? The feelings might not be on her end, but it still had an expiration date. Needed to have that date, because anything else would be too hard.

'I need to know something.'

They were almost nose to nose when she dared to meet his eye. 'Go on.' His fingers were trailing up and down her bare arm, making it hard to focus on anything but his touch. *Why did this have to be our story? Why did it have to be a story at all?*

'When I kissed you.'

She held her breath.

'Did...' *Did I want to? Yes. Do I want to again? Yes.* 'Did I cross a line?' He looked down at his hand, as if he'd just noticed the movement. 'I guess... I didn't like what that guy was saying.' He moved closer still, till his chest touched hers.

'So you wanted to shut him up?'

'Yes.' He reached up, taking a strand of her hair and running it between his fingers. 'Something like that. I'm sorry if—'

'I'm not.'

His eyes searched hers. 'You're not?'

'No.' She flashed him a grin. 'I can't stand Dean. He's almost as annoying as you.'

He laughed, and it made her heart skip. 'Oh really?' He moved his hand to her cheek, rubbing his thumb along her jaw. 'I think I might just be growing on you, Doc.'

'I doubt it,' she scoffed, but it was hollow. 'It hasn't been as bad as I thought. Dean can be a bit of a jerk. It was a good move, throwing him off like that.'

'Throwing him off?'

'Yeah, you know. He has known me professionally for a while. He knows my family. No doubt if he'd suspected us being fake, he would have told my parents. Pretending to be all jealous and passionate was definitely a good move.'

'I didn't do it for that, wildcat.'

'Then why?'

'I think you know why. We just seem to skirt around it.'

'What?' *That's it, Chloe. Play dumb. Pretend like you don't feel every minute part of this. I hate that I'm so weak. And not weak enough to ignore the world and touch him. Tell him how he makes you feel alive. And seen. And desired.* 'Skirt around what?'

His jaw clenched. 'My very real jealousy. The passion I felt kissing you. This attraction between us. I think you feel it. I sure as hell do.'

'Logan, I don't think we should read too much into that kiss. It was just a spur of the moment thing.' *It was also the single best moment of my life, bar none.* 'Part of the ruse,' she lied. She'd known the second he'd pulled her to him that he wasn't kissing her for the benefit of an audience. It was pure emotion. Just like now. She could see the frustration in his eyes as he spoke again.

'Not that spur of the moment. I've wanted to do it for a while.'

Geez. There went the butterflies.

'Maybe so, but this...' She gestured between them. 'It's not real. I'm not your girlfriend. After this week's up, we won't see each other again.'

'Who says?'

She swallowed, buying time to formulate the lies she needed to say. To put distance between them she would hate, inch by tortuous inch. 'I do. If I get the job, I'll be busy doing that, and if not I'll be looking for another placement. You'll get the movie, go back to work. We don't even live in the same city.'

'So? All of that is just semantics. I'm talking about how we make each other feel.'

'We infuriate each other half the time. It would never work. You've seen what the press are saying, the pressure from my family. It would kill anything real before it even got started.'

'I think we get on well enough to see where this goes. I know it would be hard, but I'm just saying that we could try. I'm not asking you to marry me. Just let me take you on a date. You woke me up, wildcat. I love who I am when I'm around you.'

He reached for her hand, but she folded them across her chest to stop him. If he touched her again, she was going to fold. She was going to kiss the hell out of him, and nothing good could come from that. Well, a lot of toe-curling good would come in the moment, but after? With her parents, and the media attention? She wasn't lying about that. She knew how hard it would be; the last few days had been difficult enough, even with Logan by her side 24/7. Real life wouldn't be like that. They would be apart a lot, for their work. She'd be alone again, dealing with more pressure than ever before. She wanted a normal life, away from all that scrutiny. With a boyfriend like

Logan, the spotlight would always be on them. Her family would never agree to the match. They'd do everything they could to drive them apart. Their two worlds didn't come together. That was the reality, as heart-stoppingly exciting the fantasy of them was. She'd watched this man on television for years now, daydreaming about dating Doctor Love. But daydreams were for dreamers, and she was a cold-hearted realist when it came to how she wanted to live her life. He'd get bored of the day to day, and then she'd be right back where she was. On her couch with her cat, watching someone she would never truly have. 'Chloe. Tell me what you're thinking. Please. This is killing me.'

Oh, Logan. You have no idea how much it hurts me too. She sucked in a shaky breath and braced for his reaction.

'The kiss was a mistake, Logan. We are both in this situation that neither of us asked for, that's all it is. It's not real. You're playing another role, that's all. You might like who you are around me, but that's not sustainable in real life.'

His jaw popped, his brown eyes searching hers. She turned away, not wanting to give him her secrets. The few she had left.

'That's how you really feel? That I'm playing some part with you?'

'Aren't you? Aren't we both?' She ran her fingers down her dress. 'This is not me, Logan. I am sweatpants and scrubs. I'm talking to myself and never saying what I want to say to the people in my life. I sit alone in my apartment and binge-watch TV, eating pizza. And that's when I'm not working every hour God sends to build the life I want, without people interfering or judging me. I like you, Logan, a lot – but this is just not real.'

'Bullshit. You and I, that's real. It's as real as we want it to be.' He would try, she knew. They both would, but if it wasn't enough to be worth all the hassle? Trying this and failing would hurt a lot more than not trying in the first place. She dug her heels in, stamping her feelings down underfoot as she went.

'No, it's really not. It's a long weekend of being here, being pushed to show feelings. Pretending to be something we are not. I am sick of that in my life. The lies, the deceit. Blurred lines. That's all this is, Logan. You have a big life to get back to. The movie, Belinda. You'll see that it would be too hard, when we leave here. When we go back to our own lives, you'll see that it would never have worked. We need to stick to the plan. See out the week, and then it's over. I'll make sure I stick to my side of the bargain, like you have yours.'

'I appreciate that, but I think you're kidding yourself, wild-cat. It would be hard, I know, but it doesn't mean we can't actually try this.'

'Yes, Logan,' she huffed, feeling the pressure bearing down on her. 'That's exactly what it means. Because everyone out there will stick their opinions in and tell us what they think, and it won't end well.'

He waved his hands in the air. 'Who cares what they think? I learned a long time ago that no matter what you do, people will judge.'

'Yeah? Well, maybe I don't want to be judged, Mr Big Star. Maybe I just want to be normal!'

'Normal? You couldn't be normal if you tried!' *Wow. That stung.* Logan fisted his hair, a huge sigh rattling out of him. 'That sounded awful. I didn't mean it like that.'

'It's fine.'

'It's not. I'm sorry it came out wrong. I meant the total opposite, Chlo.'

I know you did. I just can't hear it. 'It's fine, Logan. It's just the stress of the week, okay? Let's just pretend this never happened.'

'Chloe, no.'

'It's for the best. I'm going to bed. I have a full day of lectures in the morning.'

She was halfway to the bedroom when he spoke again. 'For what it's worth, I think you're extraordinary. I like sweatpants and scrubs. I love pizza, and sitting on that couch with you, it sounded pretty good to me.'

She didn't let him see the tear that slid down her cheek. She did what she always did; she ignored everything.

'I'll do what you ask. I'll pretend this never happened. I'll never kiss you again, unless you ask me to. But for the record, wildcat, I think you're the one not being real here. I'm going to the bar. Don't wait up.'

* * *

Getting to Wednesday was hell on wheels. Logan was the epitome of hot and cold. He was the perfect boyfriend in public. Bringing her drinks, being attentive, holding her hand. Carson had been a bit quieter since Doctor Jeffries and the others from the interview panel had arrived at the hotel, but he was still eyeballing her every chance he got. The guy was a total douchebag, but whenever he got close, Logan seemed to sense it and appear at her side. He was there after lectures to walk her back to their hotel room; he checked in on her in the daytime by text. Whenever she looked his way, he was always watching her. But he was a ghost when they were alone. There were no more late-night chats in the dark, no more big spoon and little spoon. Every night, she went to bed alone, and when she woke up, he was already dressed and on the couch, reading his script or talking to Pete on the phone. The press was being kept at bay thanks to the hotel, but they were still writing about them. A lot. One article said that they were secretly engaged; another said that she was pregnant with his triplets. She'd laughed pretty hard at that one. It would have been an immaculate conception, given that they'd barely kissed and were now decidedly formal with each other. The whole world seemed to love the idea of them being together, and they were further apart than ever. The irony was crushing her under its weight, and when she woke up alone again on Wednesday morning, she knew what she was going to do.

Today was her presentation and then the interview panel was going to be meeting right after, and all the hard work would be done. After that it was just the expo and the lunch on Friday. She didn't need to be there for any of that – so she was going to pack her stuff up and get the hell out of Cornwall. Logan was booked to stay for another week, so it wouldn't look too bad leaving separately. And definitely better than having to stay in that room with Logan for another few days and pretend that she wasn't dying inside. With no lectures or interview prep to pour her concentration into, she would have nothing to hide behind.

She was up at the crack of dawn that morning, sleep having evaded her till the wee small hours. She slipped out from under the sheets, trying not to ogle Logan as he slept on his back, shirtless. He looked so cute, lying there. She had to resist the urge to wake him up just to see those beautiful brown eyes of his. She missed the way he used to look at her when they lay there together in the dark. She'd never have that again now. Tomorrow she would be waking up in her own bed, back in her old life. The one without Logan in it.

The presentations started well. She had the privilege and

luck to go first, and she didn't look up once as she focused on the laptop in front of her. The slides worked; she was in the zone. Talking about private costs versus NHS costs was a gamble, but she had seen both sides of the coin for years and knew exactly what she was talking about. When she finished, applause rippled around the hall, and when she risked a glance up, she saw that even Carson was clapping. Todd Archer was on his feet, and even Doctor Jeffries was nodding in approval. She felt like a damn queen walking to her seat, and just as she was about to sit down, she saw him. Logan, standing at the back, his brown eyes looking right at her.

'Well done, wildcat,' he mouthed, his eyes crinkling in the corners in that adorable way she loved. 'You killed it.'

'Thank you,' she mouthed back, taking her seat and wishing he was next to her. When she looked back, he was gone.

The rest of the presentations went well, but they didn't get the attention hers did, and she allowed herself to hope, just a little, that she might just pull this off. That all the stress and pressure and working her arse off was finally going to pay off. Maybe then losing Logan would be bearable. *Who are you kidding, Henry? No job could do that.*

Doctor Patel's presentation was insightful, the passion for his work showing through the way he spoke. His wife, sitting in the row in front, was rapt, grinning her head off at him the whole way through. When he'd finished, she whooped. It was great to see, but it only served to remind Chloe that she was here alone. After Baldoni's presentation, which was equally as great, she had to endure Carson's effort. This was it. This was the rival to beat, and she'd never wished for a man to slip and smack his stupid face into a podium more. She giggled at the notion, stifling it with a cough and wishing Logan was here to share her intrusive thought with. She really needed to get a damn grip of her emotions. *Emotions are not the Henry way*, her mother always told her. For once, channelling her parents didn't quite suck so much. She tucked her feelings tight into herself and watched her nemesis shoot his shot.

The man was a big fan of a PowerPoint, that was for sure. The whole thing was obviously prepared by a graphics company, but he wasn't as smooth as she expected him to be. He stumbled over some of his data, and when Baldoni questioned some of the statistics, she saw him bristle on the podium.

'My data is correct, Doctor Baldoni, but thanks for the question.'

'Actually, it's not.'

Chloe held her breath as the whole conference turned to the voice at the back of the hall and looked straight at Logan Broderick.

'Er, thanks, Logan, but this is actual medical data. Not a script.' Carson bristled, his tone clearly irritated.

'It's still wrong, though. You're talking about cardiac output, correct?'

Carson's teeth clenched so tight Chloe was pretty sure he cracked a bone.

'Correct, yes. I am talking about cardiac care and how we can streamline the process of treatment.'

'Right, but your formula is wrong. You have the heart rate at 70 bpm and the stroke rate at 70 ml.'

'Correct. You can read.'

Logan didn't flinch, his smile never faltering, and she saw the moment Carson's temper started to flare when he realised that Logan wasn't backing down.

'Yes, I can read. I can also do maths, and using the formula, the result wouldn't be 3,500. It would actually be 4,900 millilitres per minute, or 4.9 litres per minute.'

Chloe did the sums in her head as the murmurs started to ripple around the room. Logan was right. She hadn't even clocked it herself. No-one had, but they had now. Carson was clicking on his laptop like a madman, his cool demeanour blown apart.

'Fuck!' he cursed, right into the microphone. Todd Archer got to his feet and started to head over as Carson turned his fury and aimed it all at Logan. 'What the hell is your problem, Logan? Defending your girlfriend again?'

Doctor Jeffries went purple. 'Doctor Carson, please! Calm down!'

Logan strode down the central walkway, stopping halfway down and looking every inch the arrogant man she'd once thought him to be.

'Oh, my girlfriend doesn't need my protection, pal. She can wipe the floor with you blindfolded with one arm behind her back. I'm a doctor on television, and I reckon my patients are safer with me working their cases than you on your best day.'

Carson jumped up and down on the spot like a toddler, and Chloe couldn't help the cackle that burst out of her.

'I'm going to kill you, Broderick! You hear me!'

Logan folded his arms, looking bored. 'Save yourself the butt cheek, Carson. Bow out gracefully.'

'Arrgghhh!' Carson exploded, knocking the podium to the floor and running towards Logan. He got three steps before security came barrelling in and scooped him up. 'No! It's not fair! Doctor Jeffries, it's not fair!'

Doctor Jeffries shook his head, turning to Todd Archer to say something before striding out of the room without a backwards glance. The rest of the place was in chaos, doctors laughing, taking photos, while the interview panel were huddled in a corner looking like they were hosting an emergency meeting. And Logan was right there, in front of her. Reaching out.

'You ready to get some lunch, wildcat? It's looking like they'll be a while here.'

Taking his outstretched hand, she stood and let him lead her to the doors. He took her bags, slinging them over his shoulder as he led them away from the chaos.

'How did you spot that error?' she asked him as he steered her to the exit. 'I missed it.'

'I do read my scripts, Doc. You pick up a thing or two. I was always good at maths.' He looked back at Carson, who was currently subdued and crying in a chair. 'I doubt that guy will even have a job at your hospital after this, never mind the top spot. Your presentation was great, by the way. I'm so fucking proud of you.'

'Doctor Henry?' Dean came up behind them, a very flustered-looking Todd Archer in tow. 'If you have a minute, we wanted to talk to you about the job.'

'Oh? I assume the interviews will be held back, in light of... events.'

'We're not going to hold interviews now.' Dean nodded. 'We have everything we need to make a decision. We will be in touch with everyone next week.'

'Is that okay with you?' Todd added.

'Yes, of course. Though in light of that, I will be leaving later today.' She felt Logan's eyes on her. 'It has been a busy week, and I am back at the hospital on Monday. I would appreciate some time off.'

'Of course, of course.' Todd nodded emphatically, smiling sheepishly at Logan. 'And Mr Broderick, we can only apologise for Doctor Carson's behaviour. We do hope it didn't ruin your time with us.'

'No, not at all. Like I told you before, I am just here in a boyfriend capacity. Nothing else. Doctor Henry is a professional, and I know that you will make the decision about the job fairly and promote the right person for the position.'

'Of course.' Dean smiled. 'We respect that. We're sorry you're leaving us today, Chloe. We'll be in touch.'

The minute they were alone, Logan took her outside. 'You're leaving today? Since when?'

'I decided this morning. There's no need to stay for the rest of the conference, and after this I doubt they will make a fuss.'

'When were you going to tell me?'

'After my interview. I think it's for the best. I'll be back at work soon, and there's my parents and the press.' And her need to run from him, to start the process of not having him in her life. The sooner she got used to it, the better. Being here, so close to Logan, was killing her.

'You're running from this.'

The way he was looking at her, she couldn't take it. He was angry and defeated, upset and unwilling to take no for an answer. She could see every emotion right there, battling within him. Because they were careening through her too. She needed to stay true to the story. The narrative she'd told herself that they would never work. That what she was doing now was for the best. For both of them. Pre-emptive surgery.

'I'm not running, Logan. The week's over. We don't need to play the happy couple at an expo, and after that fiasco I doubt the farewell dinner will be fun.'

'What if the press finds out you left early? You'll need someone there with you.'

She put her hand on his chest, and he fell silent. 'I have to face it sometime, Logan. The hard work's over. I promise, I'll be fine. I won't speak to them. Pete has my number, and you have the script to focus on anyway. It's not like we were leaving together.'

He sucked in his cheeks, his hand enveloping hers and remaining there.

'I just thought we'd get more time. What about lunch, or a dinner?'

She shook her head. 'I just want to get home, to be honest. Thanks, Logan, for everything. I mean it. I don't think I would have got through this without you.'

'Yes, you would. You're stronger than you think. Let me call you a car, at least. Get you home safe. The press will be camped outside this place.'

She nodded, not trusting herself not to break down in front of him. This was goodbye, and it felt terrible. She wanted nothing more than lunch and dinner with Logan. She wanted everything, but saying goodbye to him was coming, sooner or later. Better now while she could do it without truly knowing what it was like to be with him. For real. 'Okay. A car would be good. Thanks, and goodbye, Logan.'

'Goodbye, wildcat.' He looked down at their joined hands and pulled her into a hug, lifting her off the floor and into his arms. 'I'm really going to miss you,' he breathed into her neck.

She felt his kiss on the top of her head, and then she was standing there. Watching Logan Broderick walk out of her life without a backward glance.

Chloe shivered when she locked her front door behind her. It wasn't chilly outside, but her home felt cold. Leaving her luggage to one side in the hall, she scooped to pick up the mail that had gathered behind the door. There was a small, neatly stacked pile of parcels that she chose to ignore for the moment. Most of them were books she'd ordered, but her mind felt too empty to read. The rest were no doubt her boring bulk orders. Toilet roll, cat food, litter. Her cat sitter always took them in for her when she was on double shifts or away. It could all keep, till she had the energy to deal with it. Sliding the chain across the wood, she hung her keys on the solitary hook on the wall and shucked off her shoes.

'Meoooow!' A dark ball of tetchy fur barrelled into her feet, head-butting her bare legs and making his displeasure at being left well known. She scooped him up, shoving her face into his soft black fur as he rumbled into a loud purr interspersed with little meows of happiness.

'Aww, buddy! I missed you too, Dante.' Clicking the thermostat up on the wall, she cuddled him in her arms while she headed to the kitchen to feed him. The cat sitter would have fed him this morning, but he still acted like she'd left him to fend for himself for the week. *Drama king, living up to his name.*

An hour later, she plonked herself on the couch and stared at the recordings list on the TV screen. Her freshly showered hair was high in a messy bun, her favourite red flannel pyjamas dwarfing her frame as she tucked her socked feet under herself and dragged the fluffy blanket off the back of the couch to snuggle under.

'Perfect,' she mumbled, feeling like it was anything but. Being alone here, back in her cosy space, somehow felt strange. Lacking. And she knew why. There was a Logan Broderick-shaped hole in it. She would have been warm if he was here with her. In his arms, feeling complete like she had in that hotel room bed. 'Almost. Still, I've got you, eh, Dante?' She looked across the couch, where Dante was snuggled on top of the blanket licking his own nether regions. 'Nice. No pizza for you for that.'

She turned back to the TV, remote in hand, and flicked through the recordings for the shows she'd missed while she was away. A documentary on the state of the healthcare system, a series on Peru treks. She flicked through them all, gnawing at her lip till the flashing cursor landed on what she was looking for. *Doctor Love.* She winced as she bit down too hard on her lip. Swiping a finger across it, she stared at the red line. Blood. She'd drawn haemoglobin at the mere thought of seeing Logan again. That didn't bode well, especially since she still had another few days till she was back at work. Right now, in her little comfort fort, take-out on the way, she should feel like she usually did. Settled. Carefree, almost. Her favourite place was home, but now she realised just how... insular it was. What did she have besides work? Without Logan, it all felt... lacking. Less than fulfilling. As she glanced across at her cat, they locked eyes. He didn't stop licking his butt.

'I'm pathetic,' she mumbled, burying deeper under the blanket. 'If *Celeb News Weekly* could see me now, eh?'

The buzzer went, signalling the delivery of her usual veggie pizza, dough balls and Ben & Jerry's. She ordered from the local pizza place so often they had her card details on file and all she had to do was speak and Angelo would say, 'Chloe! *Mi bella!* The usual, on its way!' Normally, it was quite comforting, but earlier when she'd called Angelo's Pizzeria, the recognition had made her feel more alone.

'Well,' she muttered as she clicked off the TV, shrugging off the blanket to shuffle to the door. 'At least Angelo will miss me if I snuff it. Maybe he'll call the authorities before you get to eat me, Dants.'

Opening the door, she plastered a smile on her face, reaching for the bundle of food.

'Hey, Angelo.'

'Hi, gorgeous.' Logan was standing at her front door, her food in his hands. 'I hope you got enough dough balls for two.' His brows knitted together as his gaze slid over her. 'And I don't know who Angelo is, but I'm sure as hell not sharing.'

'Angelo's the pizza guy,' she managed to stammer out, feeling her face explode into a hot, red hue. Had she passed out on the way to the door? Hallucinated what she couldn't stop thinking about? 'Logan... I... er... You're here.'

'Yep, well spotted.'

'What... Why... What are you doing here?'

She didn't mean it to come out so harsh. Didn't miss the awkward shuffle of his feet as he stood there, the smile sliding off his face. He recovered quickly, overcompensating with a wide grin. 'Well, I figured I might need another career someday.' He nodded to the food in his hands. 'Pizza delivery is definitely off the list though.' His eyes locked onto hers. 'So, are you going to let me in or not?'

After pointing him to the lounge, Chloe sagged behind the bathroom door. Her chest felt like it was being compressed; she couldn't draw a breath deep enough to stop her panicking. Sinking to the floor, she willed her lungs to inflate, taking slow measured breaths, her fingers against her pulse. Why was he here? She'd assumed he'd stay at the hotel as planned, learning his lines. He must have packed up and left right after her to be here now.

Logan had followed her home. He was here, in her world, and she didn't know what the hell to do about it or how to think. She'd thought about nothing but this since she'd walked in that front door but never thought it would happen. That goodbye had felt so final. Now he was here, how was she supposed to let him leave?

On shaky legs, she pulled herself up on the sink and stared into the mirror. The reflection she saw screamed scared rabbit in the headlights.

'Oh God,' she groaned. 'I had to be in my pyjamas, didn't I. I look like a before ad for bloody sleeping tablets.'

'Chloe? You say something or sing-cursing again?' His voice was right outside the door.

Shit. 'No!' she screeched. 'No, I'll be right out!'

She flushed the chain to cover the mini panic attack he'd just interrupted, washed her hands and almost slammed right into him.

'Whoa! Sorry!'

His arms were around her waist in an instant, her hands landing on the material covering his chest. Her fingers sank into the soft wool of his snow-white jumper. His breath came hot and fast against her face. He was so close it made her think of all the other times they'd been like this. When he'd kissed her at the conference, how many times his hands had touched her body. She gently pushed him away, side-stepping him to head to the lounge even as her fingers itched to sink deeper into that wool and draw him closer. She could hear him behind her, even over the pulsing of her heart in her ears as she slowly climbed down from her heightened state of panic in the bathroom.

'Chloe, are you okay? You seem a bit... weird.'

'Weird?' she scoffed with a snort, taking up her spot under the blanket again and wrapping it around herself like fluffy armour. 'I'm not weird. Showing up here and listening outside my bathroom door is though.' She stiffened as he sat down next to her and his palm covered her forehead. 'What are you—'

'No fever,' he mused, looking at her as if she was a puzzle he needed to decipher. 'You look pale though.' He grabbed the pizza box from the stack on the coffee table, opening it on her lap. 'Eat,' he commanded, before leaving the room entirely.

'Logan, where are you going?'

'To make you some tea. I don't hear eating.'

'I don't want any tea.'

'Tough. Still don't hear chewing. Cold pizza sucks, so start eating.'

She groaned but pulled a slice from the box and took a bite. *Okay, so he has a point.* She was hungry. By the time he came back in with two steaming mugs and an approving smile, she had devoured three slices and was polishing off her fourth dough ball.

'That's my girl.'

She took the tea, not bothering to argue. The dough balls were a little dry.

'So, Angelo – that a serious thing?' He tucked his feet under him, mirroring her pose while he sipped at his own tea. 'Do I need to have a word?'

'No.' She pouted to hide the little smile his words had elicited. The more she was around him, the more she liked this jealous streak. It made her feel seen, wanted. *Desired.* 'But we have been in a food relationship for a good few years now. His pizza's the best.' She pushed the box in between them. 'There's some left, if you want a slice.'

He pushed it back. 'I think you need to finish it. This the first thing you've eaten all day?' Opening her mouth to refute his claim, she shoved another slice into it instead. 'That's what I thought. You missed breakfast and turned me down for lunch.'

The pepper slice she was chewing almost stuck in her throat. 'Yeah, sorry about that. I needed to get back. My cat sitter's nice, but she's pretty busy herself. I think she was glad to hear I was coming back early.'

'You have a cat?' His head flicked around the room. 'Where is it?'

That was a point. Where was... *Oh, crap.* 'He's, er... somewhere around here. He's a bit skittish around strangers.'

'Really.' There it was again, that assessing stare of his. 'Just like his mother.'

She swallowed the last of her crust audibly, washing it down with more of the sweet tea.

'I rang your phone but it was turned off.'

'Yeah, I thought I'd take a day, you know. Settle back in without all the noise.'

'You needed to get back to your fake cat.'

'My cat is not—'

She fell silent when the familiar rustling under the couch

came, followed by a pair of grey eyes poking up and eyeing them both.

'Hey, little guy,' Logan said, his voice low and soothing. The cat looked at him, then her, and to her surprise, jumped onto the couch arm right next to him. She watched as Logan held out a hand for him to sniff, and the little traitor nuzzled his head against his hand. 'Not so scary, am I?' Logan chuckled, rubbing his fingers along the cat's fur. Chloe heard the little shit purr and threw another dough ball in her mouth for something to do. It looked as though Logan Broderick really could charm every pussy. 'What's his name?'

Chloe inhaled half the dough ball with her gasp. Logan had to slap her on the back to dislodge it.

'Jesus, I know I said eat, Chlo, but chewing is required.' He was right next to her now, the food boxes on the coffee table where he'd shoved them aside to reach her. His hand was still on her back. She could feel the heat through her flannel top. She felt every touch as he stroked small circles across her skin. He lifted her mug of tea to her lips. 'Here.'

She coughed again, letting him touch the ceramic to her lips and drinking deep. She was still regaining her breath when he took it away again. 'Why did you leave me like that, Chloe? Was it just the Carson thing?'

'No. That was all on him.'

'Okay, but it's something. I know we've been weird around each other, but you couldn't wait to get out of there. I get it, but I wanted to talk more. What did I do?'

Nothing. Everything. She wanted to tell him the truth, but even speaking about it out loud make her feel weak. She was a Henry. They didn't get weak. They ate strength for breakfast, right alongside their Wheaties. Waking up in his arms, in that hotel room bed? Kissing him? It had freaked her out. If she'd stayed, she would have relented. Heart would have won over head, and she would have gone through with trying a real relationship. She was getting too close to Logan, and the pressure from everything was bearing down on her. It was too much. Her parents had stayed away from the conference. Hadn't contacted her, but she knew they wouldn't hold back now. They'd stayed away because they wanted to control the situation. She was in no doubt that now she was back home, they'd want to get her alone to speak about things. She was surprised she'd managed to make it back to her place without the press outside too. She lived in a secure building, with security. The doorman didn't need to deal with all that. Paul was a nice guy; he looked out for her. Signed for her parcels, brought her cookies his wife had made and told her off when she worked too hard. He was like a surrogate grandad... who had let Logan up without a second thought because the world thought he was her boyfriend. There was too much to wade through for something that wouldn't work out anyway. She didn't have many people who cared for her, but she wanted to avoid causing trouble for those few she had. Including the man sitting on her couch.

'Chloe.' Logan was looking at her expectantly. 'Talk to me. Why did you leave like that? The truth.'

'I just needed to get back. I thought since our arrangement was over...'

'It's not over. Not in my book.'

'We did the week, Logan. Or the parts that mattered, anyway. That was the deal.'

'No, the deal was I help you prove to your colleagues that you're the best person for the job, and you don't have the job yet.'

'No, but they'll make that decision. That's not down to you.'

He shrugged, pulling his hand away and wrapping her back up in the blanket. 'You done with the food?'

At her nod, he picked the boxes up, moving slowly to the kitchen as Dante eyed him like a statue sitting on the couch arm. The second he was out of the room, the little cat jumped into her lap, flexing his paws on the plush blanket to make himself comfy.

'You're dead to me,' she whispered to him, only to be rewarded with a happy-sounding mew-mew. 'No more catnip for you, Judas.'

She could hear the lid of her kitchen bin click open, Logan shuffling around her space. It was weird to have someone here, looking after her. Giving a crap whether she ate or not. The look of urgency that crossed his face when she'd started to choke. When he came back in with the tub of ice-cream in his hand, two spoons sticking out of it, she moved the blanket off the couch cushion for him to sit down.

'I'm sorry I didn't say goodbye very well.' She reached for one of the spoons, scooping up a spoonful of the cold dessert. 'I... I just had to get out of there. It was all a bit much, by the end.'

Chewing on his own spoonful, he tapped the spoon against his closed lips. 'Me, or the conference?'

'Both,' she breathed, wishing she could explain to him how she was feeling. How poorly she felt when she thought about everything she had to do, to prove. How much she'd wished for him to be here, even though she'd run from everything he made her feel. Telling him any of that felt like too much too, so she told him what she could handle divulging. 'I'm just... tired. Confused, maybe.' *Definitely. You confuse me so much, when I'm around you I can't tell which way up the world is.*

'And...'

'And?' She might have known he wouldn't buy it.

He moved closer on the couch. 'And I feel like you want to say more but don't know how to.' *Busted.*

Dante's purr was the only sound in the room as they stared at each other. His eyes always saw too much. She looked away before she spilled more of her secrets, flicking on the TV for something to distract them both. He gasped.

'You little liar,' he breathed, and she snapped her head to look at him. *How does he...* 'You do watch the show!'

Her head turned to the screen, where the recorded episodes of *Doctor Love* were highlighted.

'Bollocks,' she muttered, just as he burst out laughing.

'I knew it! You bloody fibber!'

'I... I...' She huffed out a laugh. 'Fine, I watch it.'

'Watch it? You're on season seven! That makes you a fan, Doctor Henry.' He whipped the remote out of her hand and clicked on the programme. 'Episode five next, eh? That's a good one. Want to watch?'

'Don't you have somewhere to be?'

He stuck his spoon into the ice-cream with a shake of his head. 'Nope. You?'

She looked down at herself, her loose bun bobbing with the movement. 'Do I look like I have plans?'

His smirk was downright sexy. 'No, but you look hella cute. I love the PJs. Very mountain lumberjack.' He pushed the tub into her hands and settled in closer. 'So neither of us have any plans, we've established. Episode five it is.' He pressed play, and the credits started to roll. 'I am a little cold though.' His hand reached across to rest on her blanket-covered leg.

'The heating's on,' she half whispered, feeling the ice-cream melt in her suddenly hot hand.

'Still cold,' he mumbled, pulling his hand away and folding

his arms across his chest. 'I'm not going to do anything, Chloe. We shared a bed. You slept on my chest that night you helped me read lines. I'm pretty sure you drooled on me at one point. You also made it pretty clear that nothing was going to happen between us. I respect that. I thought you'd trust me enough to know I'm not here to ravish you.'

She did know, but the fact that she hoped for it deep in her heart was an entirely different matter. Logan filled the screen, his white coat showing off the tight, muscly shoulders underneath as he strode down a corridor on screen, tablet in hand. Melodic music played over a voiceover of one of the other characters, setting the screen for the first patient journey of the episode. After a moment, she pulled the blanket taut, covering Logan with it and keeping her eyes on the screen. She heard his contented sigh as his leg brushed against hers, and without overthinking it, she leaned into him. The patient Dante Love approached was convulsing, her whole body writhing as the doctors and nurses scrambled to hold her down on the bed. When Logan's arm came around Chloe, she settled into his side, and when his fingers gently pushed at her neck, she went with it, resting her head in the crook of his shoulder. When he pulled the blanket tighter to encompass them both, her little buddy let out a disgruntled miaow.

'Shush, Dante,' she said, not thinking till she felt Logan's body still against her.

'You named your cat Dante, Chloe?' His lips brushed the shell of her ear, making her shiver despite the cosy warmth that enveloped them. 'I think that makes you a superfan.'

'Shut up,' she muttered, but her words held no heat.

'It's okay,' he rumbled, his arm tightening around her as his lips brushed her temple. 'I'm partial to a certain flannel-wearing doctor myself.'

The familiar fizzing in the pit of her stomach boiled over. Not the usual uncomfortable ache that came with the anxiety. This was warmer, heating her from the inside. A welcome bubble of pleasure that zinged through her body.

'Is that right?'

'Yeah, Chloe. That's right. I was gutted when you left. I couldn't wait to see you. I had Peter track down your address the second you left.' He sighed. 'I was planning to go to a hotel tonight, but when I got there, it was full of photographers.' He must have felt her flinch because his hold tightened. 'It's okay, they didn't follow me. I had my car turn around. I was going to come and see you anyway, before you ask. I thought they might have come here.'

'Nope. Guess they haven't found me yet.' She drew a ragged sigh. Perhaps the Henry influence had already started. 'So they're not leaving you alone? I thought things might die down.'

'They will. It's not like before. They're not after their pound of flesh this time.'

'No, just a pound of mine.'

'I won't let them near you.' His voice was so low it came out as a growl. 'My people will throw them off, Peter's already been on it. I won't let them disrupt your life any more than they have already. I just think it's best if I stay close. If I head back to London, it's too far to get to you if you need me.' There it was again, him putting himself between her and the threat. It was getting harder to not just lean into it and trust it would always be like this. The two of them against the world. 'And I want you to need me, Chloe. I know I caused this, but I want to be the one who sees you through it.'

Wow. Maybe it wasn't too bad to have people looking out for you, other than for their own ends. She forced herself to look into his eyes and saw nothing but determination and kindness there.

'I don't need you to protect me, Logan.'

He huffed out a laugh, his lips coming to rest on her forehead. 'That's the thing, Chlo. I want to do that for you, if and when you'll let me. You did it for me.'

'Not by choice.' She laughed. Another lie. She could have walked away that day, after the shower meeting. She chose not to, and she couldn't bring herself to regret that decision. Even with the pain that would no doubt be coming down the line.

'Maybe not, but you did it anyway.' Another kiss to her temple. 'I think it's about time you had someone fighting in your corner. Okay?'

Everything in her rational, stubborn mind wanted to push against his words, but they had already wrapped around her, just like his warm body under the blanket they now shared. It felt... right. They had been there for each other. It seemed only logical that it should continue. Just for now. Just till she got the job, found her footing in life again. She was so tired of battling on her own. She still had her side of the deal to fulfil. She wanted him to get the career he wanted too. She just had to try to protect her heart in the process. Remind herself that their time together was finite.

'Okay,' she said before resting her head back in the crook of his neck. Dante on the screen ordered a round of drugs as he battled to save a patient in the ER. 'And for the record, you would have killed your patient with that drug order. He already had a dose on the last round.'

The low rumble of laughter made her smile as she snuggled into him. 'Yeah, well, maybe I can take you on set one day. You can give them all what for.'

'Deal,' she murmured, feeling sleepy as his aftershave enveloped her. 'We help each other, right?'

Her eyelids were starting to flutter shut, but she felt the kiss on top of her head.

'Sure do, wildcat,' she heard him mutter as her eyes finally closed.

* * *

Her eyelashes were longer than he'd first thought. Usually he was too busy sinking into those green eyes of hers to take note, but they were another beautiful piece of her. Darker too. They were black against her pale skin, fluttering occasionally as she stirred in her sleep. If you could call it sleep. She didn't seem to relax, even in slumber. He watched her for far longer than he should have, his brows furrowing with each twitch of her limbs. She muttered a few things he couldn't make out in her sleep, but the words didn't matter. It was the sound of her voice when she spoke that made his heart clench. She was coiled far too tight, even for her. In the past week, he'd seen far more. Glimpses of a fun, feisty Chloe. A put together, smart and strong woman who was also vulnerable, guarded. He couldn't believe he'd thought her prim or snobby. She wasn't that. The opposite, in fact. She was battling her own head, just like him. The difference was, he wanted to do it all with her, and she was keeping him at arm's length. It didn't fully make sense, till the presentations had erupted and she'd run. He'd realised she was scared. Scared of wanting him. When everything around her was already crushing her, she was stubbornly refusing to take his hand and pull themselves out of it, together.

'I should have seen it,' he muttered to himself when she flinched again, pulling her closer to him instinctively. Wrapping his arm around her, feeling the warmth of her, something shifted in his chest when he felt her body react. Slowly, the flinching stopped. He stayed there for the longest time, just being in her space, revelling when he felt her relax and finally fall into a deep sleep. Something about his touch comforted her. *Do I make her feel safe?* Was that really a thing? He'd played parts like that before, when the hero was all protective and alpha. The fans had lapped it up, but in real life? He didn't think anyone had ever felt that way about him. His mother was probably the last woman who'd depended on him, but that was different. *This is different.* He thought back to the conference, how he'd felt when she'd been disrespected. It had... done something to him. Changed the way he'd acted around her. She was a strong, independent woman. She saved lives, for God's sake. Her work was tough, and important, and she thrived on it. Rose to the challenge of the job, and wanted more than that. She wanted to change things, pull others up to her level. She cared, but who cared for her? Not her parents. Her colleagues either saw her as uppity or pure competition. She hadn't mentioned any other significant people. Hell, the animal currently padding his paws on the blanket beside her was probably the closest living, breathing thing in her life.

He looked around her living room, as if the realisation was some key to figuring her out. Her place was neat, cosy. At odds to her steelier work persona. She was a complicated woman in more ways than one. As his own eyelids started to feel heavy, cocooned in her warm corner of the world, he realised something else. This was becoming much more than some PR stunt. It was to him, and to Chloe. Maybe the reasons were different, but they needed each other. Pulling her closer to his chest, he smiled as she mumbled in her sleep, settling into him like an animal into a safe burrow. That was what he needed to be for her, whether she liked it or not. He needed to be her safe place. And tomorrow, he was going to get his agent's little spies on the case. If he was going to help Doctor Henry, he needed to know about the rest of the Henry clan. Her family had a chokehold on her life, and he needed to know just what he was dealing with. With any luck, some of the Logan charm would be enough, but forearmed was forewarned. If it came to war, he had a feeling he'd be willing to go into that too. For the complicated woman softly snoring in his arms.

Jesus, he was like a damn Labrador on crack this morning. She told him so.

'Huh?' Logan cocked his head to the side comically, sticking his tongue out and panting at her. Chloe tried to keep in her laugh, but it backfired and she puffed the air right out of her cheeks in one very long and highly unflattering guffaw. 'Hah. Got you. I wondered when that morning mood of yours was going to crack. I thought the coffee would do it, but it just made you slightly less feral.'

Chloe drained the rest of her takeaway coffee cup so she could glare at him. He'd had the coffees delivered to her door, and the doorbell ringing had woken her up from her spot on the couch. For half a second, she'd thought the Unabomber had just crashed through her front door. He'd answered the door to the delivery man clad in a big coat, baseball cap and one of her novelty fabric masks left over from the pandemic that she'd kept at the door. She used to wear them on her days off over the ventilated ones, an odd way of cheering herself up when she ventured out to buy more pants or groceries. The one he'd donned was black and in red letters said *Back Up, Baby*. She would have to avoid ordering coffee deliveries for a while after that little show.

'Well, thank you, Logan. I do appreciate it, but I do have coffee in.'

'Yeah, but not coffee like this.' He raised his own cup as if that explained everything. 'Besides, you didn't have any bagels. I needed food, and you only have granola in the cupboard.'

'So?'

'So,' he teased, bouncing around in front of her like a deranged puppy. 'Granola belongs on a bird table, or on the bottom of its cage. We need energy for the day I have planned.'

'Plans? What plans?'

His proud little smile was unnerving.

'Well, I was thinking... since we pulled off the whole conference thing, we need to keep going, you know? Keep up appearances.'

Chloe nodded despite herself. He was right. They were out there in the media as a couple. He'd done his bit. Her tired brain knew it wasn't over. Maybe his cunning agent had some event she'd have to attend. Which was probably the last thing she felt like doing right now.

'I think it's time I meet your parents.'

Nope. That was the last thing they should do. Couples' tattoos, colonics on a 2 for 1 deal. Having their fingernails pulled out by pliers. Any of those were preferable to his suggestion.

'What?' The blanket dropped to her feet when she leapt off the couch. Striding over, Logan gently pushed her back to her seat. 'Not a chance. Absolutely not!'

'Yes, absolutely we have to. You said yourself your parents

hadn't been happy about... us. Well, they should meet me, and that way they can see for themselves that—'

'That I have a fake boyfriend? No way, Logan. They would see through us in a minute, I'm telling you. They know I don't date, and now they're supposed to believe I kept a movie-star boyfriend secret?'

'Well, technically I'm more of a TV star. The movies are the next thing.'

'Logan!' He looked positively gleeful. He was enjoying this.

'Okay, okay. Semantics, I know.' He finally turned serious, and that worried her even more. 'Look, I know you've been dreading fielding questions from your parents, and it got me thinking – they know a lot of people in the hospital, right?'

Chloe sighed, sagging into herself. He put his arm around her and brought her back up to face him. 'Right. Yes, they do.'

'Exactly, and those people have just seen us together. They're going to ask your parents questions.'

Chloe put her head in her hands. 'Oh God, and they are going to say that they know nothing about it.'

'Exactly, so I say we organise a lunch. Today, somewhere where the paps won't take over, and we can present our relationship to them and take the pressure off things.'

'You haven't met my parents.'

'That's kinda the point, Doc.'

'No,' she groaned. 'You don't get it. I know you spoke to my dad, but in the flesh? That's a whole other nightmare. My parents aren't like normal parents. They're not going to ask about marriage, or babies. They will grill you on your job, who you hang around with. Your family make-up. You ready for all that? Because I'm not. I don't know enough about you to pull this off, and they're sharks. When they smell blood in the water, it's all over.'

Logan sat back against the couch cushions, bringing her with him. 'You do realise you just described your folks as cold-blooded predators, right?'

'Yeah, that was intentional. And true. There's more than one reason I haven't dated, Logan. A few years ago, one of the male nurses from a neighbouring hospital asked me out. He'd been moonlighting on the bank rotation for extra cash. We went on two dates, and his bank shifts dried up. Turns out my father called the agency and told them that he was unsuitable for the hospital.' And they hadn't had years of articles to use as ammunition against the nurse. With Logan's life being out there for public consumption, they would be fully locked and loaded. Logan had enough to deal with without the Henry level of scrutiny and derision. She couldn't take watching him go through that. Seeing that, why would he stay? No-one else bothered to stick around. Why would Logan Broderick bother with all the hassle, just for someone like her?

'He didn't do that! Seriously? That's next-level meddling, wildcat.'

Sure was, and she wasn't emotionally invested in dating the guy in the first place. It was two dates, and the guy didn't make her feel a tenth of what Logan did. No sparks. It didn't hurt to lose him. At the time, her parents' interference in her life was the pain point. Losing Logan that way would be agony.

'He did, and I didn't go on any more dates with him or any other guy after that. Not in the medical profession anyway. It didn't matter though; with the job and them, it just wasn't worth it in the end.'

'And the guy, he just walked away?'

'Pushed is more the word, and yes, he did, but I wasn't invested in the first place. I think I was just going through the motions, you know.'

He nodded slowly. 'Yeah, I understand that. His loss. Sounds like he didn't have it in him to keep you in the first place.' His gaze turned to sexy smoulder, and she felt her face heat. He smirked the second he clocked it. 'Well, you're going out with a TV doctor now, surely that will count for something?' He winced when she groaned even louder. 'Okay, maybe not. But I still think we need to do it. It will make things easier in the long run. We could call them right now, if you like. Get it over with.'

'Does it have to be today? I was hoping to get some rest before work starts again.' *Suspending reality for another day can't hurt, right? Another night on the couch sounds pretty amazing right now.*

His hand covered hers, slowly, as if he was waiting for her to pull away. She didn't. Even if she did hate his idea. She had to face her family some time, and with Logan there, it would go one of two ways. Either they would behave, or Logan would be belittled. A fake doctor would not be their choice of suitor. After him standing up for her, he would no doubt be public enemy number one in the Henry household.

'I will make sure you get some rest, but I think we need to do this. We could book somewhere quiet; Peter can make that happen.'

'I doubt my parents would deem to show up at a place they can't control.'

'Well, if they want to see you bad enough, then they will make the effort, right?' He was already on his phone, tapping away. 'Okay, so Pete's going to handle everything and let us know. Want him to contact your parents too?'

Chloe could barely breathe. No-one had ever taken control of them like this, and knowing that she was going to see them soon? She couldn't take it.

'Yes,' she practically panted. 'Fine. They won't like it, but I have to see them some time. Maybe this way it won't be so bad.' It definitely would be, but Logan would be there. Selfishly, having him by her side taking fire right along with her was the better option. As long as her parents played fair, because watching Logan get ripped apart was something she was not going to stand for.

Logan wasn't wrong when he said Peter would set things up. When they pulled up that night in the car Peter had sent, she didn't even see a restaurant.

'Do we have the right place? This looks like a residential street.'

'It's down that alleyway there, off the street.' Chloe looked through the tinted window at the lamplit alleyway. She'd driven down this street many times and thought it looked like a nice place to live, but a restaurant in an alleyway? It looked kind of shady. Her parents were going to disapprove right away. The tension in her stomach amped up to an uncomfortable level. Logan was oddly calm. 'A friend of mine, Antonio Carlucci, actually owns the place. It's very exclusive. He used to run some of the special events for the cast back in London, but he considers himself Mancunian so he came back to set this place up. I've been wanting to come here for a while, and tonight's perfect. One thing your parents won't be able to fault is the food. He cut his teeth in some of the best London restaurants when he was newly qualified. He's a great guy, really.'

'So he's a good friend?'

'A great friend. He moved here from Italy when he was a teenager. He didn't really know many people when he started school so we kind of bonded. I missed a lot of school stuff because of the acting classes. We stayed in touch over the years.'

'And you're going to subject his pride and joy to my parents? This could be the end of that friendship, you know.'

'Nah. It will be fine, trust me on this. This restaurant is select, and we can have a nice meal in a safe place.' Logan's smile slipped a little when he saw her expression. His arm slid around hers, and she let him pull her closer across the back seat. 'Chloe, if you want to leave and cancel this whole thing, now's the time.'

'I can't, my parents are probably already in there.'

'So? We can say you're sick, go back to your place. Get some comfies on, watch your favourite fake doctor on the TV.'

'That actually sounds like heaven to me, so don't tempt me with a good time.'

'I'm serious. I know I pushed you into this—'

'Not for the first time, either.'

His smirk was so cute she couldn't help but smile.

'Well, that worked out, right? At the end of the day we still have to keep this up till you get that dream job. Pete said that the producers for the movie are talking about me again. We're close to pulling this off. I don't want your parents to use me as ammunition against you. That's the opposite of what we were trying to do.'

'I know, and I do appreciate you doing all this. Just remember that later when you're all torn and bloody from the battlefield.'

'Hey.' Logan grinned, dropping a kiss onto her temple. 'It will be good practice for the war movie. Let's go in, get you a wine.'

'A bottle with a straw?'

'Whatever gets you through it, wildcat.'

The restaurant was beautiful. Just down the alleyway, there was an ornate cream wooden set of doors, with the sign *Carluc-*

ci's above it, and as they knocked, the doors immediately swung open.

'Wow,' Chloe breathed as Logan took her hand and led her through the doors. 'This place is so beautiful.'

Logan walked her through those huge doors to a beautifully lit place. High-ceilinged cream walls were lit by beautiful sconces, and past the reception desk there was a bar on one wall separated by a small dancefloor and tables all along the right-hand side. They headed over to the desk, and Chloe let Logan take the lead as she took in the restaurant. She'd never seen something so stunning tucked out of the way like this. Almost every table was taken, and the bar was full of people laughing and ordering drinks. The atmosphere was happy, and peaceful. For now. She scanned each table for her parents, but there was no sign of them.

'Party of four, under the name of Chloe Henry?'

The hostess smiled at them both. 'Perfect. The rest of your party has already arrived and you are seated in the private VIP dining area this evening. Would you like champagne for the table?'

'What do you think, honey?' Logan said, turning to her. She felt him squeeze her hand to bring back her attention. 'Champagne?'

'That would be lovely, thank you.'

As the server led them to the back of the restaurant, Chloe's legs were shaking so badly that she could barely put one foot in front of the other. Thankfully, she'd selected a pair of black kitten heels to go with one of her new dresses. She'd chosen a little black dress, pairing it with one of her favourite shawls. Logan had choked on his coffee when she'd walked out of the bedroom wearing it, so she assumed that she looked good. Right now she was wishing she'd donned a flak jacket too. This was going to be difficult, to say the least. Logan was going to have his work cut out for him tonight. She was not ready for it.

The server opened another set of cream wood doors, and there they were. But they weren't alone.

'Chloe! How nice to see you!' Her sister was sitting there as bold as brass, next to their parents. 'Logan Broderick, wow! You're taller than you are on television!'

The server made a swift disappearance, returning with a bottle of champagne and a tray of glasses as Logan pulled out a chair for her, taking the one next to her. The minute he was seated he took her hand under the table. Not one out of the three of them had risen to meet them, so Logan had taken charge. Which was a good thing because Chloe's legs were barely working.

'Ooooh. Mr TV Star is pulling out all the stops tonight to please the in-laws, huh?'

Chloe didn't miss the shit-eating grin her sister had on her face. Well, part of her face. At this point she was 50 per cent Botox and sneers. To his credit, Logan let her comment bounce right off him.

'Thanks for coming, Mr and Mrs Henry,' he said smoothly. 'Elizabeth, it's a nice surprise to see you here. Is your husband coming?'

Lizzie pouted, clearly put out that she hadn't made a dent in his smooth exterior. 'He couldn't make it, he's working. A nice family dinner is always good though.' Her smile towards Chloe felt feral. 'We missed you, Chlo.'

'Yes.' Her mother finally spoke, but her face was closed off. 'We were a little surprised to be summoned here tonight, weren't we, Archie?'

Her father, sitting there buttering a bread roll, eyed her and

Logan over his glasses. 'We were. A phone call was in order, Chloe. At the very least.'

And there she was, feeling like a tantrummy teen all over again. Her mother, father and sister were all sitting there staring at her like she was the problem. She gripped Logan's hand tighter, and when she felt him squeeze back, she felt better. Stronger.

'Well, I was busy with the conference and when we got back, we wanted to spend some time together before I go back to work.'

Lizzie blanched. 'Wait, so where are you staying?'

'I'm staying at Chloe's,' Logan cut in. 'With the show being wrapped, I want to spend every moment I can with my girl. We have to spend a lot of time apart, with her job and mine. It's been nice, hasn't it, baby?'

Her mother's lip curled, but Lizzie was taking the role of queen bitch right now.

'I bet. You're pretty busy in London, with the nightlife and everything.' Shots fired.

Logan laughed as if he didn't have a care in the world. 'Well, you know the media. They love to make a good story when there isn't one.'

Lizzie pursed her lips. 'I'm sure, although seeing my sister half-naked on the front pages was a shock. Not exactly a good look, Chlo.'

'Indeed,' her father chipped in. 'A lot of damage control was needed. I assume that's why we are here, to address the problem.'

The server came in, stopping the conversation. After the orders were placed and the champagne was poured, the doors closed once more and the silence was deafening. Logan took the lead.

'If I may, I would like to raise a toast.' He turned to Chloe, pulling her chair closer to his with his free hand. 'To Chloe.' Crickets rubbed their legs together. Logan looked at her family pointedly, and they reluctantly raised their flutes. 'Thank you for sticking with me when the press overstepped. I live this life, but it was something that you never asked for or wanted when you met me.' Chloe met his eye, knowing that every word was sincere. Everything else melted away, and she let his words wash over her. 'I know how hard you have been working lately, and I just want you to know that I am so proud of you. Whether you get this promotion or not, I know that your future is bright.' His smile was pure adoration, and she wished it was real. That all of them were real, in that moment. Having him in her corner lately had been amazing, and she would miss it so much when it was over. 'I can't wait to share all of your successes, and I can't wait to see what the future holds for us.' He raised his glass, turning to the table. 'I'm so pleased that your family could be here tonight, to celebrate you with me.' Lizzie looked like she was going to shatter the glass in her grip, and Chloe stifled a laugh at her mother's tight-lipped expression. They were all hating this turn of events, and she was here for it. 'Everyone, please raise their glasses, for my beautiful girlfriend, Chloe Henry!'

Logan didn't give them a chance to say anything. He put his glass in the middle of them, held aloft till every single one of them chinked their glass against theirs.

The starters came out right after, as if the heavens were aligned. Everyone started eating and Chloe felt herself starting to relax. Logan winked at her as he filled her glass up with more champagne, and she let her smile fly free. Leaning close, she dropped a kiss on his cheek.

'Thank you, Logan.'

'Anytime, wildcat.'

'Wildcat?' Lizzie of course heard that. Her bat ears were legendary in the Henry family. 'What an odd nickname for our little wallflower.'

* * *

Wallflower? Was this mean girl kidding with this? Logan saw Chloe flinch and her whole demeanour deflate in front of his eyes. Her parents didn't react; her mother even smiled. It had taken so much for him to organise this, to get her here. Now he knew why she was like she was. They were family, but it was like they were waiting for her to fail. Her sister was a hater, and he wasn't having it.

'Wallflower?'

Lizzie grinned. 'Yeah, our little Chloe wallflower. It's our nickname for her, you know. Because she's so...' She waggled her finger in a circle. 'Well, you know.'

'No, actually, I don't know. I call Chloe wildcat because she's full of fire and passion. She works hard and cares deeply. Nothing about that screams wallflower to me, so I think the comment wasn't necessary. We are all here tonight for Chloe, and I won't have her talked down to.'

Lizzie's smarmy smile slid down her face into a scowl. 'Oh really? Well, I think my sister can speak for herself. We came here at your summons, but this isn't the Logan show.'

'Lizzie,' Yvette cut in, looking bored as she picked at the last of her starter. 'Don't make a scene.'

'Me make a scene?' she practically screeched. 'Tell him!'

'Cool heads are needed, Elizabeth. We've had enough of our private affairs being out there in the world.' Archie placed his cutlery down on his finished plate. 'Which is why I think we need to discuss things moving forward.' He waved a finger between Logan and Chloe. 'If this, whatever it is, is going to continue then I think we need a discussion on how to manage the situation. The foundation was not happy about the news coverage.'

Logan felt Chloe sink down further in her seat under her father's scrutiny. Lizzie was loving every minute, her grin sly. The woman looked like a damn fox, and not in a good way.

'We are just concerned, Chloe. We need you to make the right choices, because what you do reflects on us as a family, and the foundation as a whole. We have had a lot of calls to field, and we do not appreciate you ignoring our attempts to sort out the situation. Having tantrums and getting your... *boyfriend* to speak for you? It's not acceptable, Chloe, and you have been raised better than that.'

'This doesn't need to be an argument,' Logan cut in. Chloe's mother turned her attention to him, and her words came out clipped. Haughty.

'With respect, this isn't your business, Logan. Suffice to say, we do not approve of you dating our daughter. Archie and I expect more from our daughters. You are not the type of man Chloe should be involving herself with.'

Wow. They didn't even have the dessert course yet and things were going south. They were like a pack of hyenas, attacking their own. Chloe was frozen at the side of him the whole time, but she bolted upright when the approval barb hit.

'Mother,' Chloe muttered. 'Please, stop. You can't talk to him like that. This is Logan's friend's restaurant and you are making a scene.'

Yvette clutched her pearls, turning to glare at Archibald as if he needed to cut in. This was an ambush, pure and simple.

Lizzie was pouring more wine, a happy smile on her features. Any minute she was going to ask one of the servers for popcorn.

'Us making a scene?' Archie huffed indignantly. 'Come along, Chloe. You must realise that your chances of getting the job now are over. We saw some of the photos people were posting at the conference. You were clearly not there working. Gambling, gaudy dresses? What's the back-up plan when you don't get that promotion?'

'Exactly what I was saying,' Lizzie cut in, downing yet another glass of champagne. 'This is not the Henry way, sister.'

Logan couldn't believe his ears. They spoke about her like she was some kind of aimless underachiever. 'Why does she need a back-up plan exactly? She's a doctor, making good money.'

'Not the kind of money she could be making. At least being a head of department is more money, status, but it will never compare to private practice.'

'I don't care about all that, Dad.'

'Well, you will later. Having a husband in the arts is not exactly stable, especially when raising a family.'

Chloe flushed all the way to her neck, and Logan was about done.

'I make a good living, actually. I would provide for my family, I always have. Chloe would be very well taken care of, as my wife or as my girlfriend, if she ever needed it. Which your daughter won't because she can take care of herself. She doesn't need someone to look after her, but I will, all the same. Your daughter is safe with me.' She squeezed his hand, and he squeezed right back. *Sparks, sparks.* There they were again. Those zaps of pure... everything that jolted through him whenever he touched her.

'Well, you make good money now, but that might not always be the case. Acting is a tough business.'

'I'm aware, but I have other interests, actually.' He waved a hand around the room. 'This restaurant, for one thing.' Lizzie spluttered on her bubbles and Chloe tried not to let her jaw drop. 'I invested a few years ago. My buddy needed some capital, and we made a deal.' Steepling his fingers, he sat back in his chair. 'Growing up, I knew what it was like to do without, Mr Henry. Coming from money doesn't make a person any better than someone without.'

'I do think morals count though. Tell me, Chloe, when he came to the hotel to win back your affections, like the papers said, did you not think that all the bar antics were a bit much?'

'No,' Chloe huffed. 'I didn't. Same as I didn't think I was engaged, or pregnant, when I read about myself in the papers this week. Because it's all just noise. People are not perfect. That's what makes them human. Logan is a good man, Dad. I know you like to think I'm some idiot who needs to run every decision by you, but it's not the case. I became a doctor despite your expectations, not because of them. If I don't get this job, I will find something else that fits *my* plans for *my* life, not to carry on some family name for someone else.' Throwing her napkin on the table, she got to her feet. 'You know what being with Logan has taught me? That no matter what you do or say, some people will never care about what you want or need. I love you all, but this stops now. I won't be apologising for living my own life. If I am a disappointment to you, then I think that's on you, because you know what? I am starting to realise that I am pretty great. Call me when you decide that being in my life is more important than controlling it. And if I hear anything about me or Logan coming from your mouths, I will not be answering your calls. Ever. Enjoy the rest of your meal.'

When she looked at Logan, he was already watching her, a look of pure pride written across his face. She was absolutely amazing. His beautiful wildcat. 'Come on, Logan, it's time to go home.'

Taking her by the hand, he flashed her family one last killer smile. 'Tonight's on me. You know where we are.'

* * *

Walking out of the restaurant, Chloe felt like she had just shed a ton of weight. Her shoulders felt so light her kitten heels were barely grazing the floor. Logan was as steady as a rock next to her, and when she got into the back of the car, she let out the first easy breath in hours.

'Are you okay?' he asked as he slid in next to her. 'Do you need a minute, or do you want to go?'

'I'm fine. I just want to get home.' *With you, and Dante. And the sofa blanket that still smells of you.*

'No problem, wildcat.' He gave the driver the instructions, and the dividing screen closed up, leaving them alone. 'You were amazing in there. I'm so proud of you for standing up to them. I'm sorry I put you through it. I never thought a family could rip into each other like that.'

'Well, it sounds like you had an amazing mother. I'm glad you had that, but honestly I am used to it by now. I just didn't like how they spoke to you. That's why I snapped.'

Logan didn't say anything at first. He just stared at her, his full lips quirking into a smile.

'Thank you.' He slid across the back seat, wrapping his arms around her. 'We really have each other's backs, and that means a lot. I know this is all hard, but that took a lot, Chlo. You should be really proud of yourself.' He kissed her hair. 'I know I am. I swear, the longer I know you, the more I see things I really like.'

'Not such a wallflower any more, eh?'

She met his eye, and lust punched her in the gut. She was gone for this man. A sucker for those big, all-seeing brown eyes. She'd miss so much about him. She'd miss him.

'You've never been that, Chlo. You'll always be my wildcat. I really think your parents will back off now. If we present a united front, there's nothing they can do to ruin anything.'

'Except the hospital board. Even if I get the job—'

'When you get the job, we will deal with that.'

'You won't be here by then. This whole thing will be over. You'll be off being a big movie star.'

'Hey, even movie stars make time for their life-saving girl-friends.' His gaze dropped to her lips. 'The more I say that the more I like it. It's been nice, doing this with you. I spend a lot of time on my own usually. Pete runs my schedule, but these days with you in your place have been great.'

'Fake in-laws not included.'

'Oh, honey,' he murmured. 'They are definitely not included in my feelings.' His gaze dropped to her mouth again, catching her smile. 'That's better. I love seeing you smile. It makes my day.' He swallowed audibly. 'Seeing you like this is my goal lately. Jobs and films come and go but seeing you happy makes me happy.'

'Me too.'

The driver pulled up, and the two of them reluctantly let go of each other. Once they were inside her flat, he pulled her into his arms again.

'Want to watch a movie in our comfies, or you need to sleep?'

'Comfies sound good. Don't let me fall asleep on the couch again.'

His laugh rumbled in his chest. 'I don't know, you're pretty cute when you're asleep. You go get changed, I'll get us some wine. Do you want popcorn?'

She rubbed her belly. 'I couldn't eat another thing after that meal, but wine sounds good.'

He was already on the couch when she emerged from the bedroom. He looked right at home in a black T-shirt and grey shorts, Dante purring on his knee as they sat together. She pulled the blanket off the back of the couch, and he moved Dante to snuggle under it with her. He let out an indignant yowl and settled down next to Logan, making biscuits on the blanket with his paws and shooting them both the evil eye.

'Dante is not happy,' he told her with a chuckle.

'He's sulking for definite. He's a real diva.'

'Dante by name, Dante by nature.' Logan scratched him under the chin and his purrs increased. 'Action movie or chick flick?'

'Well, I actually thought about this. I thought maybe *Pearl Harbour*?'

Logan's brows shot up. 'Really?'

'Yeah, it would be great research for you. Lost loves, war time?' She waggled her brows. 'Plus I kind of have a thing for Josh Hartnett.'

'Really? Ben Affleck was Batman!'

She pressed play on the film. 'I will forget you just said that. Call yourself a movie star? Everyone knows Michael Keaton is the one true caped crusader.'

'Agree to disagree.' He laughed, passing her a glass of wine. 'You don't even know half the movies I have excellent trivia knowledge of.'

'Well, I spent my time working and studying! I never watched a lot of movies, and my parents aren't exactly the cinema types.'

'More country club and bending the knee type stuff?'

'Yep.' She swilled the wine around in her glass. 'Honestly, my parents make the Lannisters look like the Brady Bunch.'

Logan almost snorted wine out of his nose. 'Well, now you say it... I was half expecting someone to come in and cart me off to the dungeons.'

'Oh no, they would just take you out like a spy would. All stealthy, quick and clean.' Her phone rang in her purse, and she groaned. 'I bet that's one of them now.' The old feelings of dread and panic were there, but less glaring somehow. *Huh. How about that.*

Logan refilled her glass. 'Ignore it, you don't need that right now. Let them cool off.'

She almost let it ring off, but something in her tonight had strengthened.

'No.' She smiled. 'No more hiding.' The screen said 'Manchester General'.

'Answer it!' Logan yelped when he saw it. 'This is it, baby!'

'Hello, Doctor Henry speaking.' Chloe managed to keep her voice even, though she was sure the caller would be able to hear her hammering heart.

'Chloe!' Todd's jovial voice came through, making her heart thud. Logan was right there with her, holding her tight as she looked into those beautiful brown eyes and thanked her lucky stars that he was here for this. 'Apologies for the late hour, but the interview panel and I were keen to get everything in order.'

'No problem, I understand.'

'Good. I am glad that you were able to handle yourself so well during the outbursts of Doctor Carson. This is obviously

confidential, but Doctor Jeffries is aware of the situation and
has decided to let Doctor Carson go. He won't be returning to
Manchester General, and we would like to formally offer you
the position of head of department.' Logan's grin widened to
epic proportions as he squeezed her tighter. 'It's yours if you
want it, Doctor Henry. Your presentation was just what the
board is looking for in terms of progressive thinking in these
turbulent times for the NHS. We really feel that under your
leadership the department will flourish.'

'You're offering me the job.' This was it. She should be
thrilled, right? The pinnacle of all her hard work. But all she
saw was Logan, who was dancing around the room, trying to be
quiet. When they locked eyes, she saw nothing but pride in his
eyes. He was so happy for her, and all she felt was pain. Taking
this job was a step closer to goodbye. As usual, he saw the hesitation on her face, his brows narrowing. 'Take the job, wildcat,'
he mouthed. 'You can do this, baby.' Todd was still waffling on
in her ear. *This is it, Chloe. This is what you planned for.*

'...time, but we do need an answer pretty quickly.'

Logan gave her an encouraging nod, and a thumbs up, and
her heart broke a little as it swelled with affection.

'I accept, of course. I would be honoured to take the job.
Thank you.'

'Great! Well, we do need to appoint another doctor to
replace Doctor Carson, so if you have any input we would of
course take that on board.'

An idea flashed in her head. 'Well, I know Doctor Baldoni
wants to move to London ideally, but I do think that Doctor
Patel would be an excellent addition. We worked well together
at the conference.' Baldoni and Patel had seen straight through
Carson, and she had respected both doctors for their work
ethic.

'Okay, well, we will get in touch with him and let you know. Of course, we are keen to make the transition as soon as possible. When are you back at work, Monday?'

'Yes, that's right.' Her jaw dropped. 'So, I'm starting then?'

'If you're up for the challenge! We will courier the contract over first thing tomorrow. Any problems please do get in touch. And thank Logan too. He certainly made the conference enlightening and highlighted some issues that we weren't aware of.'

'He did?'

'He did. He spoke very highly of you, Chloe, and I can only apologise if you ever felt that your family name was ever a part of our discussion. I can promise you that going forward, it is your department to run and we will not be interfering. We trust in you, we just ask that you do the same. The board will back you 100 per cent.'

'You've got it,' she managed to choke out as his words washed over her. Her department. Finally. She was going to make the changes that were desperately needed, and not a Henry shadow in sight. *The spectre of Logan won't be as easy to shake though.* Running a department with a broken heart was definitely going to be more than she'd bargained for. 'Thank you, Todd. I won't let you down.'

'Thank you! We'll see you next week. Enjoy the weekend, celebrate!'

She ended the call and stared at Logan. 'I got it, I can't believe it!'

'I knew you would! Baby, I am so proud of you! Come here!' She went willingly into his arms, and he crushed her to him. 'You did it, Chlo. I knew they would see it.'

'What did you say to them?'

'Nothing that wasn't true. I pointed out that you were

already doing the job, how good you were. They were already starting to see Carson for the dick he was, I just pointed out that you weren't a Henry. Not in your intent, or your actions. I just told them what I saw, Chloe. A woman who deserves the fucking world.'

'You really see me, don't you.' *You're the only one who ever has. And the last, because I will never find this again.*

He brushed away the tear that fell down her face, his voice soft. Tender. Something felt wrong, even though his touch was so right. She thought of her first day on the job. The press intrusion, and her parents. What her colleagues would have to say about her new relationship. The pressure built in her chest again, taking her breath away. This was not how she wanted her life to be. She wasn't Camilla, at ease showing off her perfect life. She just wanted to be seen for her, but now she'd be thrust into being Logan's girlfriend – for real. It would overshadow everything.

'I see you, wildcat. I always have. Listen, I know we have a lot to deal with, but I really like you.'

'I like you too, but it's just a lot to take in. I never expected this, but...' The words caught in her throat. Hadn't she done enough to be able to make her own decisions at this point? Being with him would be the right decision for her heart, she knew that in the marrow of her bones, but the foundation was built on something she'd had no real choice over. She would never truly know if this was meant to be, if they carried on right now, with everything going on. She just wanted to work at her job, step into herself. And that meant... what? Being with Logan would be perfect, if they were just like this all the time. But life wasn't like that. 'We can't do this, Logan. As much as I want to, we've only spent days together. Amazing days, but real life is just too much right now. We're going to be apart, a lot. You live in London, I live here. The world is going to be watching us, and I don't know if I can bear that right now. I just feel like I've got control of my life for the first time.'

'I know.' He nodded, his eyes wet, his voice hoarse. 'I don't want that for you, and if I get this movie I will be away for a while. I'll be honest; I thought we could do it, but seeing your face just now, I can see the fear. I hate that everything I come with put that on your face. I came here to beg you to be with me, for real. Being your boyfriend was never a role to me. In the space of a week, I am a changed man.'

'I don't think you changed, Logan. You were always this man. The best man. You have shown up for me so much. I feel like we've known each other forever.' She sighed, running her hand along his cheek, his lips. 'In a different world, I really think we could have been something.' The tears fell again, and she let them. Leaving him in Cornwall had been so difficult; even for the few small hours they'd been apart, she'd wanted nothing more than to run back to him. To tell him that she was in this, that she felt everything with him. He annoyed her, challenged her, turned her on. The man had quite literally dragged her out of her hiding place and shown her the light. But then reality had snuck in. There was so much media attention, people crawling out of the woodwork who wanted a piece of her, of them. She finally had her next step, but the noise around them would never let her fully embrace her new job. She was a doctor, first and foremost. She had worked so hard to be the person she saw in the mirror now. The same person that now other people saw. She was finally out of the Henry shadow, and it felt great. She just couldn't step into someone else's. Not now, when she was only just seeing the light. 'I will always support you, Logan. I just can't do it by your side. We both have too much to go out there and do. I know our fake relationship helped save your career, but you deserve to show people the real you too. People need to see what I do. You're going to get this film; the papers are all talking about it. The studio is going to call at any moment, and I can't wait to see you shine.' The sob came ripping out of her, and he shushed her. Comforted her with his touch, whispered to her that it was okay. That he'd got her. 'I'm your biggest fan, Logan. Always.'

His lip wobbled, and when his own tears stared to fall, it broke her heart in two. 'You just can't be with me, I know.'

She looked at the man she was falling for and wanted to tell him something different. She wanted to tell him that she was ready to take on the world with him. To go into this and be his girlfriend for real, but she was on the cusp of her new life. A life he'd helped her to get. If she stayed with him now for real, she would never truly know who she could be as a person in her own right.

'I want to be. I really do, but I can't. I am so used to living with the opinions of others and not doing what I want. We're so public, I just feel like the noise of everyone will wreck us before we even start. Our next steps need to be for us, to focus on what we both wanted going into this agreement. I want you to get what you want, Logan. I want you to do that movie, and for people to see what I see. We're just on different paths; we both have so much going on.'

'I understand.' He sniffed, letting her wipe away the salty tears from his handsome face as they cried together. 'I wish to God I didn't, but I knew when the call came that you need to do this. I need to do this. My next step is this movie, and doing that with your new job, the media? They are going to be following me, waiting for me to fuck up. I can't bear the thought of you seeing some messed-up story that I'm with some woman, because it will not be true. I don't want that for us. I never want to put you under that pressure when you have just got everything you ever wanted.'

'Not quite everything,' she countered. 'The thought of you leaving is killing me, Logan. I really like you being here, with me.'

'Me too.' He sighed heavily, his breath coming out in a shudder. 'You're my favourite person, Chloe Henry. I feel like I'm flying when I look into those beautiful green eyes. I'm falling for you. Pure and simple.'

'Then kiss me,' she told him. 'Please. Kiss me, hold me. Be with me, stay with me until the end of the week.'

'Till Sunday.'

'Till Sunday. We can block out the world till then. Just me and you, right here. Till you have to go back to your life.'

He pulled her into his lap, and she went willingly. Threw her legs around him and sank into his arms.

'This is going to hurt, Chlo. Leaving you after staying here is going to kill us both. If I kiss you again, I am never going to want to leave. I'm going to want more of you. Are you sure about this?'

'I know what I'm doing,' she told him, wrapping her arms around his neck. 'I can't give you everything, but I can be with you now. We always said this was for this week, right?'

His hands cupped her bottom, squeezing tight as he nibbled at the corner of her lip. 'That was a fucking lifetime ago, Chloe. I don't even recognise those people right now. If someone had told me a month ago that I would be a goner for a badass doctor, I would have laughed in their face.' His lips kissed the tip of her nose. 'But I am, Chloe. I'm just gutted that we only get this time.'

'Me too.' Her hands raked through his hair as she stared in his watery eyes. She would be watching this man on her screen, just as she had for years, but it would never be enough again. So she remembered the way his lashes fanned those huge brown eyes. The way his eyes did that crinkly thing she absolutely adored. The way her body felt when he was holding her, like he was charging her up. Lighting her from the inside. 'Kiss me, Logan. Show me how much you're going to miss me.'

He didn't hesitate, slanting his mouth onto hers and claiming it. She opened for him, tongues meeting, exploring. Tasting each other as if their lives depended on it.

'Jesus,' he muttered against her mouth, delving back in with gusto as she pulled on his hair to drag him closer, closer. 'You are my dream girl, wildcat. Brace yourself.'

He gripped her tight, wrapping her legs around his waist as he stood. Dante yipped from somewhere in the room, making him laugh.

'Mummy's busy, bud.' Dipping his head, he kissed from the back of her ear to her collarbone, making her shudder. 'Bedroom, baby. Now. I need to be inside you.'

'Lead the way,' she whimpered, grasping the hair on his nape and tilting his head up to lick up his neck. They managed to make it to her bedroom door, and the second they were inside, he slammed her up against the door. Pushed his whole body against her, till she felt him at her core.

'God, you're beautiful. You feel so good, baby.'

She groaned, grinding her hips against his hard length. 'We need less clothes, Logan. I need to touch you.'

'Whatever you want, wildcat. You can have whatever you want.'

They stood before each other, taking turns to undress the other. Garment by garment, touching the skin they uncovered as they mapped each other with kisses and licks. When they finally stood before each other naked, she took in the man she knew by heart, and fell for him all over again.

'You're fucking stunning,' he breathed. 'Chloe Henry, you are my dream girl. Come here.'

Dipping before her, he lifted her onto the bed like she was precious. Pushed his weight on her as he hovered above her. Kissed the spot where her heart resided, beating fast. Stared into her soul with those perfect, dark eyes. She could feel him shaking as she ran her hands down his back.

'So,' she teased, kissing his chin and loving the feel of the stubble against her lips. 'Is this better than the first time you saw me naked?'

His laugh burst out of him, making her smile beneath him. 'Well, I was scared for my life back then. I thought you were going to murder me.' He kissed the top of each breast, making goosebumps bump out on her skin. 'I thought you looked hot, yes. All wet and angry like that. My wildcat.' He kissed her again, pulling back swiftly with a mischievous look on his face. 'Turn over.'

'What?' Heat flooded through her at his commanding tone. Wetness pooled between her legs.

'You heard me. Turn over, I want to see something.' He lifted off her, and she rolled onto her stomach. 'Jesus, you're perfect, Chloe.'

'Are you perving, Mr Broderick?'

'Nope.' He chuckled. 'Yes.' He kissed each of her cheeks, his mouth moving up her spine till he reached her tattoo. 'Ever since that day, when I first saw that flash of ink on your shoulder, I wanted to see it. Fantasised about what it said, how it felt.' Her tattoo was of a heartbeat line on a monitor, triangular lines rising up and down on a line. Underneath, in swirly words, it read *Life still happens between the beats.* She felt the moment he registered the words, felt his body still. Just for a moment. 'Baby,' he muttered. 'Do you have Dante's most famous line actually tattooed on your body?'

She smiled in the dark as he pushed her hair to one side from her back. 'Yes. It spoke to me. I've watched you for years, Logan Broderick. That line, it killed me.'

'Do you want to know something?'

'Anything.' He lifted her arms and linked his fingers through hers, pinning her to the bed. She felt the hard length of him against her and wiggled against it. 'Tell me.'

'That line was mine. Not the writers'. I read the scene and asked them if I could add it. I can't believe you have my words inked on your body, Chlo. It's fucking insane.'

'You really said those words.'

'Yeah, and it just sums us up, baby. This is killing me, being with you like this. Everything in me tells me that this is not something I can walk away from. I know I have to, but knowing that you're out there' – he kissed the tattoo again – 'with my words on you, I am never going to be the same, wildcat.'

'I know.' She sniffed, feeling the emotions thrumming through her body. 'Stay with me now, Logan. Stay between the beats.'

'Anything you want, I'll do it. I just don't want to take advantage of you.'

'You're not taking advantage. I want this. I want you. We have till Sunday, so be with me. Please.'

She looked over her shoulder at him, their hands still linked together, and when their eyes met, the dam broke. He picked her up effortlessly, spinning her around until she was facing him again. They came together, touching and kissing like it was their last night on earth. He reached into his jeans pocket, sliding on a condom before coming back to cover his body with hers.

'Between the beats,' he murmured, a promise on her skin as he kissed her lips. He moved his hips, till he entered her, inch by delicious inch. Fed himself into her until he bottomed out, never breaking contact with her mouth as he withdrew and plunged back in. Her walls quivered around him as she met each thrust with the passion he was making her feel. 'You're perfect, Chlo. You feel so good. Taking me like this. It's everything.'

He groaned as she squeezed his length, their tempo increasing until they were nothing but skin and pants and building electricity. She could feel herself coast the edge, and when he shoved his arms under her legs, bending her in half, she screamed. Feeling every inch of him in her, all around her as her orgasm crested and exploded.

'Yes, Logan. Jesus, I'm coming. I'm coming!'

'One more,' he growled, keeping up the pace as he sucked on a nipple, nipping at her skin and laving the pain away with his tongue. 'I need one more from you, baby. I want to come with you. Fuck!' His movements grew erratic as he pounded into her, reaching between them to massage her clit as he drove every inch of himself into her warmth. When she came again, he tipped right over the edge with her, moaning deep as he buried his face into the crook of her neck.

When he'd disposed of the condom, he came back to bed, reaching for her the second he got under the covers and dragging her across the bed to curl his body around hers. They lay there in the dark, cuddling together in the silence. 'Till Sunday, we sleep like this. You right here, in my arms.'

'Sounds good to me. That was perfect, Logan.'

'You're perfect, wildcat. You know, I think I'm fa—'

'Don't say it,' she whispered. 'I know what you're going to say, but I can't hear it. Not now, not after this. I feel it too.'

'You don't feel this, I can guarantee it.'

'I do. I feel it.' She placed his hand over her heart. 'In here.' Moved it down to her stomach. 'And here.' Tapped the side of her head with her free hand. 'And here, too. I'll never forget you.'

'Good,' he murmured, tucking himself back around her. 'Because the echo of you will stay with me forever, as sure as the ink on your skin.'

* * *

He'd wanted to say those words to her that night. He was desperate to get them out, but he knew she was right. Once they spoke them out loud, leaving would be even more impossible. For once, he hated his career. What it brought to him, because the one thing he wanted more than his acting career was the woman he was staying with. They did everything together, right there in her bubble. Avoided the press, didn't turn on the news. The press was camped outside, but the doorman was keeping them out and accepting their many deliveries of food. And condoms. It was the first time he'd had to order contraception to the door before, but they couldn't get enough of each other. He'd bent her over the counter one afternoon while she was making him a damn sandwich, for God's sake. He was a total horndog around her, and making her orgasm was his new favourite thing to do. The heat between them never abated, and they were always touching each other. They did other things too, of course. Things that made him wish they could do it forever. Being with Chloe was everything to him. No matter what they were doing, he was just happy being with her.

Reading through his script, checking the work contract that had been couriered over for her – it was bittersweet. Working on their plans together, even though they would have to do them without the other by their side. It really was her dream job; the second she'd got it he saw the light in her eyes. She'd earned it, and he was so sad that he wouldn't be around to watch her do it. Pete stayed in touch, updating them and confirming his itinerary for Monday. The studio wanted to see him asap, and Pete was making it sound like it was a done deal. They loved him for the role, and all of the qualms and reservations they had experienced had gone away. Helped no doubt by the fact that Belinda had offered him a new contract on *Doctor Love*. She'd bought the love story between them, and Logan would have felt like shit if it wasn't secretly and absolutely the truth. He was head over heels for Doctor Chloe Henry, and when Belinda had told Pete that his turnaround had given her hope for her own future, he felt so bloody proud. People were seeing the difference in him. And he got it now, why they couldn't be together. He needed to be out there on his own as much as Chloe did. He needed to show the world the man he really was, without the booze and the women and the cocky persona he had developed over the years to thicken his skin. It wasn't their time. Right woman, wrong time. The love story he never expected to happen without being in front of a camera.

So they stayed in their bubble, eating pizza on the couch and watching movies. Taking sexy showers together, lying together in the dark wrapped around each other. He'd taken a photo of her tattoo one night as she slept soundly next to him, vowing to get one of his own to match. Right over his heart, so he could carry her with him.

When Sunday dawned, it was without fanfare and fuss. Standing at her doorway, he felt like he'd cut himself in half and was leaving the best parts behind.

'My car's here,' he told her, pressing the words he couldn't say out loud into her hair with his lips as he held her to him. 'I'll say goodbye here. Pete is getting some security in place for you, and he's spoken to the hospital about ramping up things there.'

'When is he going to make the statement, about us?'

About us breaking up. She didn't need to say it. He didn't want her to.

'A few weeks, probably. Once the studio contract is signed. I'm due there tomorrow to meet them in London. We shoot in Toronto in a couple of weeks, if it comes off.'

'It will,' she told him, conviction clear in her tone. 'That part is yours. Go and kill it.'

'I will, for you, wildcat.'

She drew back, those beautiful green eyes nailing him to the damn floor. 'Do it for you, Logan. Let them see the man I do.' She wiped at her tears, rising to her tiptoes to kiss him. He kissed her with everything he had, his lips telling her everything his words couldn't.

The buzzer went on the intercom, and she sighed, resting her forehead on his chest for the last time. He smelled her hair, wishing that he could take her scent with him. To sustain him as he learned to survive without the girl he'd had for a week and wanted to keep for every week after.

'That's your cue, Mr Movie Star.'

Kissing her again, he swallowed down the huge lump in his throat. 'Goodbye, Doctor Henry. Save lives, and kick ass.'

'I will. Goodbye.'

He walked backwards down the hall, not wanting to take his eyes from hers until the last moment. The second she closed the door, his heart broke in two. Pulling on a baseball cap and covering it with his hoodie he prepared himself for the next step. London, Toronto and a life without his wildcat.

15

Doctor Love and War

TV Star Logan Broderick cut a lonely figure today on the streets of Toronto. Pictured on his own outside a tattoo parlour, Logan was then seen emerging two hours later and heading straight back to the Alberta studio in Canada, where he is currently filming the upcoming war movie, *Love and War*. Since leaving the home of his girlfriend, Doctor Chloe Henry, in Manchester, Logan has seldom been seen other than training with his personal trainer in London's Hyde Park. It looks like his bar-hopping days are over.

Chloe closed the article, pocketing her phone and heading to the scrub room to prepare for her patient. Her Google alerts for Logan had been going crazy since he left, but she checked each and every one with her heart in her mouth, dreading the day that she would read something she didn't like. *He'd got a tattoo?* She remembered the photo he'd taken of hers when he'd thought she was asleep, the way he kissed it every time he stood behind her. She wanted to text him to ask him whether he'd gotten one like hers, but they'd barely spoken. Weeks ago, they had agreed to cut things off. Just to check in with the other if they needed to. He'd texted her about getting the movie. Had sent her flowers to the hospital for her first day at work, making the nurses swoon. When she'd gotten home, there was a package for her. Inside were treats for Dante, and the hoodie he'd been wearing the day he left. The note inside read:

> *I miss your smell. The flowers were for appearances, Pete's idea. I wanted to send you a piece of me. It doesn't smell like you any more, and I hate that, but knowing you will be wearing it makes me happy. Tell Dante Dad sends his love, and to be good for his beautiful mum.*
>
> *Ever yours between the beats,*
>
> *Logan*

She'd cried herself to sleep that night, wearing his hoodie. It smelled just like him.

There had been no bar-hopping articles. Everyone was talking about how much he'd changed, how big the movie was going to be. He'd renewed with *Doctor Love* for another season, and his career was well and truly flying. She was so happy for him, but it didn't make it hurt any less. Especially since today was the day that the news of their break-up was due to drop. Pete had been in touch with a list of things to say and not to say. How the statement was going to read. It put all the blame on Logan, his schedule driving them apart, and she was not happy with it. At all. He was taking the blame when it had been her driving this. He'd left for her, and she knew it. She'd felt it that week, the way he always protected her. He went to bat for her every time. Talking to her colleagues, going after Carson. Being

her rock and giving her what she needed before she even knew it was exactly what she needed.

Work was amazing. She'd settled in well, and without the spectres of Carson and Doctor Jeffries around, she finally felt like herself. In the six months since the conference, she had well and truly settled into her own skin. She was still a Henry, but now it was just a surname. Something that she had, but didn't define her. She was trying to move on but today felt like another death. The true death of their relationship. After today, she wouldn't be known as Logan Broderick's girlfriend any more. The hashtag of theirs, #doctorsinlove, would be no more.

She'd tried to fill her life without the Logan-sized hole in it. She'd been out with her friends, had danced and drank and lived it up. She'd weathered the press and had even made friends with a couple of the snappers who seemed to live outside her building. Brought them coffee home on occasion, when they were standing out in the cold waiting for her to get home from work. She'd signed autographs for patients who'd asked, feeling like a fraud as she smiled and thanked them. Fielded questions about how they were navigating long distance. She was managing to keep up the façade, because it made her feel connected to him. Like he was still in her life. She'd even had dinner with her parents and sister. It was stilted, to say the least, but they weren't as bad as they had been before. She didn't take any crap from them anymore, and they knew it. Had heard how well she was doing at work. Her father had almost sounded impressed with her, which was a jarring experience to say the least. Her sister was a tougher nut to crack, but Logan had managed her too. All the way from Canada. He'd shared some of her videos to his socials, and her followers had exploded overnight. Lizzie was thrilled, and all of a sudden the woman was Team Logan. Chloe had laughed hearing that. Because it was so him. Selfless, caring. Doing what he could to protect her from thousands of miles away.

She focused on her day, her phone on silent in her locker as she operated. The OR was usually her happy place, but her mind still drifted to the storm cloud that was looming. The one that would finally cleave the two of them apart, like a bolt of lightning through a tree. When she finally got out of surgery and sat in her office, she couldn't stop checking her phone. Nothing. The announcement hadn't dropped yet, but it would be soon. She thought of Logan out there in Canada, probably waiting for the same thing, and suddenly she was reaching for a number and dialling.

'Pete, it's Chloe. Henry.'

'Chloe! How are you? Everything okay?'

'Not really, no. Have you leaked the announcement yet?'

'Er... no. Logan instructed me to wait till you were back at home, with the security downstairs.'

'He did?' Her heart thumped in her chest. 'But how does he know when I'm home?'

'Security report to him. It was part of the conditions he asked for when he employed them.'

'He wants me to be in my safe place before it comes out,' she half whispered. Typical Logan. That infuriatingly gorgeous man was keeping watch, from half a world away.

'Of course,' Pete confirmed. 'He cares about you, Doctor Henry. I've never seen him like this with anyone before.'

'He told you that.'

'He didn't need to. He's been a wreck, to be honest. The film's going well, he's killing it – but I don't know, he's not exactly happy.'

Her heart clenched, thinking of him out there, missing her. She knew exactly how he felt, because she was pining for him

too. She'd watched every movie and every season of *Doctor Love* in her downtime. Twice. Went to sleep most nights with his voice in her ear. Yet he'd never told her, had never put that burden on her. She asked the question anyway.

'Why didn't you tell me that? We've spoken. He never told me.'

'You wanted to cut contact, and he wanted to do the right thing for you, Chloe. He's a good man.'

'I know,' she sobbed, gripping the phone tight and trying to pull herself together. 'Listen, this is kind of why I called. I need you to cancel the announcement.'

'What? But—'

'I want to say my piece for once. You've wanted me to talk to the press, and I think it's time. I stopped hiding the minute I met Logan, and I can't let him throw himself under the bus for me. Not again. He deserves better. And you can't tell him about this conversation. I don't want him to know any of this. He needs to focus on his movie. I want him to get what he wants. He deserves the world, and everything in it.'

'Okay,' Pete said, and she could hear him smile through the phone. 'Tell me what you need.'

* * *

Logan had been filming all day, and they were due to wrap tomorrow. The film had been a dream to be a part of, and the Hollywood buzz was already building. Talks of Oscars were already in the mix, which was amazing. He was due back in London to start filming *Doctor Love* again soon. Life was fricking good, but he didn't feel any of it. Because today was the day that the news of his fake break-up was going to drop, and he felt hollow. He felt like the day he'd walked away from his wildcat. That goodbye had killed him, but keeping up the pretence had helped to keep him together. People were still talking about them, about how well they were doing long distance. About how much he'd changed as a person, and he knew he had. Since he'd met that screaming naked woman in the hotel room that day, he'd come alive. She had pissed him off, challenged him, brought out things in him that he didn't know existed. Since being away from her, he couldn't fucking breathe. He'd stalked her through security essentially, wanting to know where she was and that she was safe. He'd heard from Doctor Patel that she was thriving in the job, and hearing that and knowing that she was safe were the only things stopping him from abandoning everything and getting on the first plane to Manchester. He really missed her, but she still felt connected. Today, that final link between them was going to be broken. In a few weeks, the press would move on. His security would no longer be needed. He would lose her for good, and the thought of it made him want to rip his skin off. If he could be anyone else on the planet right now, he would be that person. As long as she loved him. And she did love him, he knew it as sure as he knew his own name. He'd felt it, in that week together. Logan Broderick, the supposed lothario, fell for a woman in a week and left pining for her forever. Dante Love had nothing on him.

Logan waved to the sound guy he passed on the way to his trailer.

'Hey, Charlie. Good day, huh?'

'Er... yeah.' He looked up from the phone in his hand and shot Logan a sympathetic look. 'Are you okay, man?'

'Yeah, why...?'

Charlie lifted his phone up. 'Well, the break-up, dude. Must

be tough. I'm sorry, man. I was rooting for you guys, I really was.'

Logan didn't answer him. He took off for his trailer, locking it behind him and running to his phone. Pete had rung him a few times, and his notifications were in the triple figures. He dialled Pete.

'What the fuck, man? I told you not to drop that shit till later! It's, what, 4 p.m. in Manchester? She better be okay, Pete, or I swear to God you're fired!'

'Hey, hey! Take a breath, okay! Where are you?'

'In my trailer, we just finished filming for the day.'

'Good, good. I sent you a link, okay? So before you fire me or break all your shit, just watch it and call me back.'

'Watch what? Pete?' He'd hung up. 'Fuck!'

Whirling through the messages, he found the link and, taking a beer out of his fridge, downed half of it before sitting on his couch and clicking on it. His broken, tattered heart stuttered to a stop when Chloe's face filled the screen. She looked absolutely beautiful. Powerful, in her work uniform of scrubs that made her gorgeous green eyes stand out all the more. She was in her office, he could tell from the picture she'd sent him on her first day, but the camera looked professional. What was she doing? This wasn't the announcement they'd planned. He was going to murder Pete when he got his hands on him. He was going to tear him apart limb from limb and bury the damn pieces under the Hollywood sign for this. She didn't want this life. What the hell had he said to her to get her in front of that camera?

Keeping his anger in check, he steeled himself for what was coming and hit the play button. The camera slowly panned out, showing Chloe sitting at her desk. A familiar voice started to speak, and Logan's stomach clenched.

'Thank you for agreeing to speak with us today, Doctor Henry.'

'No problem, and please, call me Chloe.'

It was Miranda from BBC News. He recognised the voice from their past interviews. She had not been kind to him in the past, and Chloe knew that. They'd spoken about it. *This is bad. Tiny little pieces, Pete. Wait till I get home.*

'Chloe, thank you. Now, I know that you have been pretty quiet so far about your relationship with Logan Broderick, so I guess our viewers are wondering, why today?'

He watched Chloe take a deep breath, her hand reaching over to the opposite shoulder as if she was brushing her tattoo for strength before she spoke. He covered the one on his chest, wishing he could make her feel it.

'Well, I guess I wanted to set the record straight. As you know, Logan is no stranger to the press.' Miranda let out a little laugh, and Chloe smiled at her. A feline type of smile, with a little teeth. 'And I don't want him to be destroyed again, because he doesn't deserve it. The truth is, I care deeply for Logan, and the man I know is the man that you have recently started to see. He has always supported me, since day one, and my career. Sadly, to the detriment of him, and us.' She swallowed, and he wanted to jump through the damn screen and scoop her into his arms. 'Unfortunately, I have ended our relationship.'

Miranda gasped. 'You've broken up?'

Chloe nodded grimly. 'We have. He is currently filming *Love and War* in Canada, and with my job being so demanding, I felt like I couldn't give Logan the time and love that he was showing me. We discussed it, and Logan, being the gentleman he is, was going to take the pressure of the media for me, as he knows what a private person I am.' She looked straight into the camera. 'And I am not accepting that. I will not take kindly to

Logan being blamed for this. It was me. He has this big, beautiful life, and I have my career, and as much as I love him—'

'You love him, still?' Miranda cut in. Chloe nodded, taking in a shuddery breath. 'I do.'

Logan sucked in a breath. *She loves me?* She just said it out loud, for everyone to hear. 'I think a lot of fans out there can agree with me that Logan's a pretty easy man to fall for. Dante Love, that's Logan. The sweet parts, the caring parts? It's all Logan. He's never just playing a role, I realised that very early on.'

'So, if you still love him, then why the break-up?' *Yes, Miranda. Good question.* He watched his girl lick at her lips before replying.

'With Logan's career being so big, and getting bigger, I am still in a relatively new role at Manchester General, and the press intrusion was a lot. I felt like things were too much at times, and I don't envy Logan for what you and others have put him through over the years.'

'Me? Er...' Miranda's voice was decidedly shaky.

'Yes, you. I think sometimes journalists and people who comment on people in the public eye often forget that there is a person behind the persona. A person with wants, and needs and feelings. I know Logan was born to be an actor, he is so special and brings that to every role, but he's also a human. He cares deeply for those around him and I think that impressions of people can be wrong.'

'So that's why you're here.'

'Yes. Logan had nothing but respect and understanding for my decision. He still supports me to this day, helps me to feel secure. I'm here today for him, and to ask the public to have a little grace for a man who deserves the world and everything in it.'

'Right,' Miranda said, and Logan could hear the grudging respect in her tone. 'Well, I think you've given us all something to think about today, Chloe. Thank you for your candour.'

'Thanks for having me.'

'If I could just ask one more question. If Logan were here right now, what would you say to him?'

Chloe sighed, biting her lip. Logan couldn't breathe. He'd forgotten how. He'd died right here, his body just hadn't caught up yet. She loved him. She'd said it out loud. She was doing this for him. Putting herself out there and protecting him on national television. 'That's my wildcat,' he breathed, wishing she was here right now, with him. Like he had for every day since they'd parted.

'If Logan were here right now, I would tell him to keep being exactly who he is. That people will keep on loving him for it. Between the beats, life still happens, and I can't wait to see where yours leads you next.'

'Wow, well. Thank you, Chloe, for talking to us today. I wish you all the best.'

The video ended, and Logan sat there, head in his hands, replaying everything she had told him. Told the world. She'd done it for him, had come through for him. She knew the contents of their original planned announcement and had stopped it in its tracks. She'd taken the fall for him. Looking at his phone, he started to scroll through the notifications. #doctorsinlove was trending, along with some new ones. #doctorheartbreak was right there, second from the top along with #weloveLogan. Chloe's interview had been sent to him thousands of times and retweeted, shared. The comments were full of support for him, for Chloe. Their relationship break-up was well and truly out there now, and all he wanted to do was call her and beg her to be with him.

I stan Chloe and Logan. The media needs to back off
The paparazzi needs to be accountable for this
My heart will never recover. Poor Logan
Putting her career over Logan frickin' Broderick. Is she
crazy?
Logan, I will have you. Call me!
Hot doctor dumps a movie star. I would let her operate on
me any time
Such a shame they couldn't make it work
I feel sorry for her. You can tell she's broken up about it
She loves him! Why can't they just make it work?
Okay, these two need to get back together. Like now. Where
do I sign the petition?

He dialled Pete. He answered on the first ring.

'Okay, so how mad are you? Do I need to start brushing up my résumé?'

'Why didn't you tell me, Pete?'

'She told me not to, Logan, and I have to say, I agreed with her decision. You've changed, man, you don't deserve all that noise in your life, not now.'

'You spoke to her? Is she okay? She looked good, but did she mean it? Should I call her?'

'I can't tell you what to do, but you're still in Canada. You have the whole press tour to do, you're not going to be home for a while yet. I don't know. She still has her job to concentrate on, and the press are not just going to walk away from her now. I've already had calls asking if I have her as a client. People want more interviews.'

'No,' he growled. 'Not a chance. She doesn't want that, Pete. Doing that, just now? That took a lot.'

Pete didn't say anything for a beat, and Logan filled in the silence with the ramblings in his head. Nothing had changed. Not really. The media storm would be huge now. They'd had a taste of her, and they wanted more. If they got together now, the pressure would be intense. He was months away from being back home. He wouldn't be able to be there for her.

'I can't call her, can I?'

'If you do, this won't end, mate. All the things that kept you apart will still be there. You're not even in the same country.'

'I know, I know. Dammit. I want to call her. No, I want to be there, with her.' He sighed, feeling the weight of everything thick and heavy on his chest. 'Just, look after her, okay. Whatever she needs, do it. Don't pull the security, not until things get back to normal for her.'

'Do you want to respond to the press? I don't think you need to, but this could be a good time to say your piece.'

'No.' He didn't want to talk about it. The connection had been severed. They'd ended their agreement. Nothing had changed. If he spoke to the press right now, he would end up messing it up. Declaring his intentions to make her his and no doubt bawling like a baby to boot. 'I just want to work. Load up my schedule with anything we need to do, but instruct the press that I will not be speaking to anyone about Chloe.'

'Okay, man, you got it. Listen, you'll be okay. You're doing the right thing.'

'Yeah.' He huffed out a hollow laugh. 'I know. Still fucking hurts though.'

'Get some sleep, okay? I've got her this end. She'll be safe.'

'Good.' He nodded, running his hand over his tattoo. 'Just do me a favour. Don't send me any more updates from security. Direct them to yourself.'

'You're sure?'

'Yeah.' He couldn't hear about her again, not now. He'd have to burn his passport to stop himself hopping on the first plane to her as it was. 'Unless there's an emergency, I can't hear it, Pete. I just can't. I have to stick to the plan. Finish the movie, the press tour.'

'And then?'

'I don't know. Depression? I might buy myself a cat.'

'About Chloe Logan. You're really going to let that woman go?'

'I have to, Pete. This life is not for her. With her family and everything she went through, you saw her. She's finally living her life, and I want that for her.'

'And if she meets someone else? What then?'

He traced the words inked across his heart.

'Then he better look after her, because I just trained in combat manoeuvres. I won't need a damn scalpel to make him pay.'

Pete chuckled down the line. 'Get some sleep and keep your phone on in case anything pops off.'

Pete rang off, and he was left alone with his thoughts. *A few more months.* He repeated it over and over in his head. A few more months away from home. He could handle that. He could do this. He was doing it. For now, knowing that she truly loved him would have to be enough. No-one had yelled 'cut' yet. Their story wasn't over until the credits ran.

He'd play the long game. See everything through, follow her wishes till he could get back to her. And when he got the chance to see her again, his tattooed heart would know what to do.

Doctor Chloe Henry was seen out today in Manchester, for the first time since announcing her break-up from global film and TV star Logan Broderick.

A source close to the Henry family have asked that Chloe be given privacy in the wake of her break-up. Sister Elizabeth Henry, YouTube star and Harley Street doctor, recently uploaded a video applauding her general surgeon sister for her poise amidst the media attention since her television interview.

'Chloe deserves the best, she is a strong woman, and seeing her go through this has strengthened our relationship. I support my sister and know that she wishes Logan Broderick the best.'

'I'm surprised they let us back here, after last time.' Chloe smirked as she sipped on her mojito. When Lizzie had got in touch with her after the interview, she'd expected a very different conversation. Being asked to meet her for dinner at Logan's restaurant was a shock, to say the least.

'Well, I did have to drop your name.' Lizzie laughed. 'I just figured that the press wouldn't find us here. I'm pretty sure Logan had extra security put on though. Did you see the burly guys out front?'

Chloe shrugged. She had seen them and had no doubt of the reason. His friend would definitely have tipped him off that Lizzie had booked a table under her name. It made her feel closer to him in a way, because he was still here. Keeping her safe.

'So, how are you, really?'

Chloe took another sip, needing the buzz of the alcohol as they waited for their pasta dishes. 'Is it you asking, or our parents?'

Lizzie sipped at her champagne, sighing as she clacked her nails on the white linen tablecloth.

'Well, they were a little shocked about the interview, but more than anything, I think they were proud of you. I think Dad might actually like Logan, after he stood up to us that night.'

Chloe almost dropped her glass. 'You're kidding.'

'I'm not. He did that shout-out for the clinic, and he called Mum too.'

'He called her?' Wow. Just when she thought she couldn't love him any more, he surprised her again. The ache for him was all encompassing. 'He really called Mum?'

'Yeah. After he left for Canada, he called to apologise for things getting heated. He said he stood by everything he'd said, but he also made it clear that the way we've been treating you was wrong.'

'He didn't! What did Mum say?'

'Well, she was fuming at first, but Dad went kind of quiet when she told him.'

'That's normally a bad sign.'

'Yeah, but this time it wasn't, Chlo. He called a family meeting, and we kind of agreed that he was right.' Chloe almost choked on the mint garnish. 'You've always been different to the rest of us, Chloe. We just thought you were being stubborn, but I get it now. I do. Honestly, I wish I was a little more like you.'

'Lizzie, come on.'

'No.' She grinned. 'I mean it. When you stood up to us all, going for that job, dating Logan fricking Broderick? That took guts, sis. Real guts. I have to say, I'm really sorry. I was a total bitch to you.'

Chloe looked at her sister, the pain on her face. She knew it had taken a lot for her to say those words. Lizzie got her stubborn streak from their father. They both did. It had cost them both, in very different ways. She wished Logan was here right now, so she could tell him how thankful she was. He'd stitched her life together in more ways than she ever thought possible.

'Not a total bitch.' She pressed her tongue into her cheek as she smiled at her sister. 'Not all the time, anyway. The free face creams were a nice thing to do.'

'Face creams I got for samples? Wow. If that's the only nice thing you can say then I am worse than I thought.'

The waiter brought their food, and Chloe twirled the linguine on her fork, giving herself a minute to process the many bombshells dropped. 'Okay, so you were a bitch, and our parents were horrible. Yes, all true. But I get why. It's the Henry way, but I never wanted to be a person just doing things because of their surname. It doesn't mean that I didn't love you all, I just wanted my own life.'

'We know. We get it now. Seriously, and I am sorry. I would really like it if we could do things like this more often. We've never really been close, but I would like to try, if you want to.

Not because of Logan. He made us see things through your eyes, but honestly, even before that, I guess I missed you. We were close when we were little, before the pressure got to us all. Mum and Dad weren't always like this. I think we all have some growing to do, like you have. And nights like this? Me and you, I figured it's a good start.'

'I'd like that,' Chloe beamed. She could let go of the past. She never hated her family, she just wanted to be accepted for who she was. 'A little sister time sounds good to me, and you can start by paying for lunch and getting me another drink.'

'Deal.' Lizzie grinned. They ate their food, chatting about work. By the time their desserts came, Chloe was a little buzzed and actually happy to be out with her sister.

'So.' Lizzie flashed her a coy look as she forked a piece of raspberry cheesecake. 'What about you and Logan?' Just hearing his name wiped the smile off her face. Stabbed fresh pain into her already bleeding heart.

'What about us?' She tried to be nonchalant, but she knew her sister saw through it. 'We broke up.'

'I know, but you love him. You told the whole world. I saw it that night. The way you looked at each other. I swear, you were so protective of each other, I was a little jealous. I've never really had that.'

Chloe felt her head snap back in surprise. 'You're married! Things change when you're together a while.'

'Nah.' Lizzie shook her head, nodding to the waiter when he asked if she wanted another drink. 'Another one?' she asked, nodding to Chloe's third empty mojito.

'Yeah, sure, I'm not driving. I left Dante in front of the TV; he'll be good for a while.' The waiter left, and Lizzie sat staring at her. 'What?'

'You didn't answer my question. I love my husband, but we

both know it was a decision made from the head and not the heart. You and Logan, you're so different, but it worked. I saw it, that night. I could see it on your face when you did that interview. That type of love is what all the songs are about, Chlo. Why can't you just be together?'

'Who are you all of a sudden? Cupid?'

Lizzie blushed. 'Well, no, but I am a fan of *Doctor Love*.'

Chloe banged the table. 'No way!'

'Yes way.' She pouted. 'It's my guilty pleasure. That other actor in it? Doctor Desmond? He's so hot. Although, he did bodge a face lift the other day. I swear, in real life that woman would have looked like Sloth from *The Goonies*.'

The pair of them exploded into cackles of laughter. It felt so good, so normal. She sighed, thinking of Logan again and how somehow, he had made this happen.

'I do love him,' she confessed. 'I do. I miss him so much. I am a total sucker for Logan, for Dante. All of him, but I don't know if I can handle all that. I've spent a lot of time hiding, Liz. Being out there in the open all the time? I don't know how he does it.'

Lizzie huffed, bringing up something on her phone and showing it to her. 'You are already doing it. Look.'

There was an article about her in today's news, accompanied by a photo of her out shopping for cat food and ice-cream. The headline read *Doctor Henry nurses heartbreak with comfort food*.

'Oh, Christ. I never saw them.'

Lizzie shrugged. 'It's okay, you looked great. Those heels are killer, by the way.'

She smiled again, her eyes watery. 'Logan got them for me.'

Lizzie flashed her an 'uh-hum' look. 'Okay, so this is how I see things. You can run from this, sure, but I don't think that's you, Chlo. You stood up to our parents and me, and everyone else. You went out there and got that job. You spoke to the press in a TV interview and slayed. You can do this, if you want to. You just have to go for it.'

'I did get an invitation to the premiere.' It was sitting on her nightstand right now, after she'd spent half the night poring over every word.

'Fantastic! This is your chance! Go! I'll do your make-up if you like.'

'I don't know. I think Pete sent it; he might not even want me there. We agreed no contact, and I haven't heard from him since the interview.'

'So go anyway, support him. See his movie. You might not even see him. Those things are pretty big and the movie is, like, everywhere. It's one night, sis. Just go and see what happens.'

Chloe sighed, sagging against the tabletop. 'I'm going to need another drink.'

'Now that I can sort right now.' She lifted her glass, and Chloe met it with hers. 'A toast. To sisters.'

'To sisters,' she echoed. 'And all the free face creams I want.' They were still laughing two drinks later, and when they left, Chloe felt lighter. She would go to the premiere. She needed to see him again, even if it was across a red carpet. She wanted to be there, to cheer him on. One night, and then she would move on.

'Thanks, Lizzie.' She grinned, hugging her sister as their cabs pulled up. 'And thanks for paying.'

'No problem. I'm proud of you, you know that.'

'I think that's the champagne talking.' But she knew it wasn't. She finally had a sister, someone she could share her life with. It felt good. Normal.

'Maybe, but I mean it all the same.' Her sister winked. 'Go

see him, Chloe. Find out once and for all what you want to do. If it's too much, get a taxi and leave, okay? Just find out, or you will always have that little voice inside you wondering why you didn't.'

'Love you,' she told Lizzie, meaning it.

'Love you too. I'll call you, okay? Mum wants to do a lunch.'

They both pulled a face at the same time, dissolving into fits of giggles together.

17

The flashbulbs were going off outside the car door. The minute they'd pulled up, it was like she'd entered another world. Logan's world. All day she had been sick to her stomach, hiding in her hotel room like she was some Dante groupie. Since she'd received the invitation to the premiere in the post, she'd been in a spin. The second she'd opened that shiny golden envelope, she'd played it down in her head. That perhaps there had been a slip-up in the PR team mailing list, and she'd been sent it by accident. There was a hotel room booking attached, along with details of a car service that was going to take her to the premiere and back to the hotel. It all looked like a standard invite, with all the VIP treatment, but that was Pete. Organised to a tee. She figured it could very well be a standard PR thing. Pete's way of keeping up the 'conscious uncoupling' bit for the media. Till she got home from the restaurant and read it again. This time she'd seen the note tucked into the envelope, in Logan's distinctive handwriting.

Wildcat,

I would love for you to come.
I wouldn't be here without you.
Love, Logan

She'd read those words over and over. Tried to read between the lines of script to see what he was trying to say. It was polite, friendly. Just like their sporadic texts had been since they'd parted ways. They'd both known the score. Their relationship was for the media, to get his reputation to a place where he would land his dream role, and to navigate the media storm that had almost derailed her job. She'd helped him, but he'd done the same for her in so many ways too. He'd given her the confidence to finally stand up to her parents and sister and stand out of the imposing Henry shadow. She had her job, and Doctor Jonathan Carson was gone. The trustees respected her, and she was finally running the department just how she wanted it to be run. She'd never fully have the relationship with her family she wanted, but through Logan she'd realised that she was lucky to have them regardless. Logan had braved the world on his own for so long with no-one really seeing him for the gentleman he was. The kind, funny man that she knew so well now, but still felt so apart from. They'd spent so many nights being in each other's company and sharing a bed. Dante had sulked for days when he'd left. Avoiding her attempts to pet him, yowling at the door like an abandoned animal. She knew just how he felt. She'd spent all of her nights off rewatching her favourite episodes of him, wishing he was there on the couch with her again.

Now, she was going to see the movie-star version of him, and she couldn't define any of her emotions at the moment. The note didn't give her any clue as to his state of mind. He'd seen the interview but hadn't contacted her. Would she still recognise the Logan Broderick she knew when she set eyes on him? Her hands were shaking as she gripped her purse and tried to pull herself together. There was no RSVP on the envelope so she'd comforted herself with the fact that she probably wouldn't see him. He probably didn't know she was coming in a car ordered by Pete. It was a huge premiere in the heart of London, and the screening would be full. He was the male lead, so he'd be the one in demand. If things went badly, she could just leave. Hop on the Tube and be back in her hotel room in minutes. Tomorrow, she would be back in her flat with Dante, back to her old life. No harm done.

Liar.

The driver lowered his window, checking in with a woman manning the queue of cars with a clipboard and headset on.

'Name?' she asked, her sparkly emerald-coloured dress twinkling in the lights around them.

'Miss Chloe Henry.'

The woman ticked something on her list with a smile. 'No problem, pull up onto the red carpet when you're ready. Miss Henry will be following the roped-off entrance to the left for the welcome drinks reception and be directed into the screening from there.'

Oh shit. So she wasn't just going to be able to skulk in some corner. She was on the damn list and heading to the VIP area. Her toes curled up in her high heels as she cowered in the back of the car. The driver gave his thanks, and then they were slowly following the line of sleek cars as they all dropped off their passengers in turn. The crowd were going wild in the distance, but she couldn't see what they were screaming at from her position. There was a huge billboard-type wall on the far side, where the majority of the press were camped out behind barriers. The rest of the press pack were photographing the people coming out of the cars. She felt sick, thinking about them taking her photo. She was about to be at a premiere for her supposed ex, and it was going to play out in front of the whole world. If this went badly, she was going to pull a Camilla and leave the UK, for sure. Dante would have to get used to being moody in a mud hut halfway around the world if the press embarrassed her again. She couldn't do it. Not without Logan by her side.

'Miss Henry, are you ready?' The driver was looking at her through the divider, a look of concern on his face. 'We're next.'

'We're next, really? Oh God, I can't believe I'm doing this.'

'You look great, Miss Henry. Every single person I drive to these events panics in the backseat. You'll be fine.'

'Any advice for the press?'

'Just take this one step at a time. Smile, and don't fall on your ass.'

'Oh God, can you imagine? I feel like I'm back in a towel.'

'You were invited here, Miss Henry. Just remember that and enjoy your night. Wait till I open your door, okay?'

'Okay, okay. Thanks.'

'No problem, Miss Henry. Enjoy your evening.'

The car moved forward, and then she saw the red carpet. The photographers all waiting to see who emerged from the car. *This is it*, she told herself. *The moment of truth.*

Her driver flashed her a wink as he pulled up the partition, shielding her from the onlookers as he got out and came to her door. Chloe took a last deep breath in the relative quiet of the car, and then the door opened to the chaos. She took her driver's hand, holding her shimmering green dress in one hand to cover the slit in the thigh as she placed both heels on the floor and felt the red carpet beneath her feet. The photographers all whirled around as the driver stepped back. She was blinded by the flashes as she steadied herself. 'Good luck, head held high,' the driver whispered into her ear. 'If you need an out, you have my number. I will wait by the rear entrance, just let security know.'

She smiled at him, but it felt like it was frozen on her face as she watched him get back into the car. The flashes were going off all around her and she could hear her name being called over and over.

Chloe, look this way!

Doctor Henry, have you spoken to Logan lately?

Doctor Henry, how do you feel?

Miss Henry, who are you wearing?

Chloe, turn to your left a bit for me, please?

She took a couple of steps towards the doors on the red carpet, trying to smile without looking terrified, but all she could think about was Logan. He was here somewhere, and the thought of seeing him was giving her palpitations.

'Chloe,' a photographer shouted. 'Have you seen Logan yet this evening?'

'Chloe, does Logan know you're here?'

She kept smiling, not wanting to answer any questions. Especially those that she didn't have an answer for. Some of the fans were cottoning on to the fact that she was there and moving away from the commotion down the way to try to get photos. Camera phones were everywhere, flashing away, recording. She tried to take a step away, but the cameramen were all around her. She had to focus simply on staying on her feet as she tried to keep some distance. She could see the crowd amping up and the noise decibels increase. She felt the familiar tendrils of panic trying to snake through her, clinging to her nerve endings and triggering her fight or flight. There were so many people shouting her name and asking questions she had no idea how to answer.

'He's over there, doing the cast photos!' she heard someone shout, and it all clicked into place. The commotion further down was due to the cast doing press against the photo wall. She didn't even want to look in that direction, she just wanted to get out of the melee. 'Logan! Logan!'

The fans were shouting his name now, and she noticed that they were turning back to the wall. *This is my chance.* Keeping the smile on her face, she turned with a wave and started to walk towards the entrance. She was almost at the ropes as the screaming reached a crescendo behind her. Over the noise, over the chanting of Logan's name, she heard hers being called. She knew that voice. *Logan.* As she turned, he was running right at her. He side-stepped a cameraman, not breaking his stride as he came for her. He looked every inch the film star. His hair was perfect, his tuxedo fitted to every contour on his body. Her heart was in her mouth watching him eat up the distance between them. A pap leaned over the ropes, his camera right in her face. She flinched as the flash went off, blinding her.

'Step back,' she heard Logan boom, and then his arms were around her, shielding her. 'That's not cool, man. Step away from her.'

When she blinked away the flash from her eyes, she found herself staring right at Logan. He was furious, and for a second she thought it was because of her. Security appeared at his side, and Logan pointed to the intrusive pap. 'I need him removed, please, Mac. Take his camera and film too.' Then his eyes were back on hers, his deep brown eyes searching. 'Are you okay? That guy was a jerk.'

She tried to open her mouth to say something back. That

she was okay, or that he looked so good. Anything, but what came out was straight from the heart.

'I missed you, Logan.'

His eyes crinkled as he pulled her into a hug.

'I missed you too, wildcat. I've been a mess without you.' His voice was sweet in her ear, and she wrapped her arms around him tight. 'You look so beautiful. When I heard your name being called, I had to find you.'

'I came for you,' she told him, feeling complete in his arms. The crowd was so loud, chanting both their names. The flashes were so frequent the night sky outside the theatre was bright with light. 'Dante has been a pain without you.'

'Oh really?' He pulled back, putting his hands on her face. 'Missing his dad, huh?'

'Definitely. He's been pining for you.' She licked her lips. 'We both were. My place isn't the same.'

'I'm not the same without you, baby. I was hoping you'd come. I need to tell you something.'

She looked into his deep brown eyes and saw the tension and apprehension behind his easy smile. The way he held her cheeks in his hands, running his thumb along her cheekbone. This was her Logan. The TV star, the cheeky guy who brought her snacks and snuggled with her and Dante on the couch, and now the movie star who ran to her side, shielded her from photographers. They were all him, and she was madly in love with all of them. What came out of his mouth next was make or break. For all she knew, there was a model sat there waiting for her date to come back. Then his lips were moving, and her heart stopped beating for a second.

'I hate the fake break-up. I know Pete planned the whole thing, and we both had things going on, but it wasn't the same. It just wasn't right, not having you to come back to. I've wanted to tell you so many things over the last few months, and I realised that the best time I've ever had was with you.'

Feeling the tears sting her eyes, she slid her arms around his neck.

'I feel the same. I missed you so much. You yanked me out of my rut, and even with all this around us, the only thing that I needed was you. You've changed my life for the better, and I don't want to go back to that old closed-off person I was ever again.'

'Then be my girlfriend. For real this time. No ruse, no media circus. I'll make it work, I promise. Just us.'

'I think you picked the wrong time to declare no circus was in town.'

The media circus all around them was still in a frenzy, but they didn't care. Logan was looking at her like they were the only two people on the planet, and she was here for it. All of it. They'd weathered scandals, being thrust together and having to convince the world that they were together when they were strangers. Her parents, her colleagues, the media wanting to know every detail, and through everything they'd held fast. She ran her fingers through the hair at the nape of his neck as they laughed together. It didn't matter where they were, or where they were going – as long as they were together.

'Well.' She grinned. 'Since I love you, I think being your girlfriend could be fun.'

His eyes widened. 'You really love me? I heard you say it but I didn't trust myself to believe it wasn't for the press. You really put yourself out there for me, baby. I loved it. You really love me?'

'Yes, dummy. I really love you, and I'm ready,' she told him, knowing in the very depths of her that she was. Seeing him here had only solidified that for her. She wanted Logan. If he was the prime minister, the president, the damn bin man. She wanted him, and everything he came with was worth it if he was by her side. 'I do. I know it's soon, and hard. We have a lot to work out—'

He crushed his lips to hers, throwing all of his weight behind it as he held her fast. The crowd exploded around him, but he didn't give any sign of recognition. She opened for him, feeling the slide of his tongue against hers as they moved together. Her head was swimming with the sheer passion he was showing her, could feel the way her whole body lit up from the inside. He pulled back, only to dive in again, his soft lips claiming hers with a possessiveness that made her swoon. When he finally dragged his lips away from hers, he was breathing heavily. She could relate. She'd just kissed a movie star on the red carpet, and all she wanted to do was drag him back to her place to do very dirty things to him on their couch.

'I don't care about anything else,' he told her, his eyes shining with adoration. 'I love you, wildcat. I've never loved anything or anyone like I love you.' His gaze finally slid away from hers, and Chloe laughed at the surprised look on his face. The photographers were losing their minds; the fans were hoarse from screaming. When he turned back to her, they both burst out laughing.

'Jesus, I forgot where we were for a second. I think we'd better go in, but let's deal with this lot first.'

'Pete is going to lose his mind.' She giggled. 'He's somewhere exploding with glee right now.'

Logan laughed again as he wrapped his arm around her waist and turned them both to the crowd.

'Sorry about that.' He grinned, addressing the crowd. 'I got a little over excited to see my favourite doctor.'

'Are you back together?' one of the press shouted. Logan shot a sideward glance at Chloe, and she nodded.

'Yes, we are,' he beamed. 'I am the luckiest guy in the world, having this wonderful woman back in my life.'

'Any plans for the future?'

'All my future plans involve Chloe Henry. I will be wherever she wants me to be.'

'What do you think of his doctor skills on the show, Chloe?'

A ripple of laughter rang out in the crowd, and Chloe giggled.

'Well, I have been a huge fan of *Doctor Love* for a long time. I even named my cat Dante, so I think the show is fantastic. He's an amazing actor; an even better person, and I can't wait to see him on the big screen.'

The press was lapping it up, and Logan was squeezing her tight to his side.

'So the break-up, do you regret that?'

Logan took the lead. 'I regret anything that means I don't have the woman I love in my life. Thanks, guys, but we have to go in now.' He turned and held out his hand. 'You ready for this, Doc?'

Chloe looked down the red carpet to the doors beyond and placed her hand in his.

'Let's go, baby. This is your night.'

He dropped a kiss on her cheek as they headed inside.

'Our night, wildcat. From now on, it's you and me. The beats and every damn thing in between.'

18

'Dante, come on, dude. Quit licking your butt on the couch. You have the cat tree for that. Listen to your dad, buddy.'

Chloe chuckled as she hung up her coat, slinging her keys into the bowl on the hall dresser. Logan came to meet her, and seeing him still took her breath away. He looked gorgeous, standing there smiling at her in his grey sweats and the jumper she'd bought him on their last weekend trip away. He'd taken her to Amsterdam, and they'd spent the whole time sightseeing and blending into the crowd. Since his war movie hit the number one at the box office, his career was going stellar. Peter was over the moon with the developments, and Chloe had never seen him smile so much. It was very disconcerting, but at least he wasn't having to stage-manage their lives anymore. Now, everything was real.

Logan passed her a glass of wine and led her through to the sitting room. Dante scowled at them both from the top branch of the huge cat tree that Logan had bought him when they moved in. He'd still kept his place in London, and they stayed there sometimes, but they'd made their home together by buying a house in Manchester. She was close to the hospital, and coming home to their gated little palace, and Logan and Dante were the best thing ever. She couldn't wait to fill it with their kids one day. She'd love to have little Logans running around the place down the line.

'Did I miss it?' she asked him as he hugged her to him.

'No, you're just in time. How did work go?'

'It was good, I'm pretty tired though. Oh, you got pizza?'

The living room was their favourite place, other than the bedroom. He'd set the huge plush couch up with blankets, and wine, pizza and snacks were spread across the coffee table.

'I figured we could make a night of this. I'll even rub your feet while we watch.'

'Ooh, deal! Are you excited?'

He smushed up against her on the couch, and she settled into his nook.

'I am now you're home, baby.' The theme music started playing on the television. The new season of *Doctor Love* was starting. 'I even got us a nice dessert for after.'

'Dante and a dessert? I am a lucky woman.'

The show started, and Logan was amazing. Even better, the medical jargon was on point. Of course, they had hired a new medical consultant recently, one that Chloe had recommended, and the whole show was a joy from start to finish.

'Well.' She kissed him, because she always spent her time kissing this man. 'That was amazing. I am not sure about Dante's new colleague though. Is it me, or did he make eyes at your love interest? Do I sense a love triangle coming on?'

'Nah,' Logan said. 'Not for long anyhow. I can't spoil any details of course, but let's just say he is there to ruffle some feathers and make Dante's life hard.'

'Hmm.' She smiled. 'He reminds me of a certain someone.

Rhymed with Larson.' Logan's grin gave him away, as she knew it would. 'You didn't!'

'Well, since Belinda loves me now after our red-carpet debut, she might have asked me if I had any input on the new character she was thinking of writing into the show. Johnny Boy just popped into my head.'

'Oh my God, that's so funny! Do you think he'll recognise himself?'

'Oh, I doubt it, and even if he does, who would own up to being like that?'

'Not me. I'm just glad he isn't blighting the corridors of Manchester General any more.'

'Me too, baby. Everything worked out.'

'Yeah,' she said, reaching for his hand as he cupped her cheek. 'It really did. Time for dessert now?'

His eyes crinkled at the corners as his big brown eyes scanned her face. 'Definitely. I'll even let you open the box.'

She slid the pink box closer across the coffee table surface.

'What did you get, a cake or something?'

'Open it and see.' He sat forward with her on the couch, his arm around her as she opened the box. It was a small cake, white with blue frosting. On it was written two words. *Marry Me.*

'What?' She read the iced letters over and over. 'You want to marry me?' This was so him. Doing it like this, in their cosy space. Just the two of them. It couldn't be more perfect. She knew her answer the second she'd set eyes on the question. She wanted to keep him forever too.

'I do. I've never wanted anything more.' When she turned, he'd slid down on one knee. In his hand was a small red ring box. 'I love you, Chloe. Ever since you came running at me naked, I have been in awe of you.'

'When you weren't finding me annoying, or bugging the hell out of me?'

'That too. The truth is, wildcat, when I met you, I was lost. No-one saw the real me, and I was mad at everyone. I was a very lonely man, on the verge of losing everything. You saved me, Chloe. You made me see things so differently, and I love you for that.'

The tears were already flowing when she sank down onto the carpet next to him. 'I think we saved each other. I would never have done half the things at the conference without you there to spur me on. You helped me to stand up to my parents, Logan. You're a good man, and I will always see that good in you, no matter what.'

'So do it as my wife. Stand beside me forever. I don't know where our careers will take us, but I know that the one thing I can't do without is my wildcat.'

He opened the box, and the ring was perfect. It was so her. Pretty and understated. Beautiful and elegant. A stunning emerald, in a setting of gold with a diamond-studded band.

'It's perfect.' She held out her hand, and he quirked a brow.

'Not so fast, Doc. I didn't buy the perfect ring that matched your eyes to put in on your finger without an answer.'

She brought his face to hers and kissed the hell out of him.

'That's still not an answer, but it's a start.'

'You're such a dork.' She laughed.

'Dork?' He grabbed the back of her neck, pulling her in for another toe-curling kiss. She was gasping for breath by the time he broke away.

'Dorks don't kiss like that, last time I checked.' He pressed his lips against hers, running his tongue along the seam. 'Do I have to beg for an answer? Because I will, wildcat. I think we both know how stubborn I am.'

'Stubborn, arrogant, moody – hey!'

In one smooth movement she was off the floor. He twirled her around in his arms, Dante making little excited yipping noises at their feet.

'Do I need to do this another way? What do you fancy? Eiffel Tower, Empire State Building? You let me know, because I'll book the tickets right now, baby.' She planted both hands on his cheeks, and he stopped moving. 'Tell me what you need me to do for you to marry me, Chloe Henry, because you are it for me. You want red carpet, or private jet? I'm down. I will propose to you in any way you want, as long as the answer is yes.'

'You just did the perfect proposal, Logan. You know what I want. You, me and Dante. In our house, in our comfies on the couch. It's my favourite place in the world.'

His face melted into that crinkly eyed peaceful smile she loved so much. 'Mine too. I love you, Chlo.'

'I love you too, Logan Broderick, and I would love to be your wife. Yes.'

'Yes?' His brows shot up comically.

'Yes.'

'Yes?'

'Yes! Are you going to put me down now?'

'Hell no. I'm never putting you down again.' Leaning down, he swiped the ring box from where it sat on the carpet and headed to the stairs.

'Where are we going?' She laughed as he headed up the steps, his arms tight around her. He dipped his head and kissed her again.

'I'm going to take you upstairs, strip you naked and see if the ring I bought you lights up in the dark once it's on your finger. Any objections?'

Her heart full, she looked into the eyes of the man she loved and wondered how she got to be so lucky. How one hotel room mishap had led to all this.

'None.' She grinned, running her fingers through his thick dark locks. 'Lead the way, Doctor Love. Show me your bedside manner.'

'Oh, wildcat,' he growled, kicking open the bedroom door. 'Don't threaten me with a good time.' He kicked the door shut, and for the next few hours, he showed her just how much of a good time being his fiancée could be. Dante the cat did not approve.

* * *

TV-turned-movie-star Logan Broderick wed his doctor sweetheart Chloe Henry today in a private ceremony in Manchester. Many of his co-stars were in attendance, along with Belinda Jenkins, producer of Doctor Love. She attended with her new beau, real-life doctor Anthony Baldoni. Baldoni met Jenkins on the set of the hit medical show when he was appointed as medical consultant. Sources close to the couple say that it was actually Chloe Henry who recommended him for the job, after working together at Manchester General Hospital, where Doctor Henry is head of the general surgery department.

The Henry family were also in attendance, along with Elizabeth Henry, sister of the bride. Three of the nurses she works with at Manchester General were reportedly her bridesmaids, and Logan's agent Peter Simpkin was the best man. Cameras were banned from the event, and the couple have turned down several lucrative magazine deals for the rights to the wedding photos. Logan did post one photo on his Instagram the following day, showing the couple at the altar exchanging rings. The caption read simply – My heart, my home, my wife. His wife, Chloe Henry-Broderick, is not on social media, and still continues to keep her life with Logan private.

The couple currently reside together in Manchester, close to Manchester General, and it is said that while Logan is the current hot property on the movie market, he is loyal to the character Dante Love and is keen to work any offers of lead roles around shooting of the new series. Doctor Love *recently had its best season's ratings to date, blowing the competition out of the water in the prime-time Thursday night viewing slot. The network has signed a multi-million-pound deal for another two seasons, and Belinda Jenkins recently accredited much of the success to Logan Broderick, and his passion and dedication to the show.*

The couple's honeymoon location was kept under wraps, and at the time of writing, no details have emerged. Peter Simpkin is thought to be cat-sitting the couple's cat, Dante. Sources close to the agent have confirmed that Dante is not amused.

* * *

MORE FROM RACHEL DOVE

Another book from Rachel Dove, *Don't You Want Me, Baby?*, is available to order now here:

https://mybook.to/DontYouWantMeBackAd

ACKNOWLEDGEMENTS

Thank you for reading! As ever, a book is not made by one person alone. Huge thanks to Emily and the whole Boldwood team for all their hard work. A shout-out to my ever-loving family and friends, and last but not least, to my wonderful readers. Thank you for sticking with me all this time. I love you all!

ABOUT THE AUTHOR

Rachel Dove lives in leafy West Yorkshire with her family, and rescue animals Tilly the cat and Darcy the dog (named after Mr Darcy, of course!). A former teacher specialising in Autism, ADHD and SpLDs, she is passionate about changing the system and raising awareness/acceptance. She loves a good rom-com, and the beach!

Sign up to Rachel Dove's mailing list here for news, competitions and updates on future books.

Follow Rachel on social media:

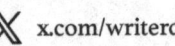 x.com/writerdove

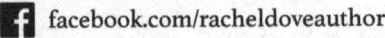 instagram.com/writerdove

facebook.com/racheldoveauthor

tiktok.com/@writerdove

ALSO BY RACHEL DOVE

Boldwood
EVER AFTER

XOXO

JOIN BOLDWOOD'S
**ROMANCE
COMMUNITY**
FOR SWEET AND
SPICY BOOK RECS
WITH ALL YOUR
FAVOURITE
TROPES!

SIGN UP TO OUR
NEWSLETTER

HTTPS://BIT.LY/BOLDWOODEVERAFTER

Boldwood

Boldwood Books is an award-winning fiction publishing company seeking out the best stories from around the world.

Find out more at www.boldwoodbooks.com

Join our reader community for brilliant books, competitions and offers!

Follow us
@BoldwoodBooks
@TheBoldBookClub

Sign up to our weekly deals newsletter

https://bit.ly/BoldwoodBNewsletter